MRS. JEFFRIES
HOLDS THE TRUMP

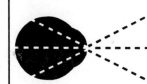

5| 3

MRS. JEFFRIES HOLDS THE TRUMP

EMILY BRIGHTWELL

WHEELER PUBLISHING
A part of Gale, Cengage Learning

GALE
CENGAGE Learning

Detroit • New York • San Francisco • New Haven, Conn • Waterville, Maine • London

GALE
CENGAGE Learning

LIBRARY OF CONGRESS CATALOGING-IN-PUBLICATION DATA

Brightwell, Emily.
    Mrs. Jeffries holds the trump / by Emily Brightwell.
        p. cm. — (Wheeler Publishing large print cozy mystery)
    "A Victorian mystery."
    ISBN-13: 978-1-59722-840-4 (alk. paper)
    ISBN-10: 1-59722-840-0 (alk. paper)
    1. Witherspoon, Gerald (Fictitious character)—Fiction.
2. Jeffries, Mrs. (Fictitious character)—Fiction. 3. Police—Great
Britain—Fiction. 4. Women domestics—Fiction. I. Title.
    PS3552.R46443M67 2008
    813'.54—dc22   2008032191

Published in 2008 by arrangement with The Berkley Publishing Group, a member of Penguin Group (USA) Inc.

Printed in the United States of America
1 2 3 4 5 6 7 12 11 10 09 08

*This book is dedicated to the one person
who said from the beginning that
I could do it —
my mother, Ella Ruth Lanham.*

CHAPTER 1

"Got the first one of the day for you, Doctor," said Harrigan, the porter, as he wheeled the rickety gurney into the ground-floor surgery of St. Thomas' Hospital. "Mind you, it's not as bad as some we've had lately. He's not covered with blood or brains like that bloke you did last week."

Dr. Bosworth nodded absently as he hung his overcoat on the peg and tucked his hat onto the shelf. The mortuary room was chilly, but he was used to the temperature. As the police surgeon for the B district of the Metropolitan Police Force, he spent more time here than he did working on the wards upstairs. He was charged with the grim task of doing postmortems on every suspicious death in this district, and recently there had been no shortage of corpses needing his attention.

He turned and stared at the body outlined beneath the gray sheet, while Harrigan pushed the contraption toward the mortuary table in the center of the room.

"I expect they called you in early today because this poor fellow is wearing a posh suit of clothes," Harrigan continued amiably. "You know how the police are; they get right nervous when a toff ends up in the river. At least this one didn't freeze to death." He stopped as a cough racked him hard enough to send a shudder through his thin frame. His complexion, which was naturally ruddy in color, flushed an even-brighter red.

"Harrigan, that cough is dreadful. When we're through here, you must come upstairs with me to one of the treatment rooms so I can have a look at your chest and throat," Bosworth ordered. "And this time I'll not take no for an answer. I think the hospital can afford a few minutes of my time and a bit of medicine to keep you from coming down with pneumonia. What the board of governors doesn't know, won't hurt them." He knew that the porter had neglected getting medical attention because, even with the reduced fees offered to the hospital staff, he couldn't afford to pay. Bosworth was having none of that.

"Thank you, sir, I'd appreciate you havin' a look-see. This ruddy cough won't go away." Harrigan started moving again. The gurney groaned and squeaked as he rolled it across the concrete floor.

Bosworth went to the sink, turned on the water, wet his hands, and picked up the carbolic soap. He always scrubbed before he did a postmortem. The dead carried just as many diseases as the living, sometimes more. "What have we got here?"

Harrigan tried to get the gurney as close to the table as possible. "Police said the man drowned. They pulled him out of the river early this morning. I heard one of the coppers that brought him in sayin' it was an accident."

Dr. Bosworth dried his hands on a clean towel and pulled his surgical apron off the peg next to the sink. He slipped it over his head as he walked to the table. "Where did they find him?"

"Off the Chelsea Vestry Wharf," the attendant replied. "He was spotted floating off the side of a piling. Miserable way to go, especially this time of year." Harrigan pulled the sheet away, exposing the face.

"Oh my Lord." Bosworth gasped in shock. "I know this man. It's Michael Provost. I was supposed to see him Friday next."

Harrigan's eyebrows shot up. "He was a friend, then? Should I go get another doctor? Gracious, sir, you've gone quite pale."

Bosworth didn't reply. He closed his eyes and took several long, deep breaths.

"Doctor," Harrigan prompted, his tone anxious. "Are you alright, sir? Should I go call the matron?"

"There's no need to call anyone." Bosworth swallowed heavily. "I'm fine. I simply needed a few moments. It's a shock when it's someone you know lying there." He paused. "Let's get on with it."

They pulled off the shroud and positioned the body on the table. For the next ten minutes, they struggled to get the sodden clothes, now made heavy by the water, off the body.

Harrigan, who'd never assisted with a drowning victim before, wrinkled his nose. "You can smell the stink of the river on 'em." He held up the man's undergarments before placing them on the top of the pile stacked on the gurney.

"I'm assuming the police searched all the pockets," Bosworth said, moving around to the far side of the table, where the trolley containing his surgical instruments and a lamp was at the ready. "But just in case they missed something, look through them again."

"Yes, sir." Harrigan pushed the gurney toward the sink. "I'll give these a good wringing out before I put them on the shelves." He now kept his back to the mortuary table. He was quite glad to help get the clothes off and that sort of thing, but he didn't fancy seeing what he knew the doctor might be doing next. "When they're dry, I'll bundle them up for the next of kin."

"He doesn't have any family," Bosworth muttered. Harrigan was more honest than many hospital porters, but he wasn't above helping himself to anything he thought might not be missed. "I expect his housekeeper will come to collect his clothes. Let me know if you find anything in the pockets."

"Yes, sir." Harrigan picked up the wool drawers from the stack and twisted them over the sink, making a face as the smell hit his nostrils.

Bosworth stared at the now-naked body of his friend. Provost's hair, prematurely white for a man in his midforties, had dried and feathered around his face, almost like a halo. Bosworth bent closer and then gently tugged the dead man's chin to the right, revealing an ugly gash along the side of the head, just above the left ear.

"Did you mention you heard the police say this was an accident?" Bosworth asked suddenly.

"That's what one of them was tellin' the matron when they brought the body in. He said the man probably had too much to drink and took a tumble off the wharf." Harrigan folded the garment, laid it on the wooden shelf next to the sink, and then reached for the undershirt.

"Michael Provost didn't drink to excess, and if he had imbibed too much, he'd have taken a hansom home." Bosworth reached down and parted the hair along the slashed flesh. He probed gently along the wound, grimacing as his fingers found the spots where the bone had cracked and separated. "His skull has been fractured."

"Maybe he bashed it on one of the pilings," Harrigan suggested helpfully.

Bosworth grabbed the lamp and moved it closer. The scalp was discolored and darkening. "Half the side of his head is bruised, and I don't think it was because he smacked it on a piling."

"What do you think caused it, then?" Harrigan turned and looked at Bosworth, his expression curious.

"He was hit with something," Bosworth replied. "I'll know more when I open him up. Luckily he wasn't in the water very long."

"How do you know that?" Harrigan turned back to the pile of clothes on the gurney. Even smelling the rank water of the Thames was better than watching the doctor work on that poor bloke.

"Oh, that's simple: His body isn't bloated and the fish haven't been at him. And look at the marks on his shoulders and neck — they're very distinctive."

Harrigan kept his gaze firmly on the task in front of him. But the good doctor didn't notice he'd lost his audience.

Bosworth shifted position so that he could splay his fingers on the dead man's right shoulder. "Just as I thought," he muttered.

He moved to the other side of the table and did the same thing again, only this time he splayed his left hand over the marks on the left shoulder. "And this is a fit as well."

The porter cleared his throat. He didn't want to look, but he was curious. "What's a fit, sir?"

"My fingers, Mr. Harrigan. They fit the bruises almost perfectly."

"So you're sayin' it wasn't an accident?"

"That's correct. Someone hit Michael Provost in the head with something hard enough to stun him and then shoved him into the water. His killer held him down with enough force to leave very clear hand impressions on the skin. In other words, Provost was murdered."

"I hope the inspector isn't late tonight. I've lamb chops for dinner, and they get tough if they sit too long." Mrs. Goodge set the plate of freshly made shortbread down on the table and eased into her chair. The portly, white-haired woman was the cook for Inspector Gerald Witherspoon of the Metropolitan Police Force. It was half past three in the afternoon, and the household servants had gathered for their tea.

"His current caseload is very light," said the housekeeper, Mrs. Jeffries, as she slipped into her spot at the head of the table. She reached for the teapot and began to pour. She was a short, plump woman who favored brown bombazine dresses and sensible black shoes. Her once-auburn hair now had more than a few strands of gray in it, but her porcelain skin was still smooth, with only a few laugh lines around her brown eyes. "So, unless something unexpected comes up, he ought to be home at his usual time. But, then again, he does have that embezzlement matter."

Wiggins, the household footman, snorted

in derision. "I don't know why they gave our inspector such a silly case. Embezzlement is about as interesting as watchin' paint dry."

Mrs. Jeffries stared at him in surprise. The lad generally had a sunny disposition and rarely complained. "I beg to differ. To the victim, embezzlement is a very serious matter. You wouldn't like it if someone stole everything you'd worked hard to acquire."

Wiggins looked down at the tabletop. A red flush crept up his round cheeks, and he shoved a lock of brown hair off his forehead. "Sorry, Mrs. Jeffries. You're right. I oughtn't to 'ave spoken like I did. It's just, I'm used to our inspector havin' big, important cases."

"But his current case *is* important," Mrs. Jeffries said, her tone a bit kinder. "And we can't always expect to have something to investigate."

Betsy, the pretty blond-haired maid, spoke up. "We could have a peek at the embezzlement case," she suggested. "Surely there's something we could do to help our inspector."

"That's right." Wiggins nodded eagerly. "We could get out and about like we do when we have us a murder. You know, askin' questions and finding out bits and pieces that would help him settle the case."

"I don't see how," Mrs. Goodge interjected. "Embezzling isn't at all like murder. There's no body and no witnesses."

"And that's why we ought to 'elp 'im," Wiggins continued doggedly. "He's already got a suspect, and that fellow might 'ave talked in front of the servants. They might know something . . ."

Smythe, the coachman, interrupted him. "James Windsor, if that's even his real name, lived in rented rooms. The inspector's already told us the man kept to himself and that no one in the lodging 'ouse knew anything about him."

Smythe was a tall man in his late thirties, with broad shoulders, a muscular build, black hair, and harsh, almost brutal features, except for his kind brown eyes. He and Betsy were engaged to be married.

"That doesn't mean we couldn't find out anything useful," Betsy insisted. "Wiggins is right. We shouldn't just sit around doing nothing."

Mrs. Jeffries stared at them sympathetically. Betsy and Wiggins both had a bad case of the winter doldrums. Christmas had come and gone, the days were overcast and bleak, and it had been more than a month since their last murder. The maid and the

16

footman were both bored, and frankly, if Mrs. Jeffries was truly honest, she was a bit glum herself.

Not that she'd ever want a human being to die simply so that she and the household would have an interesting puzzle to solve; that would never do. Of course, their inspector was now the most famous detective on the Metropolitan Police Force, and it did seem a shame that his talents were being wasted on what was really a very straightforward embezzlement investigation. Witherspoon hadn't complained about the case. In fact, it was just the opposite. At breakfast that morning, he'd told her that he quite enjoyed his current work. Apparently, searching through ledgers, reconciling accounts, and comparing invoices were interesting to him. "I think our inspector is quite happy with this assignment," Mrs. Jeffries said.

"More's the pity," Betsy sighed. "Now even if there is a murder, he'd not want it, and I don't understand that at all. He's solved more homicides than anyone."

"You're forgettin' that our inspector never really wanted to become such an expert on solving murders," Mrs. Goodge said softly. "He was satisfied working in the Records Room, until Mrs. Jeffries came along and

17

made sure he caught that horrible Kensington High Street killer."

"We helped with that as well," Wiggins added. "We just didn't know we was 'elpin'."

The footman was referring to Inspector Witherspoon's first homicide. It had been several years earlier, right after Mrs. Jeffries had been hired as the inspector's housekeeper. The case hadn't been assigned to the inspector, nor had the household shown any interest until Mrs. Jeffries made it the main topic of conversation every time they'd sat down at the table. Before any of them understood what she was up to, she had them out and about asking all sorts of questions. By the time any of the household had realized what she was doing, Mrs. Jeffries had managed to feed their inspector enough clues to catch the killer.

In the years that had passed, Inspector Witherspoon had solved more murders than anyone in the history of the Metropolitan Police Force. His superiors were amazed by his uncanny ability to unravel even the most complex of cases.

Gerald Witherspoon was as surprised by his ability as anyone else, but that was only to be expected. The poor man had no idea that his entire household helped him and that they did it gladly.

Their inspector was one of nature's gentlemen. He treated them with courtesy and respect, paid decent wages, and most important, never forgot that they were human beings. Of course, that wasn't the only reason for their willingness to assist him. All of them loved being "out on the hunt," so to speak, as it was far more interesting than domestic work. Every one of them felt that bringing murderers to justice gave their lives a genuine sense of purpose. But they were especially proud of the fact that their efforts had saved a number of innocent people from the gallows. Each of them contributed in his or her own special way.

Mrs. Goodge did her part without even leaving the kitchen. She had a vast number of "sources," as she called them, trooping in and out the back door on a regular basis. Delivery lads, chimney sweeps, fruit vendors, laundry boys, and tinkers were all welcomed into the warm kitchen. The cook was relentless in her pursuit of information. As she plied her sources with tea and treats, she'd drop the names of suspects and victims into the conversation as easily as she dropped ripe cherries into an empty pastry shell. By the time her guests were ready to go, she'd have dug out every kernel of gossip there was to be had. If that method didn't work and she couldn't get enough information for her liking, she also had a large network of former colleagues she could call upon for help.

Mrs. Goodge had worked in some of the grandest houses in all of England and knew the names of every important aristocratic or rich family in the kingdom. Luckily, many of their cases involved the upper classes. But even if it wasn't an "upper-crust" murder, as she liked to put it, she still found a way to do her part.

The cook was glad that her efforts helped bring killers to justice, but more important, she'd discovered that even this late in her life, she was capable of making fundamental shifts in her point of view. Murder affected everyone, even the people who investigated. For most of her life, she'd been sure the current social order was right and proper, and that everyone should know his or her place and stay in it. But fighting for justice had changed her in the most basic of ways. The world wasn't as black and white as she'd once thought. Sometimes there were shades of gray. Sometimes justice had nothing to do with the established order and everything to do with what was right.

Betsy, who'd come to the household by collapsing on the doorstep and then stayed on as a maid, had become skilled at getting shopkeepers to talk. She'd trot along to a suspect's or a victim's neighborhood, step into a greengrocer's or a butcher's shop, flash a wide smile at the clerk, and start dropping names.

She was also good at following people, a skill she didn't mention too often in front of her fiancé. Smythe tended to be ridiculously protective, and she was certain he'd lecture her on the dangers of trailing murder suspects.

Smythe had originally been the coachman for Inspector Witherspoon's aunt, Euphemia Witherspoon. Then he'd gone to Australia and made a fortune. When he'd returned, he'd stopped in for a quick hello and found Euphemia dying.

He'd also found her home full of greedy servants taking advantage of the sick woman. Only the very young Wiggins had been trying to nurse the poor lady properly. Smythe had tossed the other servants out the front door and sent Wiggins to find a decent doctor, and between the two of them they had nursed her in her last days. But even the best physician couldn't stop nature from taking its course, and Euphemia Witherspoon's time upon this earth had been nearing the end.

As she lay dying, she'd made Smythe promise he'd stay on and see that her nephew, Gerald Witherspoon, was settled in properly and, crucially, wasn't taken advantage of the way she had been. Smythe had agreed.

By the time the household was arranged to Smythe's satisfaction and he could have left, it was too late. He'd gotten involved. He'd liked Mrs. Jeffries' insight and intelligent conversation from the first time she'd presided over the supper table. Add to that Mrs. Goodge's wonderful meals and the way Betsy had made him feel from the first time he'd laid eyes on her, and it was no wonder he couldn't leave.

Then the group had started solving murders, and Smythe had realized that Betsy, despite the difference in their ages, had feelings for him as well. But he'd made a big mistake in not telling the others how much money he had. Now the time never seemed right. It would be awkward.

Betsy knew about his wealth, of course, and Mrs. Jeffries had figured it out, but Mrs. Goodge and Wiggins had no idea that Smythe was as rich as a robber baron. He couldn't for the life of him figure out exactly how to let them know the truth. He hated the idea that they'd think he'd deliberately kept it a secret from them, when it hadn't really been that way at all.

But his money had proved useful. When it came to investigating murder and getting people to talk, greasing their informants' palms with silver came in right handy.

Mrs. Jeffries chuckled as she recalled their first case. "I wasn't all that certain about what I was doing myself," she admitted. She'd come to London after the death of her husband. He'd been a policeman in York. She'd a bit of money — his pension — and as they'd had no children, she'd decided to move south, do a bit of traveling, and enjoy the life of the city. But within days she'd been bored silly.

The shops on Regent Street were crowded, the theater was interesting but one couldn't sit through a play every evening, and several day trips to the South Coast had convinced her that travel often left one with a headache and a nasty case of indigestion. Then she'd heard of an available position as housekeeper for a policeman. That had piqued her interest.

She'd come along, chatted with the inspector, and been offered the position. She'd been the one to insist he check her references. She'd soon seen past his hesitant manner and noted that he was no fool. He was capable of so much more than simply being in charge of the Records Room at Scotland Yard.

She smiled softly as she remembered those early first days in the household and their very first case together. "Considering that we were more or less dashing about in the dark, I think we did rather well."

"We solved the case," Mrs. Goodge reminded her. "Or, rather, you solved it. The rest of us hadn't a clue about what was going on till it was almost over."

That was Mrs. Jeffries' special talent. She could put together the pieces, take all the seemingly unrelated facts and gossip, and come up with the right solution. Most of the time.

"That's not quite true." The housekeeper chuckled. "I think you were all on to me a lot earlier than you cared to admit. You were simply afraid if you said anything, I might get worried about the inspector finding out and call off the hunt. Remember, we didn't know each other very well back then."

"I think it's the best thing that ever happened to me," Wiggins declared. "It's given us something right important to do with our lives, and not everyone gets a chance at that —" He broke off, interrupted by a loud knock from the back door. "Who's that? You expectin' any deliveries, Mrs. Goodge?" He got up and crossed the kitchen.

"Deliveries come of a mornin'," the cook replied.

The room went completely quiet save for Wiggins' footsteps as he hurried down the long hallway to the back door. Fred, the household's black and brown mongrel dog, woke from his warm spot on the rug in front of the cooker and leapt up. He raced after the footman.

A moment later, they heard the door open. "Well, 'ello. I wasn't expectin' to see you," Wiggins exclaimed eagerly.

"I wonder who it is," Betsy whispered.

"Come on in, then," Wiggins continued. "You've arrived at a good time. We've just sat down to tea, and Mrs. Goodge has made shortbread."

Seconds later, Wiggins reappeared. He was followed by a tall red-haired man with a long, bony face and deep-set hazel eyes. "It's Dr. Bosworth come to see us." The footman grinned broadly. "I've invited 'im for tea."

"But of course he must have tea with us." Mrs. Jeffries rose to welcome the doctor. Betsy got up and went to the cupboard for another tea setting.

"I'm sorry to just barge in like this, but I

needed to see you." Bosworth smiled apologetically. "And I wouldn't say no to a cup of tea or to some of Mrs. Goodge's delicious shortbread. I could smell it as soon as Wiggins opened the door."

"Then you sit down and help yourself." The cook pointed to an empty chair.

Bosworth sat down next to Wiggins and nodded his thanks as Betsy put a plate in front of him, then handed Mrs. Jeffries his teacup.

Even though they were all curious as to why he'd come, they waited politely until after he'd had a sip of his tea and taken a bite of shortbread. As soon as he swallowed, he said, "You must excuse my manners, but I'm very hungry. I've spent the day trying to convince the Metropolitan Police that a man has been murdered."

"Have you had any luck?" Mrs. Jeffries asked. She was fairly certain she already knew the answer; otherwise, he wouldn't be here.

"No, unfortunately. The killer very cleverly made it look like an accident. The police are of the opinion that the man had too much to drink and tumbled into the Thames, where he drowned."

"And you're convinced it wasn't an accident?" Mrs. Jeffries said.

26

"One doesn't accidentally hold oneself underwater with enough force to leave handprints on one's arms and shoulders," Bosworth said bitterly. "I've spent the last two hours arguing with some half-witted inspector that Michael Provost didn't drink to excess and that he wasn't stupid enough to have accidentally tumbled into the river on a cold winter's night. I tried to show the fool the handprints on the corpse's arms, but he wouldn't even bother to come have a look. He kept insisting it was an accident or, even more ridiculous, that the death was a suicide. I'm at my wit's end. I even called at the Ladbroke Grove station to find your inspector, but he was out on another case. As I was close by, I thought I'd come and tell all of you what I've learned. Oh dear, I am babbling, aren't I? Forgive me, please, but I've been up since early this morning and I've had very little to eat. I'm quite light-headed." He took another quick sip of tea and shoved the rest of his shortbread into his mouth.

"Then you'll need more to eat than just this little bit of food," the cook said. Without waiting for a reply, she got up and hurried to the dry larder. Betsy rose as well and went to the sideboard.

"Tell us what's happened," Mrs. Jeffries

said. "Start from the beginning and take your time. You can eat as you talk."

Mrs. Goodge reappeared with a loaf of bread in one hand and a plate of sliced beef in the other. Betsy had already pulled a clean plate off the top rack and set it on the counter next to the butter pot.

"We'll fix you a nice roast-beef sandwich," the cook said. "You just do as Mrs. Jeffries says and tell us everything. We'll take care of the rest."

Bosworth smiled ruefully. "I shouldn't put you to so much trouble, Mrs. Goodge, but I'll not pass up a chance to eat something you've cooked. I'll try to be brief in the telling, as it's getting late and I know you've chores. I got called in early this morning because a dead man had been pulled out of the Thames. It was the body of a healthy middle-aged man named Michael Provost."

"Where was he pulled from?" Smythe asked.

"The old Chelsea Vestry Wharf. It's just below where the new embankment ends." He tried not to watch Mrs. Goodge as she slathered butter on two thick slices of bread, but he was so hungry that his stomach growled.

"And was he fully clothed?" Mrs. Jeffries asked. She wasn't sure why that question popped into her head, but the moment the words were out of her mouth, she knew it was important.

"Indeed he was." Bosworth licked his lips as Mrs. Goodge forked a slice of beef onto the buttered bread. "Which is one of the reasons I knew immediately it wasn't a suicide, even though that fool tried to suggest it might be. But would he listen to me? No, he most certainly did not. I tried to tell him I've handled over half a dozen suicides both here and in San Francisco. Most of them had taken their shoes off. That stupid fool of an inspector tried to tell me that the fellow might have kept his shoes on so his feet wouldn't get cold. Absurd idea. People intent on taking their own life by jumping into the Thames in the middle of winter aren't overly concerned with whether or not they get chilled!"

Mrs. Jeffries nodded in understanding. "My late husband once pulled a suicide out of the river, and she too had taken off her shoes. Nothing else, only her shoes. I don't know what prompts people to remove just that item of clothing. Do you have any idea how long your victim had been in the water? Is it possible to determine such a thing?"

Bosworth almost wept in gratitude as Mrs. Goodge put his freshly made sandwich down in front of him. He glanced at Mrs. Jeffries, gave her a polite nod, and then tucked in to his food.

"I like to see a body enjoyin' their food," the cook murmured as she slipped back into her chair.

Bosworth held up his hand. "Sorry," he muttered, "but I didn't realize how hungry I really was until you started making my sandwich. It's delicious, by the way."

They waited patiently until he'd eaten the whole thing, washed it down with tea, and then leaned back in his chair. "That was wonderful," he said. "Now, in answer to Mrs. Jeffries' question about determining how long a body has been in the water, the answer is both yes and no."

"What does that mean?" Wiggins asked.

"I can't tell you exactly when the poor man was put in the water, but I can tell you he'd not been there long enough for the gases to form in his internal organs and float him to the surface. That process takes several days. When someone drowns himself, the body generally sinks."

"Then how did he get spotted if he didn't float up?" Smythe asked.

"He never sank," Bosworth replied. "His coat caught on a nail or a piling, and that kept him from going to the bottom."

"Who called in the alarm?" Mrs. Jeffries asked.

"A policeman spotted him in the wee hours last night. He was brought into St. Thomas' mortuary room at six."

"Are you sure the marks on his body were really handprints? Maybe he was just bashed up against the pilings," Smythe said.

Bosworth shook his head. "The marks were bruises, and they were most definitely handprints. He was held under the water until he drowned. I'm certain of it."

"The death was caused by drowning?" Mrs. Jeffries clarified. Dr. Bosworth had helped them on a number of their other cases, and he had some rather unusual ideas about what one could learn by a serious study of a victim's body. Bosworth had, among other things, spent some time in San Francisco, where he'd worked and studied with an American doctor and had become quite an expert in gunshot wounds. He was of the opinion that a careful examination of bullet wounds could actually give one a clue as to the kind of gun that had been used in the shooting. Thus far, he'd proved to be an invaluable help to them in their work.

But this victim hadn't died by gunshot. Mrs. Jeffries trusted the good doctor's opinion, but she needed to make sure he wasn't seeing murders everywhere.

"Definitely. There was water in the lungs. Not only that, but there was a wound on the left side of his head that indicated he'd been struck with something hard enough to stun him; then he was forced into the river and held under." Bosworth frowned heavily. "I told all this to the officer in charge of the case, but he'd already decided it was an accident or a suicide. He refused to listen to me."

"Who did you speak with?" Mrs. Jeffries asked.

"A fool by the name of Inspector Nivens." Bosworth snorted faintly. "He was in such a hurry to be off, he barely listened to what I had to say. Goodness, the man wouldn't even come and look at the body. I couldn't believe his behavior. It was outrageous — outrageous, I tell you. That's why I tried to see Inspector Witherspoon. He'd understand; he'd listen . . ." His voice trailed off as he saw the expressions on their faces. "What is it? What's wrong?"

"We know all about Inspector Nivens," Mrs. Jeffries replied. "And you're right: he is a fool."

Nivens had been a thorn in their sides almost from Witherspoon's first case. He'd made it perfectly clear that he thought

Witherspoon was an incompetent who had lots of help on all his cases. That was true, of course, but just because the household helped a bit didn't mean Gerald Witherspoon wasn't up to the task at hand.

But Nivens could be dangerous, so they had to tread carefully. He had powerful political connections in the Home Office. He was always running to the chief inspector with one tale or another and trying his best to prove that Inspector Witherspoon wasn't doing his job properly. Nivens thought he'd been very hard done by because Witherspoon now got most of the homicides, even the ones outside his own district.

"But Nivens is so eager to prove himself as a homicide detective, I'm surprised he didn't take you seriously. He'd like nothing better than to have a murder drop into his lap," Mrs. Jeffries said thoughtfully.

"He wasn't very interested today," Bosworth replied. "Apparently his lunch engagement was more important than his duty. Honestly, Mrs. Jeffries, the man seemed afraid to even look at the body. But it's my duty to ensure that a proper investigation is done, and I know this was murder, not an accident or a suicide."

"Can't you just tell 'em that at the inquest?" Wiggins suggested helpfully.

Bosworth shook his head. "I don't want to go before a magistrate with the police saying one thing and me saying another."

"You're afraid that a coroner's magistrate won't take your methods seriously and they'll come back with the wrong verdict, aren't you?" Mrs. Jeffries asked.

"That's correct. If that happens, then whoever killed Michael Provost will have got away with the crime. Once the verdict is set, it's very difficult to convince the police to investigate."

"I shouldn't worry about that, Dr. Bosworth," Mrs. Goodge said easily. "No matter how the magistrate rules, if it's murder, we'll suss it out and catch the killer." She pushed the plate of shortbread closer to him. "Now, do you know anything else about our victim?"

"As a matter of fact, I do," Bosworth replied. "I was acquainted with him. I had an appointment to meet with him next Friday at St. Thomas'."

Surprised, Mrs. Jeffries stared at Bosworth. "You knew him?"

He looked down at the tabletop and then lifted his eyes, meeting her gaze squarely. "I know I should have mentioned it straightaway, but I was afraid you might react the way Inspector Nivens did when I told him I knew the victim. He seemed to think that meant I couldn't be objective, that I couldn't do my job properly, and that's simply not true."

Mrs. Jeffries glanced at the others and saw confusion and consternation, the very emotions she felt, reflected on their faces. "I assure you, Dr. Bosworth, that no one here is at all like Nigel Nivens. However, this is a very pertinent bit of information."

"I know, and I should have mentioned the fact immediately," he replied.

"Was he a close friend?" Betsy asked softly.

"No, not really. Provost was more of a business acquaintance than anything else, but I had known him for years. When I mentioned that to Inspector Nivens, he seemed to feel that was evidence that I couldn't be objective about the matter."

"How, exactly, did you make the victim's acquaintance?" Mrs. Jeffries asked.

"Through my father," Bosworth admitted. "Provost owned a medical supply company. It's a very successful enterprise. I met him years ago when he used to come around to my father's surgery to sell him equipment."

"Why were you going to meet him?" Smythe asked.

"He'd asked me to introduce him to the

procurement manager at St. Thomas' Hospital. Provost's company manufactures excellent instruments, so I was quite willing. He'd always treated me well, and my father had a great deal of respect for him."

"When was the last time you saw Mr. Provost?" Mrs. Goodge asked.

"Two weeks ago. He dropped by my office and asked if I could arrange the introduction. He'd done business with the hospital on previous occasions, but our current manager recently took over the procurement position and Provost thought it easier to be introduced to him through a staff member such as myself rather than just sending the fellow a letter." He shook his head, his expression rueful. "He was in my office for less than ten minutes, and it wasn't an overly important issue to either of us; it was simply the most convenient way to do a bit of business. I can't recall the last time I saw him prior to that. So, as you can tell, he wasn't such a close friend that seeing him on a mortuary slab would render me incapable of performing my duty properly, nor would I be inclined to see murder where one doesn't exist."

"But, still, seeing someone you've known for years lying there must have been very difficult for you," Mrs. Jeffries said gently.

"When the porter pulled the sheet back, I was very shocked," Bosworth admitted. "It made me realize how terribly upsetting murder must be for the family and friends of the victim." He paused and took a deep breath. "But my personal relationship with the man has nothing to do with my conviction that he didn't accidentally fall into the river or commit suicide. Provost was murdered. There are bruises shaped exactly like handprints on his arms and shoulders."

"I'm sure you're right," Mrs. Goodge said briskly. "So there's no time to waste. What sort of person was your Mr. Provost? Was he married? Did he have many friends? In other words, have you any idea who might have wanted him dead?"

Bosworth smiled faintly. "He was a widower and he had no children. His wife died of cholera less than six months after they married. He never remarried. Oh, and before I forget, he was a qualified doctor. He studied in Edinburgh but never practiced."

"Do you have any idea why?" Mrs. Jeffries asked.

Bosworth thought for a moment. "I'm not certain of this, but I think I recall hearing my father say that Provost never got used to the sight of blood. But in his case, he made the right decision. He made far more money from his business than he would ever have made as a doctor. As I said, he owns a very successful manufacturing enterprise, and before you ask, I've no idea who might inherit it. I do know that he lived in a rather large house and that he had a goodly number of servants. I remember going there once years ago to pick up a set of syringes he wanted my father to test for him."

"And where is this 'ouse of his?" Wiggins helped himself to another piece of shortbread.

"He lived at number eight, Maude Grove Road in Chelsea. That's why I'm certain his death wasn't an accident: He walked along the river all the time," Bosworth insisted.

"Where is his business located?" Mrs. Jeffries asked. "Here in London?"

"Yes, it's on Gray's Inn Road, just down from the Royal Free Hospital," Bosworth replied. "The workshop, warehouse, and offices are there. But my main concern now is getting the police to admit that the poor fellow was murdered. Honestly, if I can't get them to accept that those marks on his arms and shoulders are handprints, then I don't know what to do."

"What about the fact that he was coshed on the head?" Smythe asked. "Wouldn't that be evidence of a sort?"

"Inspector Nivens claimed he probably received the injury when he fell and hit his head on the wharf." Bosworth snorted. "That's nonsense, of course. The wound was caused by Provost being smacked with a heavy object just above his left ear. But as my methods aren't universally accepted by the medical or legal profession, I've no way of proving it was murder."

Mrs. Jeffries was also very apprehensive about this. Nivens wouldn't like to admit he was wrong, but for him to ignore evidence that pointed to murder, a murder that would go to him as the senior officer on duty, meant that something was wrong.

However, before she could express her qualms and suggest they proceed with caution, Wiggins spoke up. "Oh, don't worry, Dr. Bosworth. Mrs. Jeffries is right good at that sort of thing. She'll come up with something to make them all see it was murder." He glanced proudly at the housekeeper. "Won't you, Mrs. Jeffries?"

"You can't expect her to come up with an answer this quickly," Betsy interjected. "Give her a few moments to think it through."

"Well, let's see," Mrs. Jeffries murmured. Really, she was flattered by their faith in her abilities, but rather at a loss as to the best way to proceed. "Uh."

"You could always contact his solicitor with your evidence," Smythe said to Bosworth. "You know where Provost lived. Finding out who his lawyer is shouldn't be too hard."

"I thought of that," Bosworth admitted. "But I wasn't sure if that approach would be very effective. I'm not certain that I can get his solicitor to take my evidence seriously if I can't even convince the police."

"But you must try," Mrs. Jeffries argued. "If you can convince his solicitor to press the police, even Inspector Nivens couldn't stop an investigation."

"I just don't understand why Nivens wouldn't want it to be a murder," Betsy muttered. "He's always complaining that our inspector hogs all the murders."

"Yes," Mrs. Jeffries agreed. "That is puzzling, and I expect we'll find out the answer one way or another. But in the meantime we can start having a good look at our poor Mr. Provost." In her experience, the best way to find out who committed a murder was by learning as much as possible about the victim.

"Good, that will be very helpful." Bosworth rose to his feet. "I'm glad I stopped in to see you. Tomorrow I'll see about talking to Provost's solicitor, and if I can't convince him to help me, I'll go along and see the chief inspector myself. Providing I can get the police to listen to me, it would help if Inspector Witherspoon takes this case."

"But didn't you say that Inspector Nivens would be in charge?" Mrs. Goodge asked, her expression confused.

"Had he acted properly, he would have been," Bosworth said. "But as I shall make it clear to both the chief inspector and Provost's legal representative that Nivens was derelict in his duty, I don't see how they can give the case to him."

"But that won't mean that Inspector Witherspoon will get it," Mrs. Jeffries warned.

"I understand that, Mrs. Jeffries." Bosworth smiled wanly. "But we can hope for the best, can't we?"

As it turned out, Dr. Bosworth didn't need to convince Provost's solicitor of anything. When the police went to the dead man's home to inform his household of the tragedy, his housekeeper, a sensible woman who knew her employer very well indeed, immediately sent for his solicitor,

Anthony Tipton.

Tipton went straight to New Scotland Yard and was in the chief inspector's office at the very moment that Dr. Bosworth was at Inspector Witherspoon's house in Upper Edmonton Gardens.

"The very idea that Mr. Provost would accidentally fall into the Thames is absurd. For the past thirty years, he's taken a walk along that river every single night, and he knew the neighborhood like the back of his hand," Tipton proclaimed.

"But you just stated that he was deeply concerned about some problem," Chief Inspector Barrows said. "Perhaps he was distracted and slipped on a wet patch."

"Rubbish," Tipton interrupted him. "He was fleet of foot and sound of mind. He might have been concerned about some matter, but that's how he did his thinking, by walking along the river." Tipton rose to leave the chief's office. "I expect a full investigation of this matter. I knew Michael Provost. He was a meticulous, careful man who did not have accidents."

"I assure you, sir, we'll investigate Mr. Provost's death as thoroughly as possible." Relieved that Tipton was leaving, Barrows leapt to his feet as well. "I'll put our best man on it."

"And who would that be?" Tipton stopped, his hand on the doorknob.

"Inspector Gerald Witherspoon."

Tipton nodded and pulled the door open. "Good. Keep me informed. Provost wasn't just a client; he was my friend."

"Don't worry, Mr. Tipton. Inspector Witherspoon will get to the bottom of this straightaway."

CHAPTER 2

Inspector Gerald Witherspoon handed his wet bowler to Mrs. Jeffries and popped his umbrella into the blue and white ceramic urn by the front door. "It's pouring out there, Mrs. Jeffries. The traffic on the Holland Park Road was dreadful."

"Traffic is always worse when it rains," she commented. She shook his hat gently to get the water off.

He unbuttoned his black overcoat. "It wasn't just the rain and traffic that delayed me. Late this afternoon I got summoned to the chief inspector's office. I had to go all the way over to the Yard. I do hope my tardiness tonight hasn't inconvenienced the staff."

Witherspoon was a man of medium height and build. He had thinning dark brown hair that was turning gray at the top and temples; a pale, angular face; and a nose that was just a shade on the long side.

"Not at all, sir." Mrs. Jeffries hung the hat on the coat tree and then waited for him to take off the coat. "Mrs. Goodge has made a lovely Lancashire hot pot, and it keeps quite nicely in the oven."

"Excellent. I'm very hungry. But I should love a nice glass of sherry before dinner. I'm quite chilled to the bone." He started down the hall toward the drawing room and stepped through the open door.

Mrs. Jeffries hurried after him. She went to the liquor cabinet as he settled himself in his big upholstered maroon chair. She opened the cupboard door and pulled out a bottle of Harveys Bristol Cream.

"You must join me, Mrs. Jeffries," he instructed. "Sherry is so much more pleasant when one has someone to share it with."

"Thank you, sir, that would be very nice." She poured the amber-colored liquid into two glasses, picked them up, and moved over to where he sat. She handed him his drink and then sat down on the settee. "I do hope your meeting with the chief inspector wasn't too distressing."

She wasn't at all concerned that her comment would be considered presumptuous or impertinent. The inspector had been raised in very modest circumstances and, consequently, knew that his servants were human beings. He expected them to behave accordingly.

He took a quick sip. "It wasn't so much distressing as it was odd."

"Odd, sir? In what way?" She watched him over the rim of her glass as she took a drink. He didn't look upset, merely puzzled.

"A man was pulled out of the Thames this morning. The inspector in charge at the Walton Street station was quite certain the death was an accident, and treated the matter accordingly. Apparently there was no evidence of foul play. The chief told me the fellow's watch and purse were found in his coat pocket, so he'd not been robbed."

"Do you know the man's name?" Mrs. Jeffries gave the inspector a bland, curious smile. Surely there couldn't have been two people pulled out of the river this morning?

"His name was Michael Provost, and for some reason his solicitor is certain his death was not an accident. He was so convinced of it, he went along to the chief inspector's office at the Yard and insisted we investigate the matter. Honestly, Mrs. Jeffries, I don't know what I'm expected to do now. This fellow drowned, so unless there's an eyewitness who hasn't come forward, it'll be very difficult to prove the death was anything but an accident."

"Did Chief Inspector Barrows think this Mr. Provost has been murdered?" she asked softly.

Witherspoon thought for a moment before he replied. "I'm not sure," he finally said. "I don't think he agreed to investigate the matter simply to get the solicitor out of his office. So I suppose Mr. Tipton — that's the solicitor's name — must have made a strong enough argument for the chief inspector to agree to put me on the case. Either that, or he's so politically well connected that the chief had to agree we'd look into the matter."

"Perhaps Mr. Tipton had evidence," Mrs. Jeffries suggested.

"That's possible," he replied. "But I can't think what sort of evidence there could be. The chief inspector hadn't even had time to read the postmortem report."

"Have you had a look at it, sir?" she asked. She thought of the handprints on Provost's body and wondered whether the solicitor could have found out about them.

"It hasn't been sent over from the Westminster Division as yet." He took another sip. "It was one of their lads that spotted the body, so the report was sent to the Westminster superintendent first, and he'll send it along to Walton Street station. The chief inspector told me I was to report there tomorrow morning."

"How did Mr. Tipton find out about Provost's death so quickly?" Mrs. Jeffries knew that establishing a sequence of time for the events of the case was very important. They had learned about the murder this afternoon, but only because Dr. Bosworth was the police surgeon on the case. How had the dead man's lawyer heard about it so soon?

"When the police went to the Provost house to inform everyone of his death, the housekeeper went along to the solicitor's office straightaway. For some reason, she didn't believe the death to be an accident, either."

"I take it Mr. Provost doesn't have family?" She was well aware that Provost had no relatives, but she had to pretend she knew nothing of the matter. "I mean, otherwise, wouldn't the police have spoken to them rather than a housekeeper?"

"You're quite correct: He was a widower."

"And had his housekeeper been with him for a long period of time?" She smiled. "I'm only asking because her certainty that his death wasn't an accident implies she must have known the man for some years."

"I don't really know," the inspector admitted. "But your supposition sounds quite logical."

"So you have two people, both of whom knew the victim reasonably well, who, immediately upon learning that Provost had drowned, came to the conclusion that the death wasn't an accident," she mused. "That's most peculiar; don't you think so, sir?" She held her breath, hoping he'd get her point.

"Hmm, yes, now that you've put it that way. It does make one think that the people who knew Provost the best seemed to have reason to think his life was in danger." The inspector took another sip from his glass. "In this case, both Provost's housekeeper and his lawyer are convinced someone murdered the man. Obviously, they must have an idea why someone would want him dead. Well, this is certainly a change from my usual cases."

"In what way, sir?" she asked conversationally. She wondered why Tipton hadn't shared his opinion about the reason for Provost's death with Chief Inspector Barrows. Or, if he had, Barrows hadn't mentioned it to Inspector Witherspoon.

He gave her a wry smile. "Oh, come now, Mrs. Jeffries. Most of the time, when I question the victim's family or friends, they insist he or she didn't have an enemy in the world."

"That's true, sir." She laughed. "Perhaps knowing right from the start that the poor man was in fear of his life will be of help to you."

"I certainly hope so," he replied. But his smile had faded, and now he stared at her with a discouraged, mournful expression. "Honestly, I don't know why I always seem to get the murder cases that are going to be difficult."

"Because those are the ones you're best at solving, sir." She could see he needed a bit of encouragement. Witherspoon never thought he was up to the task at hand. "But you don't know that this will be at all difficult, sir."

"It will be," he said flatly. "Obviously, there's already something odd about the case. Tipton believed Provost was murdered, but for some reason, he didn't tell Chief Inspector Barrows what leads him to think so."

As she'd just thought the very same thing, she looked away for a brief moment. "Perhaps Tipton's goal today was merely to get the police to take the matter seriously. Perhaps he was hoping you'd be put on the case. After all, sir, you are rather well-known in legal circles." She was grasping at straws, but she wanted to bolster his self-confidence.

"That's very kind of you to say, Mrs. Jeffries, but sometimes I feel rather at a loss," he admitted with a shake of his head. "As far as I can tell, Provost ended up in the Thames in the middle of the night, and there are no witnesses. I'm not even sure where to begin."

She forced herself to laugh. "Now, sir, you mustn't tease me. You're just trying to see whether I've been paying attention to your methods. Well, I'll have you know that I am an excellent student. You'll start where you always do, sir: with the victim, Michael Provost."

"With the victim," the inspector repeated. His expression brightened considerably. "Yes, yes, of course."

Sometimes he needed more than general encouragement: Sometimes when he was tired, he tended to get a bit muddled. This was one of those times. She understood the feeling; sometimes she felt muddled as well. "Are you going to start with his servants or with his firm?" She knew perfectly well what his answer would be.

"I'll begin with his household." Wither-spoon got to his feet. "After all, it was his

51

housekeeper who set things in motion. Besides, as Provost was a widower, his staff will probably be able to shed quite a bit of light on his life, and of course that will be the key to the matter. I do feel so much better now, Mrs. Jeffries. Sometimes just a bit of a chat to clarify my ideas can make a world of difference."

"Yes, sir, I'm sure it can."

"Mmm . . ." He started toward the hallway. "I can smell Mrs. Goodge's hot pot from here."

Mrs. Jeffries was up very early the next morning. There was much to be done before they could properly begin their investigation. Wiggins had slipped out before breakfast and gone to Luty Belle Crookshank's home in Knightsbridge to inform her and her butler, Hatchet, that they had a case. Luty Belle and Hatchet were special friends of the household, and they insisted on being included in all the inspector's homicides.

Luty had been a witness in one of their very first cases. As she was both smart and observant, she'd soon figured out what the household was up to as they'd surreptitiously questioned every housemaid and grocer's clerk in her neighborhood. Shortly after that murder had been solved, Luty had been faced with a pressing problem of her own that she hadn't wanted to take to the police. She'd asked the household for help, and they'd taken care of the matter. Ever since, she and Hatchet had participated in all the inspector's cases.

Smythe had gone out early to Howard's to see to it that the inspector's horses and carriage were at the ready in case they were needed. Betsy had flown through the downstairs rooms, dusting, polishing, and cleaning in short order.

The kitchen already smelled of vanilla and cinnamon as Mrs. Goodge began baking for her sources, and Mrs. Jeffries had done her part by continuing to question the inspector about the case as he ate his bacon and eggs.

By the time the inspector walked out the front door, everyone was at the ready for their first meeting. Betsy had just put away the last of the dishes when the back door opened and footsteps pounded up the long hallway.

It was Wiggins. Right behind him was a tiny white-haired woman wearing a bright green cloak with a fur collar and an emerald bonnet trimmed with peacock feathers and lace. She carried a matching fur muff. A tall, dignified white-haired man, wearing a black greatcoat and carrying a black silk top hat, brought up the rear.

"Good, you're just in time." Mrs. Jeffries gestured for them to take their seats. "The inspector has just gone."

"We got here as soon as we could." Luty slipped into her usual spot. "But the traffic was awful. Swan to goodness, it woulda been faster to walk rather than take the carriage."

"Nonsense, madam." Hatchet took off his coat and nodded a greeting at the others. "We got here very quickly. You're merely impatient to get started. Besides, the ride over gave us a chance to learn the details of the case from young Wiggins." Hatchet sat down next to Luty.

"We don't know that much as yet," Wiggins murmured.

"But we will," the cook said stoutly. "We've got a name and address. That's all we need."

Mrs. Jeffries waited patiently while everyone got settled before she spoke. "I take it everyone is fully aware of the few facts we have about this case." She looked expectantly at Luty and Hatchet.

"Unless young Wiggins left out some pertinent details," Hatchet said, "I think we know as much as the rest of you."

"I told 'em everything," Wiggins said.

"Even the bits you got from the inspector last night."

She'd given the others a full report over breakfast. "Good. Then we can get started right away. I think I'll go along to St. Thomas' and see what else I can learn from Dr. Bosworth about our Provost. Now that the doctor's had a decent night's sleep, he might be able to remember a few more details about him."

"Provost, Provost," Luty repeated. "There's something about that name that sounds so familiar, but I can't for the life of me think where I've heard it before. Oh well, I don't expect it makes any difference. The fellow was rich and owned a successful business; that means someone I know will know something about him. I'll start makin' the rounds of my social contacts today and seeing what's what."

"I believe I'll do the same, madam." Hatchet grinned cheerfully. "You're not the only one with social contacts."

Luty snorted derisively. The two of them were fiercely competitive with each other when it came to getting clues on a case. Luty knew aristocrats, captains of industry, politicians, and most of the City's bankers. She also had a string of solicitors at her beck and call.

Hatchet smiled serenely. He had an odd assortment of connections all over London. He knew artists and actors, butlers, builders, tradesmen, and merchant seamen. He also had some sources he absolutely refused to mention. But he always contributed his fair share of information and took a particular delight when he managed to beat his employer to some really good tidbit.

"I'll be off to Provost's neighborhood and see what I can get from the local shopkeepers," Betsy said. "I mean, there's no point in sitting here talking when we can be out and about."

"You're quite right, Betsy," Mrs. Jeffries agreed.

Betsy stood up and gave Smythe a quick smile. She hoped he wouldn't want to come with her. Since they'd worked out their differences and decided to go ahead with their wedding, he'd dogged her heels worse than Fred trailed after Wiggins! She loved Smythe dearly, but honestly, if he didn't let her have just a bit of breathing room to herself, she thought she might go stark raving mad.

Their wedding had originally been planned for the past summer. But only a few days before the nuptials, Smythe had been called away to Australia, and had left her. He'd come back, of course, and she understood that he'd had to go; a man's life had depended on him. But it had hurt her deeply, and when he'd returned, just before Christmas, they'd been tossed smack into another of the inspector's cases. Even though they'd realized they still loved each other, sometimes she felt a bit smothered by his constant attention.

But, for once, he didn't leap to his feet. He simply returned her smile and stayed in his chair. Betsy didn't waste any time. She hurried to the coat tree and grabbed her heavy overcoat, hat, and gloves in one fell swoop. She snatched her shopping basket off the sideboard, waved at the others, and dashed for the back hall. But she wasn't quite fast enough to make a complete escape.

" 'Ang on, Betsy." Wiggins jumped up. "We can take the omnibus together. I'll 'ave a go at seein' if I can find any of Provost's servants."

Betsy stopped at the kitchen door and stifled a heavy sigh. Blast, she'd almost made it. She would have loved to have some time to herself, but she wouldn't hurt Wiggins' feelings for the world. "All right, but hurry up. I don't want to miss the next omnibus."

Smythe waited till he heard the back door

close before he rose. "I'll be off, then," he said. He knew quite well that Betsy was getting a bit fed up with his hovering. He knew he was being silly, but he'd almost lost her once, and since he'd returned, he'd not been certain he'd ever convince her to forgive him. But she had, and he'd spent the time since then hanging on to her skirts. He'd come to his senses now, and he knew how to step back a bit. "I'm going to take a walk down to the river. Maybe I can find someone who saw or heard something the night before last."

"Do you think that's likely?" Luty asked curiously. "It was cold and wet that night. Who'd have been out in that kind of weather?"

Smythe shrugged his big shoulders as he stepped over and pulled his coat off the hook. "Provost was. Maybe someone else was takin' a walk as well." He suspected that Luty was correct, and he'd not find a soul who'd willingly gone for a stroll along the Thames on a miserable winter's night. But it never hurt to look. Besides, he had other reasons for heading toward the river. He had plans for his own investigation, which the others didn't need to know about.

Shortly afterwards, the first of Mrs. Goodge's sources arrived at the back door just as Luty, Hatchet, and Mrs. Jeffries left.

Michael Provost had lived in a five-story gray stone town house. Constable Barnes, a seasoned old copper with a ruddy complexion and a headful of gray hair under his helmet, climbed the three steps leading to the front door and thumped the knocker against the painted black wood. He worked almost exclusively with Inspector Witherspoon these days, and was glad they were back on a decent murder and off that miserable fraud case.

The door opened, and a middle-aged woman stuck her head out. Short and plump, she wore a black wool dress and a white apron. She glared at them through a pair of blue eyes. "It's about time," she snapped. She opened the door wider, stepped back, and waved them inside. "It took you long enough to get here. Quit your dawdling, now. We're all ready for you, and frankly, we've been waiting for ages."

"I'm terribly sorry." Witherspoon followed the constable into the foyer. "I'd no idea you were waiting . . ."

She cut him off and slammed the door hard enough to make him jump. "I'm Hazel Corwin, Mr. Provost's housekeeper. Come along, then." She turned and charged down the hallway. "We're all downstairs."

Surprised, the inspector looked at Barnes. But the constable only shrugged and fell in step behind her. Witherspoon hurried after them. He tried to get a look at his surroundings as he went down the corridor.

Over the course of his many cases, he'd found that one could learn quite a bit by paying close attention to the homes of both the victim and the suspects. But Hazel Corwin was moving so fast that he almost had to run to keep up with her. As he passed the open double doors of the drawing room, Witherspoon glanced in, but all he could see was that the walls appeared to be painted a dark green and the window shades had been drawn.

They followed her to the end of the corridor, down the stairs, and into the servants' dining hall. Three women, two of them wearing maids' uniforms and one with a cook's cap on her head, were sitting on the far side of a long butler's table.

"The police have finally arrived." The housekeeper shot them an irritated glance and pointed at two empty chairs opposite the servants. "Please take a seat," she ordered as she slipped into the spot at the head of the table.

"I'm Inspector Gerald Witherspoon, and

this is Constable Barnes." Witherspoon introduced them as he sat down. The constable nodded politely but remained standing. The inspector continued, "If you don't mind, Mrs. Corwin, I'd prefer to take your statements separately. Is there another room the constable can use?"

"There's the butler's pantry. It's just next door," she replied. "He can use that, but I warn you, the place isn't very clean. It doesn't get used much, so it's apt to be dusty. Mind where you sit."

The woman wearing the cook's cap got up and said, "If you've no objection, Mrs. Corwin, I'll go first. I want to get back to my kitchen before that tart has to come out of the oven." The housekeeper nodded permission, and the cook turned to Barnes. "I'm Mrs. Richardson. Come along, then, Constable. It's this way." She led him toward the back hallway.

The two maids looked uncertainly at each other and then at the housekeeper. She smiled at them. "You two run along to the kitchen and make us some tea; I'll call you when the police are ready for you."

As soon as the door closed behind the women, Hazel Corwin closed her eyes for a brief moment, sighed, and said, "This has been a dreadful time, Inspector. Absolutely dreadful."

"I assure you, ma'am, we're going to do everything possible to get to the bottom of this matter," he replied. No doubt the servants, as well as being upset over the death of their employer, were also very worried about what was going to happen to them.

"I should hope so," she snapped. "If your lot had been doing their jobs properly, he'd still be alive."

"I'm sorry?" Witherspoon was bewildered. "Doing our jobs properly? I'm not certain I take your meaning, Mrs. Corwin."

"Don't be dense, man." Her eyes narrowed angrily. "If you'd responded to his letters, he'd have not put himself in harm's way, and that means he'd not be dead now."

"What letters?" the inspector asked. "I've no idea what you're talking about, ma'am. I never received a letter from Mr. Provost."

He jerked in surprise as she slammed her fist against the tabletop. "He's been sending the police letters regularly ever since he started his investigation. So don't tell me you never received a letter, because I know you or someone else at Scotland Yard bloomin' well did. I saw them myself. He kept you fully informed about everything he found out, and you did nothing, absolutely nothing, and now he's been murdered. You ought to be ashamed of yourself," she yelled.

"Please calm yourself, ma'am," Witherspoon urged. "I can't help you if all you do is shout at me."

She flattened her hands on the table, took a deep breath, and relaxed her hunched shoulders.

He measured his words carefully before he spoke. He had no idea what on earth the woman was talking about. "Mrs. Corwin, you are understandably upset, but I assure you, ma'am, I've never seen a letter from your Mr. Provost. Do you recall precisely where he sent his letters? Did he mail them directly to New Scotland Yard?"

"I didn't look at the address. Why should I? I just know he's been sending them off to the police regular-like once a week for ages now. That means someone knew he was putting himself in danger."

"Mrs. Corwin, I want to understand. But as I know nothing about the contents of these letters, I'll have to rely on you for information. What was Mr. Provost investigating?"

"He was trying to find out what happened to his friend Ernie Grigson. Mr. Provost was sure he'd been murdered."

"Who is Ernie Grigson?" Witherspoon

asked softly. He hoped he could remember everything.

"I just told you: He was Mr. Provost's friend. They'd known each other for ages. The two of them were at medical school in Edinburgh together."

"Mr. Provost was a doctor?"

"He qualified, but he never practiced." She sank back against her chair. "His father died, and he took over the business. Mr. Grigson never even qualified; he left before taking his exams."

"But the two men stayed friends?"

"Yes, they were both in business," she explained. "Mr. Grigson owned a pub close by here. It's the Iron Anchor, down at the end of Tadema Road."

Witherspoon was getting very confused, and when that happened, he knew to go back to the basics, to establish the facts and let the complicated bits work themselves out later. "Weren't you alarmed when Mr. Provost didn't come home the night before last?" he asked.

"But I didn't know that until the morning," she replied. "Mr. Provost didn't like the staff to wait up for him. So as soon as the evening chores were finished, everyone went off duty or up to their beds. It was only when I sent May up to fetch Mr.

Provost for breakfast that we realized he'd not come home. His bed hadn't been slept in."

"What did you do then?" Witherspoon asked. "If you knew he was in danger because of this investigation he'd started, then why didn't you go to the police straightaway?"

"Because the police got here first," she replied. "Mr. Provost wasn't an early riser. He didn't need to be; he owned his own business. So I didn't send May upstairs for him until half past eight. The police arrived just after that with the news of his death."

"Mr. Provost owned a medical supply company?" Witherspoon nodded encouragingly.

"A very successful company," she added quickly. "And I've no idea what's going to happen to the firm now that he's gone."

"I expect you're concerned about what's going to happen to all of you as well," the inspector said sympathetically.

"Not really," Mrs. Corwin replied. "Mr. Provost told us ages ago that both the cook and I needn't worry about our futures. He provided for us in his will."

Witherspoon made a mental note to be sure to ask the solicitor precisely how much Provost was going to leave his servants.

Inheriting money was a good motive for murder. "What about the maids?"

"They're both young, and they haven't been here very long," Mrs. Corwin replied. "May is engaged to be married, so she'd be leaving in any case, and Hilda is a fully trained housemaid. She'll not have any trouble finding another position. But knowing Mr. Provost as I did, I'm sure he made some provision for them. He was a good man." She blinked hard and looked away. "If it hadn't been for that Mr. Arthur Conan Doyle and that detective of his, Mr. Sherlock Holmes, Mr. Provost would still be alive."

Downstairs, Barnes was having an almost identical conversation with Mrs. Richardson. "So you're saying that Mr. Provost was trying to find out what happened to a friend of his, someone named Ernie Grigson, who'd disappeared?" he asked cautiously.

He and Mrs. Richardson were seated at a scratched, rickety table in a room that had once been a butler's pantry but now appeared to be a combination dry larder and storage room. Old-fashioned glassware and odd pieces of mismatched china filled the shelves along one wall, while the shelves on the other side held various-sized tins of flour, sugar, salt, and cocoa. Dust was everywhere, and if he'd been so inclined, he could have written his notes on the tabletop instead of in his little brown book.

"That's right." She nodded agreeably. "He kept trying to get the police to take an interest in the matter, but they never responded to his letters. Of course, it wasn't my place to say anything, but I did think it a bit foolish for him to put himself in harm's way like that." Her eyes filled with tears. She pulled a handkerchief out of her pocket and dabbed at her cheeks. "Poor Mr. Provost. Now he's dead."

"Please, ma'am, don't upset yourself. We'll do everything we can to find out what happened to your Mr. Provost."

"But I've just told you what happened. He was murdered. I blame that Sherlock Holmes fellow. Mr. Provost would never have taken it into his head to go about asking questions if he'd not been such an admirer of that Mr. Holmes."

"Sherlock Holmes?" Barnes repeated. "You mean the detective in the magazine stories?"

"That's right." Mrs. Richardson nodded emphatically. "Mr. Provost couldn't wait for his copy of *The Strand* every month. He used to come flying in the front door on the day it was due to arrive, demanding to know if it was here. If it wasn't for that Holmes fellow, he'd never have decided to play at being a detective. Magazines ought to be careful what they publish. It can put strange ideas in some people's minds."

Barnes sighed inwardly. According to the cook, Michael Provost had been actively pursuing some kind of detective work on his own when he was killed. But regardless of what Provost had or hadn't been investigating, Barnes needed to find out some basic information. "Did you see Mr. Provost at all on the evening he died?"

She shook her head. "No, he went to his club that night to play whist. He played there on Tuesday and Thursday nights. Now, mind you, I don't approve of card playing in general, but Mr. Provost was ever so pleased when he was accepted into his gentlemen's club." She took a deep breath and wiped at her eyes again. "It's really too sad. He was such a decent man."

"Whist," Barnes repeated. "Did he play for money?" Some people gambled quite heavily on whist.

"I'm sure I've no idea." She sniffed disapprovingly to show that even considering such a possibility was beneath her. "But if you're thinking he got himself into debt and then jumped into the Thames to end it all, you're sadly mistaken. He'd plenty of money; I know that for a fact."

"He discussed his finances with you?" Barnes stared at her skeptically.

"Don't be daft; of course he didn't. But I overheard him talking to Mr. Tipton last month about his will, about wanting to change it to give an extra thousand pounds to the Anti-Slavery Society. Well, he'd not be wanting to make a change like that if he was concerned about money, would he?"

Barnes wasn't sure how to respond to that comment, so he simply asked the next question that popped into his head. "Did Mr. Provost have any relatives?" He might as well try to begin sorting out who was going to benefit from the dead man's estate.

"Not really," she replied. "He had no children, and his wife died years ago. He never remarried. He'd no brothers or sisters that I know of, just a few cousins, and they emigrated to New Zealand when he was a boy."

"I see," Barnes murmured. "Which gentlemen's club did he join?"

"The Wentworth Club."

"I know the place." Barnes nodded in encouragement. The Wentworth wasn't the most exclusive club in London, but it wasn't one of the lesser lights, either. "How long had he been going there?"

"Let's see now. I believe since the autumn. Yes, that's right: He started this past September. At first we were all very pleased, but then I realized he'd not joined because he had any real intentions of making friends."

Barnes looked up from his notebook, his policeman's senses on full alert. "I'm not sure I understand."

Mrs. Richardson looked at Barnes as if he was dimwitted. "Haven't you been listening to a thing I've told you? He only joined that club because of his investigation. He seemed to think Mr. Grigson's disappearance had something to do with someone at the Wentworth Club."

"He told you that?" Barnes asked. He hoped the inspector was having a better time of it than he was.

"Of course not," she replied. "I overheard him talking to Mr. Tipton."

"His solicitor?"

"They were having dinner together out on the terrace during that warm spell we had in October." She pointed to her left. "The girls were late coming to get the sorbet, so I took it out to the gentlemen myself. That's when I heard him tellin' Mr. Tipton that

70

joining the Wentworth Club would help him find out what happened to Mr. Grigson."

"Surely his solicitor didn't approve of such an action," Barnes said.

She shrugged. "I don't know. I went back to the kitchen."

The constable thought for a moment. "Do you know when this Mr. Grigson disappeared?"

She thought for a moment. "I'm not certain of the exact date. But I know it was sometime last summer."

"When was the last time you saw Mr. Provost?"

"At breakfast day before yesterday." Her eyes filled with tears again. "I fixed him bacon and eggs."

"Did he usually come home for supper on the nights he went to his club?" Barnes asked softly.

"He did. But that day he sent Mrs. Corwin a message saying that he had some business to take care of, and he'd eat at a restaurant and then go straight to the Wentworth."

Betsy stood on the corner of Fulham Road and stared at the row of shops on the other side. There was a draper's shop and an ironmonger's, and next to that was a chemist's.

The chemist's was one of those new places with big front windows, large enough that she could see the place was filled with customers. She turned. On this side of the road was a grocer, a butcher's shop, and a greengrocer's stall. She walked toward the nearest establishment, the butcher's, and peeked through the window. But it was full, too. There were four women waiting to be served.

Betsy had learned that picking the time you went in and started asking questions was important. Even a chatterbox of a shopkeeper wouldn't speak freely if he or she had a line of customers wanting to spend their money. Betsy continued walking, passing the greengrocer's and moving toward the grocer's shop. She stopped, peeked through the window, and saw that there was only one woman in front of the counter. Betsy stepped inside.

The clerk, a young man, glanced at her as she entered, and then turned his attention back to his customer. Betsy silently prayed that no one else would come into the shop as she waited to be served. Getting information out of young men was much easier when she was on her own with them.

"Thank you, madam," the clerk said as the other woman put her purchases into her basket and left. He smiled politely at Betsy. "May I help you?"

Betsy returned his smile with one of her own. The lad was barely old enough to shave; he couldn't be more than nineteen. "I'd like a box of salt and a tin of drinking chocolate, please." She'd picked a few items off Mrs. Goodge's provision list before their meeting this morning, so she knew the household needed these things.

"Certainly, miss." The clerk turned and walked down the long row of shelves behind the counter, stopping for the chocolate first and then moving a few feet farther and grabbing a small yellow box of salt. He came back and placed them on the counter. "Will there be anything else, miss?"

Betsy put her basket on the counter, gave him another smile, and then sighed prettily. "If I might be so bold — I really shouldn't ask such a thing, but you seem like a nice, helpful young man, and if my mistress finds out I've lost the man's address, she might sack me."

"I'd be pleased to help you in any way that I could," the clerk said quickly. "Ask whatever you like."

She reached into the pocket of her jacket and pulled out an envelope. "My mistress gave me this note to take to her friend, a

Mr. Provost. He lives around here somewhere, but for the life of me, I've forgotten his address. I was wondering if you might know where he lived. It's awfully important that I deliver this to him." Of course the envelope was empty — she'd borrowed it that morning from the inspector's study — but she'd learned to be prepared.

"You mean Mr. Michael Provost. He lives just around the corner at number eight, Maude Grove. But he'll not be home this time of day: The man works. He owns some sort of firm that makes medical equipment. He's one of our best customers."

"Thank you ever so much." She smiled broadly. "I've no idea what's in this envelope, but my mistress said it was ever so important that it get delivered today." Blast, the lad obviously hadn't heard that Provost was dead. She usually got much better information when that kind of bad news had spread about the neighborhood. Whether anyone would admit it or not, people loved to gossip about the dead. Betsy hoped the clerk would keep talking.

"I'm sure it's very important," he replied seriously.

"Oh, it is." Betsy tucked the envelope back in her pocket. "Mr. Provost sounds like a very important person."

"Will there be anything else?" the clerk asked.

"No, thank you. I must be off to Mr. Provost's." She took her time paying for the goods and actually managed to mention the dead man's name two more times. But the clerk didn't take the bait. Finally, when it was impossible to dawdle any longer, she picked up her basket, smiled graciously, and headed for the door.

Her smile disappeared as soon as she stepped onto the street. What on earth was wrong with that stupid clerk? She didn't trust someone who didn't like to gossip. It simply wasn't natural.

Wiggins kept a sharp eye out as he crossed the road and started down the pavement on Maude Grove. He didn't want to run into Inspector Witherspoon or any of the other constables who knew him by sight. The neighborhood was quite posh, with big five- and six-story gray town houses on each side of the wide road.

Just then a hansom pulled up and stopped in front of the Provost house. Wiggins dropped to one knee and pretended to tie his shoelace. He saw a tall, dark-haired man, wearing an overcoat and carrying a brief-case, get out of the cab, pay the driver, and then hurry toward the Provost residence. Fearing that he might be noticed or, worse, that the inspector might be near the front door, Wiggins got up and moved quickly toward the corner, all the while watching over his shoulder.

Still craning his neck, he rounded the corner and ran straight into a young woman carrying a basket. "Watch where you're going," the girl cried as he slammed into her. She scrambled to keep the basket from falling.

Wiggins, trying to help, leaned forward and grabbed at the handle just as she moved in the same direction, causing their heads to smack together with a loud crack.

She jerked backward with enough force to lose her balance, which caused her to stumble. She flung her arms out and waved them frantically as she tried to steady herself.

Wiggins, again trying to help, leapt toward her, meaning to grab an arm to steady her, but his aim was off and he pushed at her shoulder instead, knocking her completely off her feet. She landed on her backside with a loud thud.

"Oh God, miss, I'm so sorry . . ." He leaned down to try to help her up.

She scrambled in the other direction, trying to get away from him. "Are you mad? Stay away from me."

"I'm ever so sorry," he began again. This time he had enough sense just to stand there. Aside from knocking the poor girl over, he'd obviously frightened her as well. "This is all my fault. I wasn't watching where I was going. I'm so very sorry."

"Of course it's your fault, you big oaf." The girl got to her feet, glaring at him as she stood up.

Maybe he hadn't frightened her after all. She looked more angry than anything else. He noticed that her basket was still on the ground, but he'd learned his lesson. "May I pick up your basket for you, miss? Please, I feel so awful about knocking you down."

She stared at him for a long moment, and he noticed she was very pretty, with brown eyes, porcelain skin, and dark hair tucked up under a gray hat. She wore a tight, well-fitted black jacket over a high-collared white blouse and a long gray skirt. Her clothes were nicely tailored, marking her as more than a servant girl on her day out. Yet she carried a shopping basket.

"Yes, you can pick up the basket. Mind you don't drop it. It's been bashed about enough as it is."

Wiggins lifted it off the pavement and

handed it to her. "Please, miss, I'm so sorry. I do hope I haven't hurt you."

A slight smile curved her lips. "Nothing's hurt but my pride. I'm sorry I was so angry: It was an accident. But you should pay more attention to where you're going."

He grinned, relieved that she was alright and that she was in the mood to chat. "Oh, I will, miss. May I be so bold as to offer you a cup of tea?" He whipped off his own cap as he made the offer. "There's a Lyons Tea Shop not far from here, and it's a perfectly respectable establishment. Please, miss. I'd like to make it up to you for knocking you down."

She laughed. "I don't even know you."

"I'm Wiggins." He bowed slightly. "And I work for a police inspector." He surprised himself by telling the truth. Usually, when he was "on the hunt," so to speak, he never used his real name, and he rarely admitted that his employer was a policeman. But there was something about this girl that loosened his tongue.

She studied him for a moment. "I was on my way to do a bit of shopping, but I could do with a cup of tea. My name is Catherine Shelby."

Wiggins let out a breath he didn't know he'd been holding, and took her arm. "It's this way, miss. Just up the road a bit. Do you live around here?"

"Yes, I do," she replied. "Do you?"

"I live in Kensington, just off Holland Park Road," he said, still telling the truth.

"And what do you do, Wiggins?" she asked.

"Oh, right now I'm a footman," he said. "But one of these days I'm going to be a private inquiry agent. Either that or a novelist."

And he was still telling the truth.

CHAPTER 3

Smythe walked into the Dirty Duck Pub and stopped just inside the doorway, giving his eyes time to adjust to the dim light. As it was only a few minutes past opening time, the place wasn't as crowded as usual. A couple of day laborers stood at the bar; a young bootblack nursing a pint sat on one of the benches running along the side wall; and all of the tables, save one, were empty. The colorfully dressed man at the one occupied table was just the person he'd come to see.

Blimpey Groggins, a portly middle-aged man with ginger-colored hair, a ruddy complexion, and a toothy smile, spotted Smythe. Blimpey raised his glass and waved him over. He was dressed in his usual business attire: a brown checked suit and a graying white shirt. On his head sat a grimy porkpie hat of indeterminate color, and a bright red scarf was wound around his neck.

He wore the same clothes winter or summer, rain or shine, regardless of what the temperature might be.

"You're right on time," Blimpey said as Smythe slipped onto the hard oak bench. "I 'ad a bit of a wager with myself whether you'd be 'ere this morning or wait until the afternoon."

Smythe laughed. "So you've already 'eard. Good, it'll save me time having to explain everything."

He wasn't in the least surprised that Groggins knew about Michael Provost's death. He knew everything that went on in London. That was why Smythe had come to see him. On a number of their previous cases, Smythe had used Blimpey's services. He charged a pretty penny, but he was worth every bit of it.

Groggins had started out in life as a thief, with second-story breaking and entering as his specialty. But as he was considerably brighter than the average crook, he quickly realized that thieving, especially second-story work, was exceedingly dangerous. He possessed a superb memory and the ability to connect divergent facts and come to useful conclusions, and it soon became apparent to Blimpey that he could make far more money buying and selling information than risking life and liberty climbing drainpipes or trees.

Blimpey now had sources at the Old Bailey, the magistrate courts, the police stations, the financial centers in the City, every shipping line, and all of the insurance companies. He paid his informants well and gave them a good discount if they ever had need of the services he offered. His clients ranged from banks seeking information about their general managers to thieves wanting character references for which fence was the most reliable.

But Blimpey had standards. He wouldn't trade in information that caused physical harm to a woman or a child, and he wouldn't get involved in criminal turf wars or supremacy battles. He considered violence both foolish and bad for business.

"I've already got my people workin' on the matter," Blimpey said. "But it's goin' to take a few days. From what I hear, your Mr. Provost lived a very quiet life." He crossed his arms over his chest and frowned. "But there's something about that name that's naggin' at me, something I heard. Mind you, I can't for the life of me recall what it was, but it'll come to me eventually. It always does."

"I hope so." Smythe laughed. "Knowing

things is how you make your livin'.""

"Have you got any other names?"

"Not yet," Smythe replied. "But in the meantime, why don't you have a look at his business. Maybe one of his employees had it in for 'im. The place is over on . . ."

"I know where it is," Blimpey interrupted, "and I've got someone on it as we speak."

"Good. I'll come back in a day or two with the other names that are connected to the case." Smythe started to get up, and then stopped as Blimpey waved him back to his seat.

"Have you and your lady set the date yet?" Blimpey asked.

"Sometime in the autumn," Smythe replied. He normally wouldn't discuss something as personal as his relationship with Betsy, but as he'd helped Blimpey and his wife get to the altar, he didn't mind answering the question. "We've not decided exactly when, but it might be sometime in October. Betsy is right partial to that month."

He wished Betsy would set a proper date, but every time he brought up the subject, she shied away from that final detail, and he wasn't willing to press her too hard. Not just yet.

"It's a good month to wed." Blimpey nodded wisely. "A man should be married,

Smythe. It makes him complete. Besides, if you're married, you've got someone to take care of you when you get old and feeble."

"I'm not marryin' Betsy to have her take care of me," Smythe protested. Blimpey had hit a sore spot; he was sensitive about his age in relation to Betsy.

"Of course not." Blimpey grinned broadly. "But it's a nice benefit, isn't it."

"I would have liked to have had a word with Mr. Tipton," Witherspoon said to Barnes. "It's too bad he was in such a hurry." They were in a cab heading for Provost's firm.

"He was due to consult in chambers, sir," Barnes said. "He'd only stopped by the house to give Mrs. Corwin enough money to pay the household accounts."

"Still, I should have liked to ask him what he knew about this other matter," Witherspoon said thoughtfully.

"Ernie Grigson's disappearance?"

"That's right. I suspect the real reason that Tipton went to see the chief inspector as soon as he heard about Provost's death was because he was well aware of what Provost was doing," Witherspoon murmured. "As a matter of fact, considering Mrs. Richardson's statement, I think we can assume that Tipton knew all about Mr.

84

Provost's investigation. In which case, you've got to ask yourself if his eagerness to get away from us is because he knows something more, and he didn't want me asking him too many questions before he had time to think the matter through."

Barnes was surprised. It wasn't like Witherspoon to be so suspicious. "Mr. Tipton said his appointment was urgent and that he couldn't be late. Mr. Provost wasn't his only client, sir. I don't think he was trying to put us off or be evasive."

"Hmm . . . yes, perhaps you're right." Witherspoon sighed and closed his eyes briefly. "I'm being fanciful; it's just that this whole matter is very peculiar."

"Aren't they always, sir." Barnes leaned forward to see where they were. By his calculations, they should be close to their destination.

"Honestly, Constable, some people have more imagination than they have good sense." Witherspoon grabbed for the handhold as the hansom cab hit a particularly bad hole in the road. "What on earth did Michael Provost think he was going to accomplish by making inquiries on his own? Amateurs simply don't know how to conduct a proper investigation."

"Both Mrs. Corwin and Mrs. Richardson

told me that Provost had tried to get the police interested. He'd been sending them letters all along," Barnes said. "Besides, sir, it makes our task less difficult. If he was murdered because he was asking questions about Ernie Grigson's disappearance, we've got a motive. Maybe he was getting too close to finding out the truth about what happened to Grigson."

"If your theory is correct, Constable, then we've got two crimes to solve, not one," Witherspoon said glumly. "But, nonetheless, I think our first task is to concentrate on our current problem."

The hansom slowed and pulled over to the curb. Witherspoon stepped out and Barnes followed, stopping just long enough to pay the driver.

Provost Surgical Instruments and Medical Supplies, Ltd., was housed in a two-story brown brick building just down from the Royal Free Hospital. They stood on the pavement and stared across Gray's Inn Road at the business that no longer had an owner. The structure was in excellent condition. The bricks were clean, the signs neatly lettered, and the black shutters along the front windows of the showroom freshly painted. The showroom itself was dark, but the workshop was very busy.

Through the open double doors, Witherspoon and Barnes could see several rows of men sitting on high stools, hunched over worktables. Another man stacked wooden boxes by the entrance as an empty delivery wagon backed onto the cobblestone drive.

A man wearing a long cream-colored cotton duster emerged from the shop and began speaking to the driver of the wagon.

"Mr. Provost's death doesn't seem to have stopped his business from operating," Barnes murmured as they crossed the road.

The man in the duster spotted them coming, waved to the driver, and then headed in their direction. "Good day, sirs." He held out his hand as they approached. "I'm Angus McCracken. I'm the general manager." He was a tall man with blue eyes, thinning reddish hair, and a huge mustache.

"Good day. I'm Inspector Witherspoon, and this is Constable Barnes." He shook McCracken's hand as he spoke. "We're here to speak to you about Mr. Provost."

"Of course you are, God rest his soul." McCracken nodded his head. "Mr. Tipton stopped by to tell us what happened. The men are upset. Mr. Provost was a fine man and a good guv."

"I'm surprised you didn't close out of respect for your employer," Witherspoon remarked.

"It's because we respected the man that we've kept workin'." McCracken's eyes narrowed, but he kept his tone civil. "We've orders to fill, Inspector. Mr. Provost wouldn't have wanted even one order sitting in the warehouse if a hospital or clinic was depending on gettin' it today. This is important work we do, and he'd be the first to tell you that."

Witherspoon smiled faintly. He'd learned what he needed to know. Mrs. Corwin had been telling the truth when she'd said that Provost's workers had admired and respected him. "I meant no offense, Mr. McCracken."

"None taken, Inspector." McCracken turned and walked through the doors into the warehouse proper. "Come along, gentlemen, let's go upstairs to the office. We can talk there."

The men on the shop floor openly watched them as they crossed the cavernous room to a set of narrow stairs. McCracken took the steps two at a time, with the constable and Witherspoon following at a more sedate pace. When they reached the top, the inspector paused to catch his breath.

They'd come out into a room with a row

of desks along the windows. At each one, a clerk sat staring curiously at the two policemen. "We ship our goods all over the world," McCracken said by way of explanation. "And we need a lot of clerks."

"Yes, I'm sure you do," Witherspoon murmured.

McCracken walked toward an open door on the other side of the room, but then he stopped, turned to the staff, and said, "This is Inspector Witherspoon and Constable Barnes. They're investigating Mr. Provost's death. Please give them your full and truthful cooperation if they should have need to speak to you." He then continued toward the office.

Surprised, the inspector glanced at Barnes, who shrugged faintly in return as they followed McCracken. Both men were taken aback by McCracken's statement. In most of their previous cases, very few people had ever encouraged their staffs to speak candidly with the police.

"Please make yourselves comfortable, gentlemen," McCracken invited as soon as they were inside. He pointed to two wooden chairs in front of the desk.

They did as he bid and waited politely until he'd settled himself in his own seat. Witherspoon noticed that McCracken's blue eyes were red-rimmed with fatigue. "I take it you're aware of why we're here? That Mr. Provost's death was a homicide."

"Yes, sir, I know that. But I simply don't understand why anyone would wish to hurt Mr. Provost. He was one of nature's true gentlemen."

"That's what we hope to find out," Witherspoon replied.

"Mr. Provost sounds like a very admirable person," Barnes said. "Now, sir, can you tell us when was the last time you saw him?"

"This past Tuesday afternoon. He sent the messenger lad off with his last appointment request and then said he was leaving early. He generally stayed until half past five on most days, but Tuesday he left at two in the afternoon."

"Did he say why he was leaving early?" Witherspoon asked.

"No." McCracken waved his hand in dismissal. "Of course, I didn't ask. Mr. Provost was a good man, but he wasn't one to invite overfamiliarity."

"He seems to have been well liked by his staff," Witherspoon said. "But had he had any problems recently with an employee? Had he let anyone go recently?"

"He never had to sack anyone." McCracken shook his head emphatically. "The workers here have it good, and they know it. Mr. Provost paid an excellent wage, didn't dock a man for taking a day or two off if he was ill, treated everyone decently, and gave us a bonus every Christmas."

"What about his customers? Did he have any difficulties with any of them? You know, defective products, late shipments, that sort of thing?" Barnes asked.

Again, McCracken shook his head. "They weren't just customers to Mr. Provost. He believed that we were performing a valuable public service. Without good surgical instruments and proper medical supplies, people would die. We don't send out defective goods. Every man on the floor knows that, and the only times we've ever been late on a delivery were when there was a railway strike or a flood."

Barnes nodded in understanding. "Did anyone owe Mr. Provost an inordinate amount of money?"

"All the accounts are in proper order. But I don't expect you to take my word; you're welcome to have a word with Larsen. He's our Receivables clerk." McCracken pointed toward the clerks in the outer office.

"Do you know of anyone, anyone at all, who might have wished to do Mr. Provost harm?" Witherspoon asked.

"Ever since Mr. Tipton told us what happened, I've thought and thought on why someone would do such a dreadful thing." McCracken's eyes filled with tears, and he blinked hard to keep them from spilling down his cheeks. "But I can't think of anyone who'd want him dead. All he did was come to work, go to church on Sundays, and play whist twice a week. That's all."

"He'd no friends?" Barnes pressed. "No other activities? He didn't go to the theater or the music hall?" The constable wanted to see if the rank and file here at Provost's work knew about his investigation.

"He had friends at his club, I suppose," McCracken said slowly. "But he never spoke about them."

"Had he any disputes there?" Witherspoon asked. Provost's household servants might say that he hadn't gambled, but that didn't make it a fact. "Perhaps his card playing hadn't been successful?"

"You can look at the books yourself — he didn't need money. As for his friends, I don't know much about them; he only started playing at that club a few months ago. He used to play whist at a pub down by the river, near where he lived. A friend of his owned the place, but he disappeared a while back."

"Disappeared?" Barnes repeated.

"That's right. Mr. Provost was terribly upset about the matter. One of the barmaids came here one morning last summer and said she was worried because his friend hadn't opened the pub. Mr. Provost went along and reported it to the police, but I don't think they took him very seriously."

Witherspoon asked, "What was Mr. Provost's friend's name?" He knew it already, but he was curious to learn how wide Provost's investigation might have spread.

"It was Grigson," McCracken replied. "Ernie Grigson."

"Did Mr. Provost ever say why the police hadn't taken his concerns about Mr. Grigson's disappearance seriously?" Barnes asked.

"He did, sir, and I must say, he was more than a little annoyed about the whole matter. Mr. Provost told me that just when he'd started to convince them that something awful had happened to Mr. Grigson, his sister, a Miss Edith Grigson, showed up and took over the pub."

"Wasn't she concerned about her brother's whereabouts?" Barnes asked.

"Not in the least." McCracken snorted in disgust. "As a matter of fact, she's the one that stopped them from investigating. When she found out Mr. Provost had made inquiries, she flounced down to the police station and told them they were wasting their time. She said that her brother suffered from melancholia, and this wasn't the first time he'd taken off without a word to anyone."

"Do you happen to know who she spoke to at the police station?" Witherspoon asked hopefully. The station would have records, of course, but in his experience it was simply so much easier if one had the name of the officer who'd taken the report.

"No, sorry, Mr. Provost never mentioned any names. I don't think he'd have spoken about the matter to me at all if he'd not been in such a state that day. He wasn't one to share his personal business, but he'd been to see Miss Grigson, you see, and the visit hadn't been very pleasant. By the time he got back to the office, he was in a right old temper. I've got to tell ya, it scared me a little. Mr. Provost wasn't one to lose control of himself."

"Did he say what had upset him?" Witherspoon shifted his weight.

"Oh, he did." McCracken nodded emphatically. "He knew she was lyin' about Mr. Grigson running off without a word. He said she didn't care a whit about her brother, that all she was interested in was getting her hands on his pub. A few days later, the barmaid, the one that had come and fetched Mr. Provost the day Mr. Grigson hadn't opened up the pub, came back. Mr. Provost and I were sitting right here going over the delivery schedule when she come in and told him that Miss Grigson had moved into the flat over the pub, sacked all the staff, and hired her own people."

Everyone was at their afternoon meeting on time. Mrs. Goodge put a plate of sliced seed cake next to the teapot and then slipped into her chair. "I've not got anything to report," she said glumly. "Apparently our victim wasn't particularly well-known about town."

"Don't look so downhearted, Mrs. Goodge," Wiggins said cheerfully. "We've only just got started; it's still early days yet. You'll soon be findin' out all sorts of useful bits and pieces." He'd not learned all that much himself, but he didn't care. After having tea with Miss Catherine Shelby, he'd walked her to her lodging house and she'd agreed to have tea with him again tomorrow. They were to meet at the Lyons Tea Shop on Oxford Street.

"Of course you will," Mrs. Jeffries added. "Now, let's get on with this. Surely one of you has learned something today."

"I take it you didn't get much else out of Dr. Bosworth?" Hatchet guessed.

"No. Apparently a good night's sleep didn't help him recall many additional details about our victim," she replied. "But he is still utterly convinced that Provost was murdered. He even had another doctor examine the bruises on the body, and that doctor concurred with his opinion. The marks are handprints."

"Did you tell him about the solicitor going to the chief inspector, and how our inspector has now got the case?" Smythe asked.

"Yes, he seemed very relieved. Who wants to go next?"

"I'll go, if it's all the same to everyone," Betsy volunteered. "I spoke to some of the local merchants in the neighborhood. Mr. Provost was well respected and always paid his bills on time. But no one really knew much about him. I did find out a bit from the girl at the newsagent. According to her, Provost was usually a very quiet, polite sort of person, except for one time."

"What happened?" Luty asked.

"Apparently the owner had forgot to put a copy of a magazine to one side for Mr. Provost," Betsy explained hesitantly. "When he got there that evening after work, they'd sold all their copies. She said it was the only time she ever saw Mr. Provost get angry." This was such a silly bit of information, she felt foolish to even bring it up. But there was an ironclad rule that everything, no matter how silly it might seem, had to be shared with the others.

"Did the girl remember the name of the magazine?" Mrs. Jeffries asked.

"It's *The Strand.*" Betsy shrugged. "The girl said that soon after that, he stopped buying it from them."

"You mean he was annoyed enough to take his business elsewhere?" Mrs. Goodge reached for the sugar bowl.

"Oh, no, he still came in every day to buy his newspaper. But he stopped getting the magazine," she sighed. "I know this isn't much, but there are a number of other shops in his neighborhood that I didn't get a chance to go into today. Maybe tomorrow will be better."

"Stop your frettin', love." Smythe reached over and patted her arm. "You've done a good deal better than me already. At least you found out Provost liked to read. You couldn't fill a thimble with the few bits I heard today. I walked all over the riverfront and didn't find anyone who'd been out in the vicinity of the wharf when Provost was murdered."

"It seems to me that if Provost was killed at night, you might have better luck findin' a witness tonight," Luty suggested thoughtfully.

He nodded in agreement. "I plan on popping back down to the area after the inspector comes home. There might be some night workers or river men who were about the area when Provost was killed."

"Mind you be careful," Betsy said softly.

"Don't worry, I will." He grabbed her hand under the table and gave it a squeeze. "The lads at his local pub didn't know anything about him, but I did run into a bloke who worked in the house down the road. But all he knew was that Provost didn't do anything except go to work. That's all I found out. Maybe my luck will change tonight." He glanced over at Wiggins and noticed that he was staring at the opposite wall with a dreamy, faraway look on his face. "Wiggins, are you listenin'?"

The footman didn't appear to hear him.

"What's wrong with you, boy?" Mrs. Goodge poked him in the side. "Quit your daydreamin' and pay attention. This is improtant."

"Sorry." Wiggins blushed a deep red. "I

was woolgathering."

Mrs. Goodge gazed at him sharply. "Are you feeling alright? You're flushed. You're not coming down with something, are you?"

"I'm fine," he replied quickly. "Just a little tired, that's all."

"Did you learn anything when you were out?" Mrs. Jeffries asked.

"Not really," he admitted. "I couldn't even find anyone who'd heard of Michael Provost." He didn't want to tell them that once he and Miss Catherine Shelby had gone to the tea shop, he'd found it hard to concentrate on anything else. She'd been ever so interesting, telling him all about how she'd started work at the age of twelve as a seamstress' assistant in a theater in Manchester, but had managed through sheer talent and hard work to become the assistant to the manageress of the Odeon Opera Company. She intended to make something of herself. He simply couldn't stop thinking about her. But he'd tried to do his fair share today: He'd gone back to Provost's neighborhood to see whether he could find out anything useful. It wasn't his fault that by the time he'd got to the area, no one had been out and about. "I'll go back out tomorrow and see what's what.

Someone must know somethin' about the feller."

"He sounds a right unsociable sort," the cook grumbled. No wonder she couldn't find out anything about the dead man; he was practically a hermit.

"Doesn't look like any of us is findin' out too much." Luty glanced at her butler as she spoke, and was relieved to see him nodding in agreement. Good — she hated it when Hatchet found out more than she did. "But I did hear something interestin'." She paused and reached for her teacup.

Hatchet glared at her. "Oh, come on, madam, stop being so melodramatic and tell us what you found out," he said irritably.

"I ain't bein' dramatic," she shot back.

" 'Melodramatic' was the word I used, madam," he corrected.

"Do go on, Luty," Mrs. Jeffries said quickly. When it came to finding clues, all of them tended to be competitive, but Luty and Hatchet were by far the worst. "Tell us what you learned today."

"Two days before he died, Michael Provost was trying to get a recommendation for a reliable private inquiry agent." Luty grinned triumphantly.

"And how do you know this, madam?" Hatchet stared at her skeptically.

"I know it because I'm good at findin' clues," she snapped.

"This is very interesting information, Luty," Mrs. Jeffries interjected. "I'm surprised Mr. Tipton, Provost's solicitor, didn't mention it to the inspector."

"He probably didn't know about it." Luty gave them an embarrassed smile and relaxed back in her chair. "Sorry, I didn't mean to fly off the handle, but I am good at findin' things out, and it ain't just because I'm rich, though I'll admit that helps some. But the point is, it just so happened that the first person I went to see this morning knew Provost. Seems they're both members of the same club. Let's see now, which one is it?" She broke off and frowned. "Oh, Nellie's whiskers. What's wrong with me that I can't remember that silly name? The dang thing is on the tip of my tongue."

"Don't think about it," Wiggins suggested. "That's what I always do when I can't remember a name, and then it pops right into my head."

Her face brightened. "Now I remember. It was the Wentworth Club."

"Your source actually knew the victim?" Mrs. Jeffries clarified.

Luty shook her head. "Not really, but he knew him by sight. He told me that a couple

101

of days back, he saw Provost having a serious chat with Lord Barraclough. Barraclough is a friend of mine."

"Lord Barraclough." Hatchet stared at her incredulously. "Ye gods, madam, you can't stand the man. Tell me you didn't go haring off to see him. You called him a hidebound old blowhard the last time your paths crossed."

"He knew I was just joshin'." Luty waved Hatchet off impatiently. "You know how I do love arguin' politics. Anyways, I buttered up the old fool, told him I'd come to tell him how sorry I was about our last misunderstandin'. I found out that the reason Provost and he were in a corner chattin' with each other was because Provost was asking him to recommend a good private inquiry agent."

"If Provost and Lord Barraclough weren't friends, why would he ask Barraclough for a recommendation?" Mrs. Goodge muttered. She wondered whether she'd ever been considered a hidebound old fool. She hoped not.

"Because just last year, Lord Barraclough used a private inquiry agent to track down some jewels that had gone missing," Hatchet explained. "It was all very hush-hush. But, of course, I found out all about it."

Luty snorted but didn't interrupt.

Hatchet ignored her. "Barraclough couldn't go to the police. The suspicion was that one of his relatives had helped themselves to the contents of Lady Barraclough's jewelry case."

"So Provost knew that Barraclough should be able to recommend a decent agent," Betsy said.

"I take it Lady Barraclough got her jewelry returned?" Mrs. Jeffries asked.

It was Hatchet who replied. "Indeed she did. The gossip was that the theft had been perpetrated by Lord Barraclough's younger brother, Harry."

"He's a gambler, and not a very good one, either," Luty added. "And no matter how hard you try to hush that up, it gets out. Especially when you have a household of fifteen servants."

"It would be helpful if we knew why Mr. Provost needed a private detective." Betsy took a sip of her tea. "As soon as they heard he'd died, both his solicitor and his housekeeper were sure he'd met with foul play. I think they either knew or suspected he was involved with something very dangerous."

"Or someone very dangerous," Smythe added.

"People don't hire private inquiry agents

unless something's amiss," Mrs. Goodge said stoutly. "And I'll bet you that's the reason he ended up in the river."

"Where do you think those letters might be, sir?" Barnes asked Witherspoon as they got down from another hansom in front of the Wentworth Club.

"Probably at the Yard." He pushed his spectacles, which had slid down his nose, back into place.

"But, then again, Provost might have sent them off to his local police station instead. Tomorrow I'll ask Mrs. Corwin if she can recall seeing an address. Otherwise it might be difficult to track them down; the police get so many letters. But we've sent out a notice to all the London stations, so I'm sure they'll turn up soon."

"I wonder why whoever received the letters hasn't stepped forward," Barnes commented. "By now, every copper in London knows that the drowning wasn't an accident, but a murder."

Witherspoon didn't reply; he simply charged up the short concrete walk to the front door, opened it, and stepped inside. Barnes followed at a more leisurely pace. He knew the inspector was trying to put the issue of Provost's communications to the police in the best possible light. He didn't want to admit, even to himself, that someone had made a grave mistake. Barnes would bet his next hot dinner that whoever had actually got the letters wouldn't be stepping forward anytime soon. Not if he valued his career.

A white-gloved butler came toward them as they entered the foyer. "May I help you, sir?" he asked, looking at the inspector.

"We'd like to see whoever is in charge," Witherspoon said.

"That would be the club secretary, sir," the butler replied. He looked at Barnes, and his expression darkened. "If you'll just wait here, I'll go get him."

"Thank you." Barnes grinned broadly. Exclusive establishments like this hated it when a uniformed copper was about the place. "I expect he'll be here pretty quickly," he murmured softly to Witherspoon as the butler turned and almost sprinted down the hall.

Witherspoon chuckled. "Let's get a look at the premises while we wait," he suggested as he moved toward the wide archway just ahead of them and stuck his head inside.

He looked into the common room and saw that it was huge. The bottom halves of the walls were paneled with a rich dark brown wood, and the upper portions were painted a deep sapphire blue. In the center of the room, an ornate crystal chandelier blazed with enough light for the gentlemen sitting in the leather chairs, settees, and couches scattered around the room to read their newspapers without squinting. Book-cases, newspaper racks, and footstools were strategically placed close to seating areas. Cigar smoke drifted through the air, min-gling with the scent of late-afternoon tea and cognac. An old man dozed on the love seat by the fireplace.

"The secretary will see you now," the butler said. "If you'll follow me, please."

Witherspoon spun around. The man had slipped up so quietly that neither policeman had heard his approach. "Yes, of course."

They followed him down the hall to an open doorway, and when he nodded at them, they stepped inside.

A fat, balding man dressed in an old-fashioned black suit with a wing tip collar sat behind a desk. He leaned back in his chair and studied them for a moment before he spoke. "I understand you wish to speak with me."

"I'm Inspector Witherspoon, and this is Constable Barnes," Witherspoon said. "And yes, we do wish to speak to you. We're investigating the murder of one of your members."

"What's your name, sir?" Barnes kept his voice hard and his expression harder, training his gaze on the man as he reached into his pocket and pulled out his notebook and pencil.

"My name? Why . . . I never . . . why, I'm Barnabas Bagshot. I'm the club secretary." He looked utterly stunned. He hadn't expected either policeman to be so direct.

"Was Mr. Michael Provost one of your members?" Witherspoon asked. He'd taken his lead from Barnes. Sometimes the upper class acted as if they were above the law, as if it wasn't important for them to take time out of their busy lives to answer a few simple questions. The good constable had shown Witherspoon that often, if one acted quite aggressive with these sorts of persons, one got quite good results.

"He was," Bagshot replied.

"How long had he been a member?" Barnes said quickly.

"Since last September. Mr. Provost was recommended by two of our members when he applied, and he was accepted." Bagshot's chair squeaked as he shifted in his seat. "But I don't see how any of this is relevant to Mr. Provost's death."

"So you've heard about Mr. Provost?" Witherspoon said. "How did you hear this news, sir?" The murder hadn't been widely reported in the press. There had been nothing in that morning's *Times* about it.

Bagshot's mouth gaped, but he recovered quickly. "One of our members, Mr. Quigly, told me this morning."

"Did he say how he'd heard the news?" the inspector pressed. Even without help from the press, there were a variety of ways the news could have become public. Nevertheless, Witherspoon's "inner voice," as Mrs. Jeffries called it, was telling him to find out how Provost's death had become public knowledge so quickly.

"He didn't say, and I certainly was far too much of a gentleman to ask such a thing," Bagshot blustered. "Mr. Quigly isn't one to make up tales."

"You said that two members of the club recommended Mr. Provost for membership." Witherspoon unbuttoned his top button. It was very hot in here. "Which two members were they?"

Bagshot was silent for a second longer than was polite before he spoke. "I shouldn't like to involve any of our members in something unsavory, but if you must know . . ."

"We must," Barnes interrupted.

Bagshot shot him a quick glare. "It was Mr. Percy Harkins and Mr. William Marston. They've been members here for years. They are gentlemen."

"Are either of them here now?" Witherspoon asked. "Or Mr. Quigly? Is he here?"

"Quigly is in the common room," Bagshot replied sourly, "but neither of the others are here as yet. They don't generally come in until later."

Witherspoon glanced at Barnes, who gave a barely perceptible nod, indicating he'd no further inquiries. Both policemen respected the Metropolitan Police Force's chain of command, but Witherspoon had discovered that Constable Barnes sometimes asked questions the inspector hadn't even thought about.

"Thank you for your cooperation, Mr. Bagshot," the inspector said formally. "With your permission, we'll go out to the common room and speak with Mr. Quigly."

Bagshot's mouth gaped again. "Go out to the common room — oh, no, that will never do. There's a small card room right next door. Go in there and wait. I'll have the butler send Mr. Quigly in to see you. We can't have the police barging around our common room, bothering the members."

"That will be fine," Witherspoon said. "However, we will ask that you provide us with Mr. Harkins' and Mr. Marston's addresses. We can't hang about waiting for them to appear."

Bagshot looked as though he wanted to argue. Then he shrugged and got to his feet. "Alright. Just go along to the card room and I'll send someone to fetch Quigly."

But the card room was already occupied. The butler groaned softly when he saw three men seated around one of the tables in the center of the room. "Oh dear, Mr. Bagshot didn't think anyone was in here. Usually they don't start playing until much later in the afternoon."

"Is there another place we can use?" Witherspoon asked softly. But he hadn't spoken quietly enough, and all three of the men were now openly staring at them.

"Do come in. We're not playing yet." One of the men stood up. "We're waiting for a fourth." The speaker was a tall, pale-skinned fellow in his late thirties. He had a long patrician nose, brown hair, and deep-set light-colored eyes.

"I'm terribly sorry to have disturbed you, Sir Edmund," the butler sputtered as he backed out the door. "I'll take these gentlemen elsewhere . . ."

"Good Lord, is that a policeman?" One of the other men rose to his feet, his gaze locked on Constable Barnes. He was a tall, chubby fellow with wispy blond curly hair, a ruddy complexion, and bulging blue eyes.

"Yes, I'm a policeman." Barnes stared back at the man.

"Perhaps they're here about poor Michael," the third man said.

Witherspoon turned and looked at the man who'd just spoken. The man remained seated and gazed back at the inspector with a slight smile on his thick lips. He was in his late thirties or early forties, slender, and with a receding hairline.

"You're correct, sir. We are here about a gentleman named Michael Provost. Do you know him?" Witherspoon asked.

"Of course I do," the man replied. "It's tragic what happened. But, honestly, I didn't expect the police to come around." He finally got to his feet. "I'm George Barrington. Mr. Provost played whist with us twice a week."

"Perhaps we'd better go elsewhere, Inspector," the butler whispered nervously. "Mr. Bagshot will be upset if we disturb the gentlemen."

But the inspector ignored him and moved purposely into the room. "He played whist

111

with you? Then I need to speak with all of you. I'm Inspector Witherspoon, and this is Constable Barnes."

The butler scurried after the inspector and plucked ineffectually at his sleeve. "Inspector, really, Mr. Bagshot specifically said . . ."

"Leave off," Barnes snapped. "Go and tell your Mr. Bagshot that the inspector is going to be interviewing three gentlemen in the card room, and he's not to be disturbed. You can find me another room and send your Mr. Quigly there."

Alarmed, the butler drew back so fast that he stumbled. "You can use Mr. Katzman's office. He's the general manager, but he's never here. It's right next door. Go along, and I'll see if Mr. Quigly is available."

As soon as they were gone, the inspector continued to the card table. He directed his first question to George Barrington. "Mr. Barrington, would you mind telling me how you found out about Mr. Provost's death?"

"Quigly told me this morning. Wretched business." He shook his head. "Honestly, it simply goes to show that you never really know people, do you?"

"We've only been playing with the fellow for a few months," the tall, pale-skinned man commented. He looked at the inspector. "I'm Sir Edmund Cleverly. I don't mean to sound harsh, Inspector, but we were hardly close friends with Provost. He's been our eighth only since September."

"I've no idea what an eighth might be," Witherspoon admitted. "Would you mind explaining the term?"

Cleverly smiled. "I take it you don't play whist, Inspector."

"I've never had the pleasure," he replied. He felt a twinge of guilt as he spoke. Ruth Cannonberry, his neighbor and very special friend, had tried on several occasions to interest him in learning the game. But he had no head for cards.

"When we play whist, we play two tables of four people each," Cleverly explained. "Provost made up our eighth person. We've been playing together for years. But Michael just joined us in September, when one of our members emigrated."

"And now we're going to have to find another one," the blond fellow added. "What a bother."

"What is your name, sir?" Witherspoon asked.

"Rollo Barrington." He put his hand over his mouth as he yawned. "Exactly why have you come here? Surely an accidental drowning doesn't warrant the police harassing everyone who happened to know the fellow.

If the police waste their time asking questions about stupid accidents, then it's no wonder they never catch any real criminals."

"An accident?" Witherspoon repeated. "Oh dear, I'm afraid you've been misinformed. Michael Provost's death wasn't an accident."

"Are you saying he committed suicide?" Cleverly slipped back into his seat. "Good Lord, that's even worse."

"I'm afraid that you've misunderstood." Witherspoon watched their faces as he spoke. "Mr. Provost didn't take his own life. He was murdered."

CHAPTER 4

Down the hallway, Barnes was having a very difficult time getting Mr. Quigly to understand his question. "Let me explain it again, sir," he said for the third time. "I'd like to know how you heard about Mr. Provost's death."

Quigly was an elderly man with a gray walrus mustache and a headful of hair. He was sitting on a straight-backed chair and staring hard at the constable, who was perched on the edge of the absent general manager's huge walnut desk. "Good Lord, man, it isn't a secret."

"But how did you find out about it?" Barnes pressed. The newspapers hadn't caught wind that Provost's death had been a homicide; consequently, the only mention in any of the daily papers was that the body of an unknown man had been pulled out of the Thames.

"You mean who told me?"

"Yes, sir, that is precisely what I mean," the constable replied.

"Well, why didn't you ask me that in the first place?" Quigly grumbled. "My housekeeper told me."

"How did your housekeeper find out?" Despite being perched on the edge of the desk, Barnes managed to prop his notebook in such a way that he could write.

"How the deuce should I know," Quigly snapped. "This is most unsettling, most unsettling indeed. First we have that upstart March blathering on about being shoved in front of a cooper's van; then we have that fellow Provost throwing himself into the river. Silly fool, always asking stupid questions and sneaking about, talking to the staff. I knew this sort of thing would start happening once we let their sort into the club, and I've been proved right. But will anyone listen to me? No, they will not. I shall have another word with the membership committee."

Barnes looked up sharply. "Someone claims to have been pushed in front of a cooper's van?"

"I've just said so, haven't I? It was that fellow March."

"When did this happen? Recently?" Barnes pressed.

Quigly shrugged. "I don't know the exact day. It was last week. Not that I believe for an instant that the man was telling the truth. I think he made the whole thing up so people would pay attention to him. People from his kind of background never seem to know their proper place."

"And what would that be, sir?" Barnes asked softly.

"Well, it certainly isn't here." Quigly glared at Barnes for a brief moment and then looked away. "Just because he's made lots of money in *trade,* he thinks he's a right to become a member. That fool Cleverly and those idiot Barrington brothers put his name up for membership. This is a gentlemen's club, for proper English gentlemen. If we continue to let anyone with a bit of money into the membership, the club will cease to stand for anything at all."

"Where were you the night before last?" Barnes asked bluntly.

"The night before last?" Quigly repeated the words as though he didn't understand what they meant. He looked stunned.

"Yes, the night Michael Provost threw himself into the river." The constable stood up. "You see, sir, Mr. Provost didn't commit suicide, nor was his death an accident. He was murdered."

Quigly's eyes widened. "Murdered. Ye gods, it's worse than I thought. Decent people don't go about getting themselves murdered."

"You'd actually be surprised at how many supposedly 'decent people' do end up getting themselves murdered." Barnes deliberately echoed Quigly's words. "But I'm not here to debate the subject with you, sir. You seem to have disliked Mr. Provost and resented his presence here. So I'll ask you again: Where were you this past Tuesday night?"

"Where was I? That's none of your business," Quigly blustered. "And I resent your inference. I had nothing to do with the man's death. I barely spoke to him."

"You can either answer my questions here, privately," the constable continued easily, "or I can summon Inspector Witherspoon, and we can take you down to the station to help us with our inquires." He knew the inspector would back him up on this tactic, but he hoped it wouldn't come to such drastic action. He'd asked the question only to rattle the old snob.

Quigly's mouth flattened into a thin line. "I was home all evening. My housekeeper and the other servants can vouch for the fact that I never left the house."

"What's your address, sir?" Barnes asked calmly.

"Number fourteen, Linley Walk, Bayswater." He got to his feet. "And rest assured, Constable, your superiors shall hear of my displeasure."

Barnes would have liked to ask a few more questions about this Mr. March supposedly being tossed in front of a cooper's van, but he didn't think Quigly was going to cooperate much longer. He'd find out from someone else what he needed to know. "You must do what you think is best, sir," Barnes said. "You may send your complaints directly to Chief Inspector Barrows at Scotland Yard."

Quigly's only response was to slam the door as he stomped out of the room.

"Murder?" Rollo Barrington repeated.

"Gracious, that's dreadful," George Barrington muttered.

"I heard the poor fellow had tumbled into the Thames and drowned," Sir Edmund said, his attention on the inspector. "Are you certain it wasn't an accident?"

"We're quite sure it was murder," Witherspoon replied. He knew that he shouldn't be interviewing all three of the gentlemen at once, but for the life of him, he couldn't think of a way to take their statements separately. It wasn't as if he'd come to see or speak to them specifically; they'd merely volunteered information about their relationships with the victim. He decided to be as general as possible in his questions. "If you don't mind, gentlemen, I'd like to know how you found out about Mr. Provost's death. It hasn't been reported in any of the papers as yet."

"We heard about it last night," Rollo Barrington volunteered. "We were all having dinner at a friend's home. As a matter of fact, it was a policeman who mentioned the death. Fellow by the name of Nigel Nivens — do you know him?"

"Yes, I'm acquainted with Inspector Nivens."

"He's the one who said Provost had either accidentally drowned or possibly committed suicide, but as there wasn't any sort of suicide note, he was of the opinion it was accidental." Sir Edmund added, "I'm a bit at a loss as to why the police think it's murder."

"We have our reasons," Witherspoon replied carefully. He was genuinely distressed and trying hard not to let it show in his expression, manner, or speech. It wasn't precisely against the rules to speak in public about ongoing cases, but it was most certainly discouraged. Witherspoon, of course, was discreet and only ever mentioned his cases to his staff, all of whom were very trustworthy.

He wondered whether he should mention Nivens' misstep to Chief Inspector Barrows, then decided he'd speak to Barnes about it first. Witherspoon's relationship with Inspector Nivens wasn't very good to begin with, and he didn't wish to increase the man's animosity toward him by running to their superior and telling tales. "Were any of you gentlemen acquainted with Mr. Provost before he became a member of your club?"

"I'd met him once or twice," Sir Edmund said.

"As had I," Rollo added. He glanced at his brother. "You'd met him a time or two as well."

"When was the last instance any of you saw Mr. Provost?" Witherspoon asked.

"We played whist together on Monday night," Sir Edmund murmured. "That was the last I saw him."

"Us as well," George said.

"What was his manner like that evening?" the inspector asked. "Did he seem preoccupied or upset about anything?"

"Not that I noticed," Sir Edmund replied.

"He seemed fine to me," Rollo said.

"He was his usual self," George agreed.

"Did Mr. Provost ever mention any problems, any enemies he might have had?" Witherspoon asked.

"He never spoke about his personal life to us," Cleverly replied. "At least not in my presence." As he spoke, the two Barrington brothers were nodding in agreement.

"As a matter of fact," Cleverly continued, "we didn't know him very well at all. He was simply the eighth at cards."

When the inspector got home, Mrs. Jeffries ushered him directly into the drawing room and handed him a glass of sherry. "Now, sir, you must have a rest before dinner. You look dead tired." He really did appear exhausted, and she wanted to get as much information as she could out of him before he went up to bed.

"I am rather done in," he agreed as he leaned back in his chair and took a quick sip from his glass. "It's been the strangest day."

"Really, sir?" She smiled sympathetically.

"Indeed. I don't know why my cases get so wretchedly complicated. Honestly, you'd think that just once I could have a nice, straightforward murder." He told her about his visit to the Provost household, and about the unsettling news that Provost had been investigating Ernie Grigson's disappearance and had sent letters to the police detailing what he'd learned.

"Goodness, sir, that is an odd turn of events," she replied.

"Yes, isn't it? Gracious, Mrs. Jeffries, you'd think people would have more sense than to go out and start asking questions to all and sundry about what could be a very serious crime, especially if this Mr. Grigson didn't disappear but was murdered." The inspector continued telling her about Provost's obsession with the stories of Mr. Arthur Conan Doyle, and how his housekeeper thought it was the unhealthy influence of that Mr. Sherlock Holmes character that had put the idea of conducting his own investigation into Provost's head in the first place.

Mrs. Jeffries looked down at her lap. She feared her face would give her away. She was simultaneously stunned and saddened at this turn of events. Michael Provost was doing the very same thing that she and the other members of the household did quite regularly, and he'd probably been murdered for his efforts. "Perhaps his housekeeper was exaggerating, sir," Mrs. Jeffries ventured.

"Perhaps he hadn't been quite as active as she thought."

"Oh, no, the housekeeper's account was confirmed by the cook. Then his general manager told me how upset he had been over Mr. Grigson's disappearance." Witherspoon gave her the details of his visit to Provost's company and of his interview with Angus McCracken. "After that we went to the Wentworth Club."

"And did you learn anything useful, sir?" Her mind was moving in so many directions at once that she could barely get the question out.

"I'm not sure," Witherspoon replied. He told her the rest of what had happened at the club.

When he mentioned Nigel Nivens' name, she was surprised again, but this time she didn't have to look away to keep her expression calm. She listened carefully, occasionally asking a question or making a comment.

"Poor Mr. Provost." Witherspoon shook his head sadly. "Half the people at his club believed he'd committed suicide, and the other half thought he'd had too much to drink and stumbled into the Thames accidentally."

"People often like to think the worst," she

commented. "Either that, or they jump to the wrong conclusion."

"Indeed they do," he agreed. "Considering there was no evidence whatsoever that the man ever overindulged in alcohol."

Mrs. Jeffries sipped her sherry and nodded encouragingly as Witherspoon finished his recitation. By the time he got up to go to the dining room, he felt as if a huge burden had been lifted off his shoulders — and that, of course, was precisely how she'd planned for him to feel.

Mrs. Jeffries didn't tell the others until their meeting the next morning about the added complication of Ernie Grigson's disappearance. She'd decided that there was no point in having to repeat the information twice.

"Cor blimey." Wiggins shook his head. "This is gettin' right mixed up, isn't it. Does this mean we have to suss out what might 'ave happened to this Ernie Grigson as well as figure out who killed Michael Provost?"

"I'm afraid so," the housekeeper said.

"Perhaps we'd best find out precisely when this Mr. Grigson disappeared," Hatchet commented.

"I think we ought to find out everything we can about both men," the cook said stoutly. "Seems to me that's the only way to make sense of either matter."

"I agree," Mrs. Jeffries said. "But now that we've two crimes to investigate, we're going to be spread a bit thin. We'll have to cover Ernie Grigson's neighborhood as well as Provost's."

"And so far we aren't doin' all that well," Smythe said glumly. "I spent a good two hours 'angin' about the Chelsea Vestry Wharf last night, and got nothin' to show for my efforts except wet socks and sore feet."

"What about that feller that was shoved in front of the cooper's van? You know, that Mr. Jonathan March," Wiggins asked. "Do we 'ave to count him as well?"

"Let's hope not," the cook muttered under her breath. "This is complicated enough as it is."

"The inspector is going to interview the gentleman to see if there's any sort of connection," Mrs. Jeffries replied. "But he doesn't think that's likely. According to the other members of the Wentworth Club, Jonathan March and Michael Provost barely knew one another. But even without that added wrinkle on our sleeve, we've still much ground to cover."

"Actually, the Grigson matter might be very helpful to us," Hatchet said thought-

126

fully. "It would explain why someone wanted Provost dead."

Smythe nodded. "You mean whoever got rid of Grigson might have thought Provost was gettin' too close to findin' out the truth."

"Or, at the very least, might have been getting the police interested in looking into the matter," Mrs. Jeffries speculated. "Though I am still at a loss as to how they could have ignored Provost's letters. But perhaps we'll find that out in the course of our own investigations."

"I'll bet that's why Provost was trying to find a good private inquiry agent." Betsy got to her feet. "Maybe he wanted help with Grigson's disappearance."

"That certainly makes sense," Mrs. Jeffries agreed.

"We'd best get cracking, then," Smythe warned. "Time's a-wastin'."

"The inspector will probably be late tonight," Mrs. Jeffries said. "So I think we ought to move our afternoon meeting back to five instead of four."

As they were all going to be very busy, everyone agreed that was a good idea.

The Swan's Nest pub was just around the corner from the Provost home. Smythe had already spoken to the drivers at the hansom stand on this end of the embankment. But none of them had picked up or taken any fares to or from the area surrounding the Chelsea Vestry Wharf the night Provost was murdered. He hoped his luck would change here.

He stepped into the pub. It was a half hour past opening time, and the place was already full. Gardeners, day laborers, shop assistants, and clerks sat at the small tables or along the benches. People holding glasses of gin or pints of bitter gossiped and laughed in small groups clustered around the room. He pushed his way through the crowd to the bar and eased into a narrow space between two women. He tried to be careful, but his elbow nudged the tall redhead standing next to him. "Watch it there, big fella," she cried.

"I'm sorry, ma'am." He moved back.

She turned her head, surveying him speculatively. She was big-boned and bursting out of the top of her tight white blouse. There were deep lines around her mouth and eyes. "You're a tall one, ain't ya." She gave him a cheery smile, nudged her friend out of the way, and patted the now-empty space next to her. "Come on, then. I'll not bite."

Smythe was tempted to make a run for it;

she was too friendly by half. But he wanted information, and women like her usually knew everything that happened in the neighborhood. He eased back to the counter and leaned his weight on his elbow. "Ta. What'll you 'ave?"

"That's right gentlemanly of ya." Her smile broadened. "I'll have a gin, please. My name's Bernadette Healey. What's yours?"

"Lester Phelps," he lied. "Pleased to make your acquaintance." He gestured to the barman. "A gin for the lady and a pint for me," he ordered. He never gave his right name when he was "on the hunt," so to speak. But truth to tell, it had been so long since he'd done any real sleuthing on his own, he was a bit unsure of himself. Between his trip to Australia and his using Blimpey so often, he was out of practice.

"I've never seen you around here before. I'd remember a tall one like you. What brings you to these parts, Lester?" She ran her fingers over his arm as she spoke.

He about jumped out of his skin but managed to steel himself to be still. "Everyone calls me Les," he replied. "I'm trying to find a lady."

"I'm a lady," she said coyly. "Will I do?"

"I'm sure you'd do just fine, but this lady

happens to be the sister of an old friend of mine. I'd 'eard she went to work as a scullery maid around 'ere somewhere, but for the life of me, I can't remember the address."

The barman brought their drinks, and Smythe handed him some coins.

Bernadette picked hers up and took a long, deep pull. "Good friend, was she?"

"Not really, but I've news for her from her brother. We were in the bush together, and 'e made me promise to let her know he'd be comin' home in the spring." He took a quick sip of his pint, hoping that she believed his story. "I don't suppose you know of anyone named Provost that has a house around these parts, do ya? That's the name of the man she works for."

Her smile faded, and she drained her glass before she answered. "Sorry, wish I could 'elp, but I've never 'eard of him."

He knew she was lying. Provost's murder was old news in this neighborhood by now. He'd lay odds that everyone in the pub knew where the man had lived.

"Mr. Provost was murdered," said a voice from his other side.

Smythe turned and saw a blond-haired lad staring at him. He was leaning on the bar, nursing a pint of bitter. He had a sprinkling of red spots on his face, and despite the wispy mustache on his upper lip, he couldn't have been more than sixteen.

"Murdered? Are you sure?" Smythe tried hard to sound shocked.

"I said so, didn't I," the boy replied, raising his voice a notch. "And none of the girls that work for Mr. Provost has got a brother in Australia. I know because I worked for him."

Smythe felt Bernadette's gaze on the back of his head. His story was more or less in tatters, and he knew that if he wanted any information out of anyone in this pub, he'd better do something quickly. He leaned closer to the lad and dropped his voice. "I know Provost was murdered. That's why I'm 'ere."

"Who are ya?" The youth drew back and stared at him suspiciously. "I'll bet your name's not Lester Phelps."

"Never mind that," Smythe replied. "All you need to know is, I'm a private inquiry agent and I'm lookin' into Mr. Provost's death. Now, is there somewhere a bit more private-like that we can talk?" He stuck his hands into his coat pocket and slapped a couple of coins together loudly enough for the boy to hear. He heard Bernadette's clothes rustling on his other side as she moved away from the bar. Turning his head, he saw her pushing her way through the crowd to the door.

"Don't worry about her," the boy said quickly. "She doesn't know Mr. Provost, and she's not one to want anything to do with a murder. She's got enough trouble in her life. But I'll talk to you if you've a mind to buy me another pint."

Smythe shrugged as he saw Bernadette reach the door and hurry out. There were plenty of people in London who had no reason to involve themselves in someone else's troubles, and murder generally meant trouble for someone. "Fair enough." He caught the barman's attention, pointed at the lad's pint, and nodded.

"There's a table emptyin' up over there. I'll go grab it." The boy shot away from the bar and slithered through the throng. He plopped down on the just-vacated stool and propped his leg on the empty one next to it.

Smythe paid for the fresh pint, picked up his own half-finished beer, and joined him. "So you worked for Mr. Provost." He pushed the beer toward the lad and slipped onto the stool. "What's your name?"

"Jerry Carter," he replied. "I don't work for Mr. Provost now. I mean, even before he was drowned, I only worked occasionally for 'im. My aunt is the cook there, and she sends for me whenever there's any heavy work to be done."

"When was the last time you worked at the Provost house?"

"A couple of months back." Carter took a quick sip from his pint.

"A couple of months back," Smythe repeated irritably. "If you're only there every few months, you couldn't know much about the household."

Jerry shrugged. "I know more than anyone else in 'ere. What do you want to know?"

Smythe silently cursed his bad luck, but decided that as he was here and he'd already promised the boy money and paid for the blooming pint, he might as well ask a few questions. Perhaps Carter wasn't all talk. "I don't suppose you'd know of anyone who wished to harm Mr. Provost?"

"Aunt says that Mr. Provost was a good man," Jerry replied somberly. "But she knew he was worried about something. Said he was off his food."

"When did this happen?" Smythe drank from his beer.

"A few days before he was killed," he said. "Aunt says she left his plate of Stilton and bread out for him, just like she did every other evening when he played whist, but this time he didn't eat it."

"Maybe he wasn't very hungry." Smythe sighed inwardly. Blast — he hoped that Blimpey had some decent information for him. He certainly wasn't finding out much on his own.

Jerry shook his head. "Nah, Mr. Provost liked his food. He ate everything that was put in front of him, and he always ate the food she left out for him when he was playin' cards. Aunt says it's a wonder he didn't weigh sixteen stone. Aunt says she happened to see him that night when she got up to visit the water closet. She said that instead of sitting at the kitchen table eating his cheese and bread, he was pacing about like there was something hard on his mind."

Hatchet nodded his thanks to the barman, picked up the two glasses of whisky, and carefully made his way across the Prince Alfred pub to the small table in the corner. He put the drinks down and slipped into his seat. Sunlight filtered in through the etched glass of the pub window, illuminating the deep lines on the face of the man sitting across from him.

Time had not been kind to Gideon Deere.

He sat hunched over, his elbow on the tabletop and his once-straight spine now bent with age and the indignity of illness. Deere reached for his drink with hands that trembled. The knuckles on his fingers were so swollen that for a moment Hatchet was sure he'd not be able to bend them enough to lift the glass.

But Deere managed, and put the whisky to his lips. He closed his eyes, drained the liquid, sighed deeply, and put the glass back down. "Thanks, Hatchet, I've not had a decent drink in donkey's years. My daughter is one of those Methodists, and she won't have it in the house."

"Then I'm glad I coaxed you into coming out." Hatchet pushed his whisky over to Deere. "Have mine. I'm not thirsty."

"You a Methodist, too?" Gideon snorted. "Good Lord, is everyone in this country joining the damned Temperance League?" But he was reaching for the whisky as he spoke.

"I just prefer tea," Hatchet replied. He wasn't about to explain his reasons for abstaining to this old man. He'd not liked the fellow very much when he'd last seen him, which had been forty years ago. He'd been a bit of a bully back then, and Hatchet suspected Deere's character hadn't improved with age. Hatchet had decided to contact him only because a mutual acquaintance had mentioned that Deere's last employment had been at the Wentworth Club. "But my drinking abilities, or lack thereof, aren't why I wanted to see you today. I'd like to speak to you about the Wentworth Club."

Deere frowned at him. "Why? It's a gentlemen's club. Don't you still work for that American woman?"

"I do. But I've a reason for asking."

"What reason?" Deere stared at him suspiciously.

Hatchet sighed inwardly and then reached into the inside pocket of his overcoat and pulled out his flat black leather purse. Deere's gaze locked on it. Hatchet slapped it down onto the table and said, "If you've anything worthwhile to tell me, I'll gladly compensate you for your time. All I ask in return is that you tell no one we've spoken."

"How much?" Deere didn't take his gaze from the purse lying on the table. "My time is valuable."

"I'm sure it is." Hatchet resisted the urge to laugh. As pleasurable as it would be to tell the greedy old sod that his time was worth nothing and probably never had been, that wouldn't get him any information. "But you've no idea what it is I want to know and no way of placing a monetary value on whatever it is you tell me. Now, let's just say you'll have to trust me. Would you care for another drink?"

Deere hesitated. "All right, then. You get me that drink and ask your questions. You always were a decent sort. I trust you."

Hatchet caught the barman's eye, lifted an empty glass, and held up one finger, indicating that he wanted one whisky. The man nodded and pulled a bottle out from under the counter.

Hatchet turned back to his companion. "When did you stop working at the Wentworth?"

"Last year." Deere rubbed his jaw. "They said I was getting too old to be much good to them, so they turned me out. That's when I had to go live with my daughter, and frankly, she wasn't all that happy to see me."

A young man wearing a white apron around his waist put the whisky on the table. Hatchet handed him some coins, smiled his thanks, and waited till he'd gone before he continued. "What month did you leave?"

Deere thought for a moment. "It was in July. Yes, that's right, the end of July."

Blast, Hatchet thought. That was a good

two months before Provost had joined the Wentworth. "What did you do at the club?"

"What do you think I did?" Deere shrugged. "I was a servant. I did what I was told. I fetched and carried drinks, got newspapers for the members, helped in the cloakroom. Whatever needed doing, I did. It wasn't much of a club, despite what the members liked to think. They'd only a few trained serving staff, and half the time they couldn't hang on to them as the wages were so poor."

Hatchet knew he was wasting his time. The Wentworth Club probably had nothing to do with Provost's death, but as he was already here, it wouldn't hurt to learn what he could about the place and its members. "They had several aristocrats as members, and I understand the whist games were quite good."

Deere snorted. "They had that half-witted Lord Barraclough and Sir Edmund Cleverly, both of whom have no money and not much of a pedigree, if you ask me. As for the card playing, it's not much by my way of thinking. There's generally two tables of members that play regular-like, the Octet group — that's what they call themselves. Leastways they would play, but they're such miserable people, they can't even hang on to an eighth to make up the two tables."

"You mean the eighths quit the club," Hatchet clarified. That was hardly news. People came and went at London's clubs all the time.

"Course they quit," Deere exclaimed. "It'd take a saint to put up with that whist group. Delmar and Marston weren't too bad — they'd treat a body decent-like — but some of them others were right miserable snobs. Especially the Barrington brothers."

"What was so miserable about them?" Hatchet asked.

"They're both stupid," Deere replied. "They like to gamble and play the ponies. From what I heard, they weren't very good at either activity. Gossip was that most of the reputable bookies wouldn't take bets anymore from the Barringtons or from that toff-nosed cousin of theirs, Edmund Cleverly. The last couple of years, they've had to do their bettin' with an independent, if you know what I mean."

Hatchet did. An independent was a bookie who took bets as a side business. "What about the other members of the club? Weren't any of them decent sorts?"

"Jonathan March was alright. He wasn't as demanding as most of the others, but he'd just been a member for a few months when I left. They only let him in because Sir Edmund nominated him for membership, and he only did that because he was sweet on March's sister." Deere smiled maliciously. "Mind you, I'd be sweet on her, too, considerin' that she's an heiress."

The Iron Anchor pub was a two-story wooden building at the very end of Tadema Road, almost at the river's edge. "Look, we're only a hundred yards or so away from the wharf where Provost's body was found," Barnes whispered to Witherspoon as they stepped into the establishment.

He nodded in acknowledgment. So far it hadn't been a very good day. They'd attempted to track down Provost's letters to the police and hadn't had any luck. Neither the Walton Street police station nor Scotland Yard had any record of receiving any communication of any sort from Michael Provost. As a matter of fact, the chief inspector, upon learning that Witherspoon was at the Yard, had insisted upon a full report on his current case. Witherspoon had dutifully reported most of what they'd learned thus far, leaving out only the fact that Inspector Nivens had been indiscreetly discussing police business during a dinner party. When the chief inspector found out about the letters Provost had written, letters they couldn't actually produce at the moment, he'd told Witherspoon and Barnes in no uncertain terms to keep that particular fact out of the newspapers.

The pub wasn't crowded. A couple of ferry workers stood at the bar, and a bread seller sat on the bench along the wall. The two policemen crossed over to where a woman stood behind the bar. She didn't look pleased to see them.

"Good day, madam." Witherspoon doffed his bowler politely. "I'm Inspector Witherspoon, and this is Constable Barnes. We'd like to speak to the person in charge of this establishment."

"That would be me," she replied. "I'm the owner, Edith Grigson." She was short and fat, with dark blond hair pulled back in a tight bun and a round, doughy slab of a face. She had a thin slash of a mouth and small, squinty hazel eyes. She was better dressed than most who stood behind a bar and served drinks. She wore a dove gray skirt, a fitted jacket, and a white high-collared blouse. A silver stickpin in the shape of an owl was on her left lapel. Witherpoon noticed it because the eyes of the owl looked like diamonds.

"Are you related to Mr. Ernie Grigson?" Witherspoon asked.

"I'm his sister." She crossed her arms over her chest. "Why? Has he turned up? Have you found him, then?"

"Have you reported him missing, Miss Grigson?" Barnes took out his notebook and flipped it open.

"Certainly not." She sniffed disdainfully. "I only asked because I'm not used to uniformed police coming into my place of business. This is a respectable establishment. When the two of you walked in, I thought that nosey parker that's been pestering me for the past few months had gone running to you and telling his silly, wild tales. But I'll tell you exactly what I told him: This is family business, not police business."

"I assure you, madam —" Witherspoon began, but she cut him off.

"Ernie's done this before," she cried, "taken off without so much as a by-your-leave to anyone. Luckily for him, I was able to quit my position and step in to run this business. When he does finally show up, he'll still have a roof over his head and a decent income."

"When did your brother disappear?" Barnes asked before she could start speaking again.

"The end of July." She edged away from them and grabbed a clean glass from the tray under the counter. She shoved the glass under the tap beneath the bar and hit the handle. When the glass was full, she put it on the counter and slid it to a man standing at the far end. "I've not seen nor heard from him since."

Witherspoon shifted his weight to his other foot. He felt as if he'd been standing on his feet for hours. "And you say your brother is in the habit of simply disappearing?"

She shrugged. "I've already said so, haven't I."

"How often has your brother disappeared?" Barnes asked.

"How should I know?" She reached behind her and grabbed a cleaning rag from the shelf. "I've not lived with my brother in years."

"Yet you're insisting he's done this before," Barnes said calmly.

She began wiping the counter. "He's done it at least twice that I know about."

"You mean he's just up and left his business?" The constable didn't believe that for a moment. "Pubs aren't cheap, nor are licenses easy to acquire. I find it hard to believe that someone who went to all the trouble and expense to obtain an establishment like this would just up and walk away from it."

"I didn't say he'd done it recently, did I," she snapped. "He's only had this place a couple of years. Before that, he moved around quite a bit. Ernie's never really been right. He gets the melancholia and then acts strange. That's what I told that Provost fellow when he came snooping about and wanting to know where Ernie was."

"Michael Provost came around and asked questions about your brother?" Witherspoon said. It was more of a comment than a question.

"He did. But I told him to mind his own business."

"It's too bad he didn't take your advice." Barnes looked up from his notebook. He didn't for a moment believe she didn't know about what had happened to Provost. "Perhaps if he had, he'd still be alive. As a matter of fact, we're of the opinion that it was because he was asking questions about your brother that he was murdered."

Even though they'd put their afternoon meeting back by an hour, they were all still late. Mrs. Jeffries cast a worried glance at the clock as everyone took their usual places at the table. "We'd best hurry. It's almost half past, and it would be just our luck that the inspector does come home on time tonight. Who would like to go first?"

"I've got nothing useful to report," Wiggins said glumly. "Absolutely nothing. I swear, that man didn't do anything except go to work." He didn't really know whether this was true, as he'd spent most of the day hanging around the Odeon Opera House. As he and Miss Catherine Shelby had planned on having tea together again, he'd decided it was only gentlemanly to meet her outside the theater and walk her to the Lyons Tea Shop. Then he'd needed to escort her safely back to the theater, and then, well, he'd stayed for just a bit longer trying to get another glimpse of her. By then it was already half past two, and he'd had time only to race over to the Provost neighborhood and nose about a bit. He'd learned nothing, and he felt lower than a snake because they thought he'd been out on the hunt all day.

"He played whist," Luty reminded them. "At the Wentworth."

"Yes, madam, we know all about how you found out he was trying to hire a private inquiry agent," Hatchet said sharply. "Did you find out why?"

Luty grinned impishly. "No, but I'm workin' on it. Did you find out anything?"

"Not really." Hatchet didn't bother to put a brave face on his disappointment. "I thought I'd a good possibility, but it turned out my source left the Wentworth Club two months before Provost became a member. All I heard was some gossip." He told them about his encounter with Gideon Deere.

"Doesn't sound as if you heard any better than what I did today," Mrs. Goodge commented when he'd finished. "The only thing I heard was that Isabella March — she's the sister of that fellow who claimed he was shoved in front of the cooper's van — was supposed to announce her engagement to Sir Edmund Cleverly, but it's been postponed."

"Did your source know why?" Mrs. Jeffries asked.

The cook frowned and shook her head. "Not really. The gossip was that her brother didn't approve of the match, but as she's in her midthirties and has an income of her own, I don't see how that could have stopped her if she'd really wanted to get married."

"Maybe she didn't," Mrs. Jeffries suggested. "Now, who would like to go next?"

"I'll have a go," Smythe volunteered. He told them about how he'd spoken to the hansom drivers, and then about his meeting with Jerry Carter in the local pub. He didn't mention that he'd bought a certain lady named Bernadette a drink and that she'd run off without answering a single question. Now that he thought about it, there was something strange about her leaving so fast. But still, best not to mention it, at least not in front of Betsy.

"So all you learned was that Provost was off his food?" Betsy asked, her voice skeptical.

"That's all," he replied. "But I'm meetin' some sources tomorrow, and they may know something." Now that they had a few more names and knew about Ernie Grigson, it was time to pay Blimpey another visit. "Did you 'ave much luck?"

Betsy shook her head. "Believe it or not, my luck was even worse than yours. No one, and I do mean no one, so much as knew the poor man's name. I must have gone to every shop within three miles of his house, and I learned nothing. It's very discouraging."

"I think we've got the world's most boring victim," Mrs. Goodge muttered. "Half of London tramped through this kitchen today, and all I heard was that Miss March didn't announce her engagement."

Mrs. Jeffries glanced at all the glum faces around the table. "You mustn't get discouraged. These are still very much early days. I did actually have a bit of luck. I found out that Ernie Grigson's sister took over his pub only a few days after Grigson was reported missing."

"What does that mean?" Luty demanded.

"According to my source, Edith Grigson left her position as a governess a few days after he disappeared. She came down to London straightaway, moved into his flat over the pub, fired his staff, and hired her own workers. When Michael Provost showed up and began asking questions, she told him that if he didn't mind his own business, he'd have to pay the consequences."

"Cor blimey, that's motive for murder," Wiggins exclaimed.

"That's right." Mrs. Jeffries was rather proud of herself. She was usually the one who put the puzzle together, not the one who was skilled at finding all the pieces. But a quick trip to Tadema Road and a few coins in the hand of a loose-tongued barmaid who'd previously worked at the Iron Anchor had made her feel as clever as the rest of them in "sussing out" a clue. "As long as Grigson is gone, his sister is in charge of the pub, and according to my source, the place does very well financially."

"What about his other relatives?" Luty demanded. "Ain't they worried about him?"

"There isn't anyone else," Mrs. Jeffries replied. "Just the sister."

"I wonder what happened to him," Wiggins said softly. He vowed that tomorrow he'd allow himself only a very brief tea with Miss Catherine Shelby; then he'd get out and do his part. It wasn't fair to expect the others to do it all.

"I think he was shoved in the river and drowned, just like Michael Provost," Betsy muttered.

"You may be right, Betsy," Mrs. Jeffries said. "But until we know what happened to Grigson, shouldn't we be asking ourselves another, more basic question? Mainly, how did Provost's body end up where it did? Did he walk there —" She broke off as she heard the clip-clop of horses' hooves and the rattle of a cab pulling up at the front. "Oh dear, he is home early tonight. We'll have to continue this tomorrow."

"Nell's bells." Luty got up. "The inspector comin' home means he probably didn't learn much today. That can't be good."

Hatchet grabbed Luty's cloak off the coat

tree and ushered her toward the back hall. "We'll find out in the morning. Good night, everyone. We'll be here right after breakfast."

Mrs. Jeffries made it to the upstairs hall just as the inspector stepped through the front door. "Good evening, sir," she called cheerfully. "You're home a bit early. I do hope this means you've had a productive day."

Witherspoon handed her his bowler. "I think I've learned a fair bit today." He slipped his coat off and draped it on the peg, under his hat. "But I'm not certain. Sometimes it's very difficult to see whether we're making progress or not."

"But of course you're making progress, sir. Would you care for a sherry before dinner, or would you like to go right into the dining room?"

"Oh, Mrs. Jeffries, I should love a sherry. I think that would be a very good idea, but only, of course, if you'll join me."

That, of course, was precisely what she'd been hoping he'd say.

CHAPTER 5

"We've learned a substantial amount of information about Michael Provost and a even a little bit about Ernie Grigson. But at this stage of the investigation, it's difficult to understand what is important and what isn't." The inspector settled back in his chair, took a sip of sherry, and then sighed in satisfaction.

"You'll sort it all out, sir." Mrs. Jeffries set her glass down on the table. "You always do. Were you able to track down Mr. Provost's missing letters?"

"Not as yet, but I'm sure they'll turn up soon," he replied. He hesitated for a moment, as though he wanted to say more.

Mrs. Jeffries knew there was something he wasn't telling her. "Of course they will, sir. I'm sure they're sitting in someone's desk drawer at this very moment. Probably at the Yard."

"Actually, I had a rather unpleasant discussion with the chief inspector about them," he blurted. "But I think finding them is very important regardless of whether or not the press gets wind of it."

"But of course they are important." She reached for her drink. "Surely the chief inspector must understand that." She had to tread carefully here. She could see by the expression on the inspector's face that the confrontation with his superior had upset him and that he'd not got over it as yet. "Did Mr. Barrows instruct you to stop looking for them?"

"He wasn't that blunt." Witherspoon sighed again, but this time he sounded glum. "But he made it clear that it's imperative the press doesn't find out that Provost had been trying to get our attention for weeks before he was murdered. Barrows said it would make us look as if we ignored a serious crime. Of course, that's the whole problem. Whoever opened and read those letters did ignore Provost's concerns, and now he's dead."

She wasn't at all surprised that the powers that be were upset. Since those appalling Ripper murders a few years earlier, public confidence in the police had fallen very low. Still, the letters were evidence and had to be dealt with one way or another.

"And you're going to find out who killed him, sir," she said briskly. "You're very good at that sort of thing, and I see no reason whatsoever that the newspapers should find out about Provost's letters. Now, what's on your agenda for tomorrow? No, don't tell me. Let me see if I can guess." She paused as if she were thinking. "Let's see. I'll bet you're going to find out from the victim's household how Mr. Provost got home from his club on the nights he played whist." She raised her glass and watched the inspector over the rim as she spoke. She'd tried to bring this up with the others at their meeting, but the inspector's premature arrival had stopped that discussion before it started.

Witherspoon's eyes narrowed in thought, and then he brightened. "Goodness gracious, Mrs. Jeffries, you really have sorted out my methods. That's precisely what I'm going to do." He frowned suddenly. "But I ought to have covered an elementary matter such as his movements that night well before this point in the investigation."

"This has been an odd case from the beginning. Besides, you know you must trust that 'inner voice' of yours, and apparently you were being directed toward other matters," she replied.

Witherspoon smiled faintly. "You're being kind, Mrs. Jeffries, but tracing a victim's footsteps is simple, straightforward police work. I ought to have seen to it already. Still, better late than never."

"What else did you find out today, sir?" she asked. He seemed a bit better than when he'd first sat down. Some of the worry had gone out of his face, and he wasn't holding himself so rigidly.

"We gathered statements from a number of people." He took another sip. "Then we went to Ernie Grigson's pub." He told her about his visit to the Iron Anchor pub and his impression of Edith Grigson.

Mrs. Jeffries listened carefully, occasionally asking a question or making a comment. When he was finished, she said, "She doesn't sound as if she's overly concerned with her brother's disappearance."

"She claims he's done it before," Witherspoon responded. "But, as Constable Barnes rightly pointed out, pubs and licenses are very expensive. You'd have to be completely unbalanced to just up and walk away from a good business like that one."

"It's successful?" She already knew the answer.

"Very much so. The Iron Anchor isn't one of those huge monstrosities that you see

154

nowadays, but it's nicely furnished. The fittings and fixtures appeared to be of good quality, and we found out that Grigson owns the building."

"Freehold or leasehold?" she asked.

"It's freehold," he replied. "The property alone is worth a great deal of money. It's right by the water, so they get a lot of foot traffic as well as a lot of customers from the riverboats. As a matter of fact, the pub is only a hundred yards or so from where Provost's body was found."

"And you think that's significant?" She prided herself on her ability to put the pieces together, but the inspector was no fool, and his opinion was worth noting.

He thought for a moment. "I'm not certain . . . No, that's not true. I think it is very significant. A river makes for a handy murder weapon. Which is really most unfortunate. Murder by drowning is very difficult to prove unless one has eyewitnesses."

"But you do have the bruised handprints on Provost's neck and shoulders," she pointed out. "That certainly should help prove the case, and I'm sure you'll find other evidence. Did you learn anything else today?"

"I sent some lads back to Provost's neighborhood, and they took statements from his neighbors. But none of them had any idea why someone would want to harm Mr. Provost, and on the day he died, they'd not seen nor heard anything unusual. All of them certainly spoke well of the man." He got up. "Once I find out how he went home on the nights he played whist, perhaps we'll be able to retrace his route and see if there's some clue that might help."

"Perhaps you'll even find your eyewitness, sir," she said with a smile.

"That would certainly make my life easier, but I'm not counting on it." He laughed. "Goodness, I am hungry tonight. But I shall eat quickly. After supper, I'm going to see Lady Cannonberry."

Ruth Cannonberry was their neighbor and Witherspoon's "special" friend. She lived across the communal garden and was the widow of a peer. She adored helping the household with the inspector's cases. Naturally, she was very discreet and kept her assistance to herself. Her late husband had left her not only a tidy fortune and a title, but also, unfortunately, with a number of his elderly relatives, who were always imposing upon her good nature. Consequently, she was frequently gone from London, and her relationship with Witherspoon suffered greatly.

"I thought Lady Cannonberry was at Cambridge," Mrs. Jeffries said as she got up.

"She came home last night." Witherspoon grinned like a schoolboy.

"Then I'm sure she'd welcome your visit, sir," Mrs. Jeffries murmured as she picked up the inspector's glass from the table and went to the door. "I'll bring your dinner right up."

Smythe stared out the small kitchen window over the sink. "There's a nasty fog rollin' in off the river. You can't see two feet in front of your face. Wouldn't be a nice night to be out and about."

"I rather like the fog," Mrs. Jeffries replied. She and Smythe were the only ones in the kitchen. The others had gone upstairs. While they ate their supper, she'd told them everything she'd learned from Witherspoon. They'd had a lively debate over what it all meant, but hadn't been able to come up with any answers as yet.

Smythe laughed and started for the back door. "I'd best lock up the back."

"I'll do it," Mrs. Jeffries said quickly. "I'm wide awake, and I think I'll sit up awhile."

Smythe covered his mouth as he yawned. "You sure? That lock can be a bit stiff."

"I'll manage," she interrupted. "Go on up. You look dead on your feet, and we've a busy day tomorrow."

He nodded, yawned again, and headed for the back stairs. She waited until she heard his footsteps fade; then she grabbed her heavy black cloak off the coat tree and wrapped it around her shoulders. She pulled out her chair and picked up the bonnet and gloves she'd hidden on the seat after supper; then she picked up the lantern from the sideboard and made her way down the hall, stopping just long enough to put the lantern on the shelf by the door in the dry larder.

Taking care to be quiet, she crept down the hall, slipped outside, and closed the door behind her. She hoped that, as everyone had been very tired tonight, none of them would take it into their heads to come downstairs. She stepped out onto the small terrace and went toward the path that bisected the garden.

The fog was heavy, but she could see clearly enough to make her way. A frisson of excitement swept over her, and she giggled softly. Gracious, she'd not done this in years. Nightwalking. That's how she'd always thought of it when it came to mind. When her husband had been alive and

158

they'd lived in Yorkshire, she'd done it quite often. Out in the crisp night air, she'd found that the darkness helped her to look at problems with a new perspective. It was almost as if the night sharpened her senses, enhanced her ability to put together facts and ideas in such a way as to make them clearer and more easily understood.

She stepped onto the path and hurried across the garden to the small gate at the far side. Darkness didn't frighten her. But she wasn't foolish, and she took care where she went. She kept a sharp eye out for others who might be about. She'd learned that if she kept to the small, quiet streets, stayed in the shadows, and kept her wits about her, she was quite safe.

She stuck her head out the gate and looked up and down the street, making sure she was alone before she stepped out into the shadows. The fog wasn't as thick as it had been in the garden. She turned left and went up Addison Road, listening for voices or footsteps as she walked. But the road was quiet and empty, so she continued on. When she reached Uxbridge Road, she stopped at the edge of the pavement. There wasn't any foot traffic, just a few hansom cabs heading for the train station.

She hurried across the road. By the time

she turned onto Addison Road North, the night was silent, and she felt quite safe. She slowed her steps as she started around the crescent-shaped street, taking long, deep breaths of air.

This case wasn't going very well. No matter how often she told the others it was still "early days," it really wasn't. They had two crimes, and as far as she could tell, absolutely no motive for either of them. She turned onto Queens Road and continued toward Norland Square.

Provost hadn't drunk, gambled, womanized, or had the usual packet of relatives desperate to inherit his money. So he was probably killed because he was investigating Grigson's disappearance. But what if that assumption was wrong? What if Edith Grigson was correct, and tomorrow or the next day or one day next week, her brother would suddenly show up alive and well? What then?

From behind her, Mrs. Jeffries heard the rattle of a hansom as it rounded the corner. She stepped back, away from the pale light of the nearest gas lamp, and stood stock-still until the vehicle went by. There was no point in letting anyone see a lone woman on the night streets.

The cab disappeared in the distance, and she started walking again. But Grigson isn't going to suddenly appear, she told herself. Every instinct she had was telling her that the man was dead. He might have suffered from melancholia, but that didn't mean he was foolish, and walking away from a prosperous pub on the banks of the Thames would be foolish indeed.

She stopped again as another idea popped into her head. Pubs, especially nice ones on the river in London, cost money. Edith Grigson had been employed as a governess, so that implied there wasn't a great deal of wealth in the family. The inspector had told her that the only items of value Ernie and his sister had left from their family were matching silver stickpins. So how had Ernie Grigson got the money to buy the Iron Anchor? His sister had told the inspector that he'd only owned the pub for a couple of years, and before that he'd drifted from one postion to another. So how had he been able to buy a pub?

In the distance, she heard a dog bark, and the sound got her moving.

She came out onto Norland Square and stood on the corner for a moment before cutting across the deserted street to the far side and turning toward Upper Edmonton Gardens.

Her mind wandered as she walked. All

sorts of bits and pieces swirled about like bits of paper in a windstorm. Why hadn't Tipton immediately told the police about Provost's investigation? He'd not said a word about it, only insisted that they investigate his client's death. And what was it about the Wentworth Club that made Provost think it had anything to do with his friend's disappearance? Grigson wasn't even a member of the club. Had there really been an attempt on another member's life the very same week that Provost had died? If that was true, had Jonathan March's mishap with a cooper's van anything to do with Provost's murder?

For the second time, she found herself at Uxbridge Road. As she started across, she suddenly realized something very important. Premeditated murder didn't happen arbitrarily. There was always a trigger for the killing.

She reached the opposite pavement, and her footsteps slowed as she cast her mind back to the inspector's previous homicide cases. Why had those murderers taken a human life? In some cases the killer had wanted to get rid of someone who stood in their way; or they had a rich relative and wanted to inherit a fortune; or the killer desperately wanted a secret to stay secret.

However, in each and every case, there was one common aspect: Every single murder they'd ever investigated had been precipitated by an event or a change of one sort or another.

Provost had been investigating Grigson's disappearance since the early autumn. It was now February. So what had made the killer act now and not when Provost first began snooping about? Something had precipitated Provost's murder. But what? And how could they possibly find out what it was?

She reached Addison Road. She turned the corner and slipped back into the garden. She crept back into the house and stood for a moment, listening. But she heard nothing. She tiptoed down the hall to the dry larder and lit the lantern she'd left on the shelf. As she made her way up to her room, she realized the nightwalking hadn't answered any of her questions. But at least it had given her some excellent ideas about where they ought to start looking next.

"What are the names again?" Luty asked as she pulled a pencil and a little brown notebook (identical to the one Constable Barnes carried) out of her muff. "I want to make sure I git 'em right."

163

"Provost played at the same table as Sir Edmund Cleverly. There were two brothers there as well, Rollo and George Barrington. He partnered with Cleverly. The other four members of the card group were Charles Capel, Octavius Delmar, Percy Harkins, and William Marston."

"It was Harkins and Marston who nominated Provost for membership," Hatchet reminded them.

"That's right," she replied. "And that is one of the reasons I think we ought to have a closer look at those two gentlemen."

"And we've got to find out why Mr. Tipton didn't tell the inspector about Provost's investigation straightaway," Betsy said. "I think that's very strange. Knowing about Grigson could have saved the inspector a lot of time. He could have gone to the Iron Anchor right away."

"Someone needs to find out about Jonathan March and the cooper's van," Mrs. Jeffries ordered.

"But you said we didn't 'ave to count that one," Wiggins complained. Cor blimey, he thought, all these new bits and pieces were going to make it hard to have tea with Catherine today.

"After thinking about it, I decided it might turn out to be important," she replied. "And we need to discover how Ernie Grigson got the money to buy the pub, and we mustn't forget that we need to know how Provost usually got home on his whist nights . . . Oh dear, I'm getting ahead of myself, aren't I?"

"We don't have to do all of this today," Mrs. Goodge said gently. "Besides, I thought I overheard you hintin' to the inspector that he ought to have a chat with Tipton. Why don't we see what he tells you tonight before we hare off in dozens of different directions. As you've pointed out, we've two crimes to solve now."

"Of course you're right." Mrs. Jeffries laughed. "It's just that there's so much to do."

"Should we ask Lady Cannonberry to help?" Betsy suggested. "She's usually gone when we have a murder, but she's home now."

"I think that's a right good idea," Wiggins volunteered. "She'd be ever so pleased." If Lady Cannonberry was going to help, maybe he wouldn't need to stop having tea with Catherine.

"I'm not sure." Mrs. Jeffries hesitated. "Sometimes I think that asking her for assistance might put her in an awkward position, considering the nature of her relationship with our inspector —" She broke off, not sure that she was explaining her meaning properly.

"Fiddlesticks," Luty exclaimed. "Ruth Cannonberry loves to snoop. There ain't a woman alive that hasn't kept a few secrets from the man in her life. You ought to know that, Hepzibah — you were married."

"That's very true." Mrs. Jeffries laughed again. "I loved my husband dearly, but if I'd told him everything I did, we'd have had a very miserable time of it." Her concerns evaporated. "I'll pop over to see Ruth this morning and see if she can lend a hand. Perhaps she'll know something about the members of the Wentworth Club."

Smythe looked at Betsy. "You're not keepin' secrets from me, are ya?"

"Of course not, dearest," she replied sweetly. He stared at her skeptically for a moment and then turned his attention back to the housekeeper. Betsy glanced at Luty, who was grinning from ear to ear, and rolled her eyes. All of the women knew that Smythe would have a fit if he knew half of what Betsy got up to when she was out on the hunt. But, wisely, they kept their knowledge to themselves.

"At least we've a few more names and addresses to work on, so that's all to the good," Wiggins muttered.

"And Rollo Barrington lives in Knights-bridge," Luty added. "It'll be easy to learn a few bits about him."

"I'll see what I can learn about George Barrington and Sir Edmund Cleverly." Betsy stood and headed for the coat tree "They both live in Marylebone." She also intended to have a quick trip to the Iron Anchor if she had time. Why should it just be the men who got to do the interesting bits?

Smythe got up and trailed after Betsy. "I still think it's worth finding out how Provost usually got home on the nights he played cards."

"I agree," Mrs. Jeffries said. "And I think you ought to have a go at talking to more hansom drivers. Even if Provost didn't take a cab, you might find out if there was anyone else of interest who was in the area on the night of the murder. But don't spend too much time worrying about that; I imagine the inspector will have a few consta-bles following up on that avenue of inquiry."

Betsy put on her hat and tied the ribbon firmly under her chin. "Come on, Smythe, get a move on. Time's a-wasting, and we've got a lot to do today."

He laughed as he slipped her cloak off the peg and draped it over her shoulders. "Not even married yet, and she's already badgerin' me." As they disappeared down the hall, the others heard him say, "Are you sure you're not keepin' bits from me?"

Charles Capel was not pleased to see them. "I've no idea why you think I can be of any help. I barely knew Michael Provost." He flopped down into an overstuffed chair and glared at the two policemen who'd had the temerity to invade his spacious drawing room. He was a man of medium height, with slight buckteeth, brown hair, and a small chin.

"You played whist with the man twice a week," Barnes said harshly. "I think that makes you more than just passing acquaintances. So it would be most helpful if you'd answer our questions, sir, then we can be on our way and you can be about your business." The constable was annoyed by the man's blatant rudeness in deliberately keeping them standing.

Capel was taken aback, but before he could sputter a reply, the constable continued his assault. "Now, sir, can you tell us when you first became acquainted with Mr. Provost?"

"Last September," Capel replied sullenly. "Harkins and Marston recommended him, and as we needed an eighth and he was supposedly a good player, he was elected to the club. But he usually played with the Barringtons and Cleverly. We've never had trouble keeping our fourth."

"Do you know of anyone who would have reason to want Mr. Provost dead?" Witherspoon asked.

"Of course not." Capel picked a piece of nonexistent lint off the cuff of his black coat.

"When was the last time you saw Mr. Provost?" Barnes asked.

"Tuesday evening. We'd played cards, and when the game broke up, I went home."

"Do you play for money, sir?" the constable asked softly.

"Not anymore," Capel replied. Then he seemed to catch himself as a flush rushed up his cheeks. "I mean, occasionally we'll have a gentleman's bet, but not very often. We play for the love of the game."

"What time did the game end?" Witherspoon asked.

Capel thought for a moment. "We started about half past seven, and I think we stopped about ten o'clock. Yes, I know that's when it broke up, because Rollo pulled out his watch and commented upon the time."

Witherspoon nodded. "Was everyone else still at the club when you left the premises?"

"Octavius and I left together. We shared a cab home that night," he replied. "Percy and William walked out just ahead of us . . ."

"Did they get a hansom as well?" Barnes asked.

Capel shook his head. "I don't know. We stopped to have a word with Edgar Biggleston as we were leaving, so I didn't see what they did when they left the premises. You might ask Deekins. He was on the door that night."

"And the others, sir?" Witherspoon prompted. "Were they still there?"

"The Barringtons were still in the card room." Capel's face creased in concentration. "But Sir Edmund had already gone. As soon as the last hand was played, he got up and dashed off. He said he was tired."

Witherspoon nodded in encouragement. This was the sort of information that generally proved useful. "Did Sir Edmund have his own carriage?"

Capel laughed. "No, he took a cab just like the rest of us. Do you have any idea how expensive it is to keep a carriage in the city?"

"Actually, the inspector knows precisely how much it costs," Barnes said. He knew he shouldn't do it, but he simply couldn't stop himself. Capel was really getting on his nerves. The man treated them as though they were dirt under his feet. It wouldn't have hurt him to invite them to sit down. "He's got one of his own. He keeps it and his horses at Howard's Livery."

Hatchet stood in the foyer of the elegant Mayfair town house and waited while the butler went to see if the gentleman of the house was "at home." He returned a few moments later. "Would you come this way, please."

He followed the butler down the long hallway. Seascapes, pastoral scenes, and still-life paintings of fruit bowls were prominently displayed on the walls. All of them were Reginald's work. Ye gods, his new wife must be absolutely besotted with him. The work was decent but not remarkable, and Hatchet knew the lady of the house could afford to hang Botticellis and Rembrandts if she wished.

The butler led him into a conservatory. Reginald Manley, artist and old friend, stepped out from behind an easel. "Hatchet, how delightful to see you. Have you come to congratulate me?"

"Indeed I have." Hatchet surveyed the room. Cool winter sunlight filtered in through the overhead glass. A white wrought-iron table, two wicker chairs with blue and pink floral cushions, and all of the plants were arranged on one half of the huge glass room. The other side had been turned into an artist's studio.

"Then we must celebrate." Manley looked at the butler. "Bring a pot of coffee for my guest and a glass of whisky for me."

"Yes, sir." The butler nodded and withdrew.

Manley wiped his hands on a cloth he picked up from a small wooden table next to the easel. He was a tall, slender, middle-aged man with black hair, deep-set gray eyes, and a wide, generous mouth. He had the kind of appearance that women thought handsome and men either envied or resented. He tossed the cloth down and motioned to the table and chairs. "Let's sit."

"I was very pleased to hear you'd married." Hatchet sat down.

Manley looked amused. "Thank you. Myra's a wonderful woman. I'm lucky she agreed to marry me. Let's be honest, Hatchet: We both know I made more money courting the ladies than I ever did selling my artwork. But Myra doesn't care. She loves me, and oddly enough, I love her."

"You were always a gentleman with your ladies," he replied. "Your wife is a very lucky woman. I know you'll be faithful and attentive, and treat her kindly for the rest of your days. That's more than most marriages can claim." He wasn't just buttering up Manley to get information out of him. He knew that despite Manley's reputation as a ladies' man, once he said his vows, he'd take them very seriously indeed. The man was a charmer and a bit of a bohemian, but he had always had principles. "And you actually are quite a decent artist."

"Decent isn't good enough," Manley replied softly. "But I appreciate your saying it. Now, why are you really here?"

Hatchet laughed. "You still get right to the point, don't you. Alright, I'm hoping you can help me with some information. As you've moved up in the world, I won't insult you by offering you money for it."

"Who says I'd be insulted?" Manley grinned broadly. "Don't worry, I'm jesting. Myra gives me a very generous allowance, and I do occasionally sell a painting. What kind of information do you need?"

Manley was one of many sources that Hatchet was going to tap. He'd no idea whether the man would know anything about any of the names on his list, but he thought it worth a try. "Do you know of the Wentworth Club?"

"Second-rate, tries hard to pretend they're top-drawer because they've a few aristocrats that can't afford the fees at the really good clubs," Manley replied. He stopped speaking as the butler returned and put the tray on the table.

"I'll serve us," Manley said to him. "Thank you."

"Very good, sir." Manley waited until they were alone again before he spoke. "You know, Hatchet, I always thought I'd love having a passel of servants waiting on me, but the truth is, it makes me very uncomfortable. It's unnerving." He poured the coffee and handed it to his guest.

"Perhaps you're just not used to it," Hatchet replied.

Manley tossed back his whisky in one gulp. "I'll never get used to it. It's not right; it's simply not right."

"Good gracious, you sound like one of those radicals." Hatchet eyed him warily. The last person he'd ever have suspected of harboring a soft spot for the working class was Reginald Manley.

"I'm not a radical. It's just that now that I'm living like this" — he gestured at his surroundings — "it hasn't been quite what I thought it would be. But that's not why you're here. Go on; which members of the

Wentworth Club are you curious about?"

"Michael Provost —"

"You mean the man that was fished out of the Thames," Manley interrupted. "I'd never heard of him until he died."

"Charles Capel, Octavius Delmar, Percy Harkins, or William Marston. Ever heard of any of them?" Hatchet rattled off the names and then paused.

Manley simply stared at him blankly. "Sorry, I don't know them."

"How about Rollo and George Barrington, or Sir Edmund Cleverly?" he persisted.

Manley's eyes brightened. "I know Cleverly. Rather, my wife knows him. He's been to dinner here a few times. Can't say I like him very much. He's a dreadful snob. He's only civil to me because he's scared of Myra." He grinned impishly. "One word from her, and his invitations in this town would dry up like last year's spring bouquets. Despite his aristocratic peerage, Cleverly isn't well liked. He's not amusing, intelligent, or charming, and to top it off, he's not got much money. These days, having a pedigree one can trace back to William the Conqueror doesn't mean what it once did."

"What else do you know about him?"

175

Manley toyed with his empty whisky glass. "He's supposedly engaged to Isabella March, but there's some impediment to the marriage. Odd, really, when you think of what a snob he is, that he'd want to marry someone like her."

"What do you mean?" Hatchet asked.

"As I said, Cleverly is a horrid snob, one of those types who think they're entitled to everything in life simply by virtue of their birth. His fiancée is very wealthy, but her family made it in trade. Mind you, I'm not certain that marriage is going to take place in any case. From the rumors I've heard, her brother is opposed to the match. Jonathan March is no fool; he'll not be giving his blessing to the happy couple just because Edmund was born a baronet."

"Cleverly is poor?"

"He's not a church mouse, but the family estate is long gone," Manley said. "He's managed to hang on to the house in Marylebone, and he's a bit of income that he lives on. God knows the fellow's never done a day's work in his life. As for those other two you mentioned . . ." He frowned. "The names sound familiar, but I can't recall anything specific."

"That's because they are two of the dullest men in all of London," a woman's voice said from behind them.

"Myra, darling." Manley leapt to his feet, a wide, genuine smile on his face. "I thought you were going to be out all morning."

"I got bored and I came home," she replied, her gaze on Hatchet, who'd also risen to his feet. "Won't you introduce me to your friend?"

Myra Haddington Manley was a tall, sturdy woman with brown hair, pale skin, a long nose, and slight buckteeth. She wore a high-necked white blouse with a fitted forest green jacket and a matching skirt.

"This is Hatchet," Manley said. "I've known him for years, yet I've never discovered his Christian name."

"How do you do, Mrs. Manley." Hatchet bowed formally. "I'm delighted to make your acquaintance."

"And I yours." She smiled in amusement and turned to leave. "Please don't let me interrupt . . ."

Hatchet wasn't about to let her get away. "Oh, no, madam, if I might make so bold, please join us."

Taken aback, she stopped.

Manley laughed. "Come on, Myra, be a sport. Hatchet's dying to find out what you know about the Barrington brothers."

She stared at him, her expression frankly

curious. "Why do you want to know about those two bores?"

Hatchet wasn't sure how to reply. He didn't wish to say too much and run the risk of any additional people getting wind of the fact that the inspector had a lot of help on his cases; yet he sensed this woman wouldn't be fobbed off by some silly story.

"Hatchet's the one I told you about," Manley interjected. "You know, the one who works for the elderly American lady."

"Ah, I see. You're friends with that police detective, aren't you," Myra said. It wasn't a question, more like a statement of fact.

Hatchet's heart sank. God in heaven, had everyone in London cottoned on to what he was doing? "I am acquainted with the inspector, but we're not friends by any means."

She laughed as though she didn't believe a word he said, then sat down in the seat her husband had just vacated. "Reginald, dear, ring for the butler and have him bring another chair. Oh, and I'd like a glass of whisky, too."

"But of course, dear."

She turned her attention back to Hatchet. "Don't worry, I know how to be discreet. I've met Mrs. Crookshank. She's delightful, but she is getting a reputation for asking a lot of questions, especially about people associated with murder. But then again, that would only be natural, wouldn't it?"

"Uh, I suppose it would." He'd no idea what to say. Hatchet wasn't sure whether she was sending him a warning that their activities were becoming widely known or simply making polite conversation. With women like her, it was impossible to tell. But he did as she instructed and took his seat again.

"Make yourself comfortable," she continued. "And I'll tell you what I know about George and Rollo Barrington."

"I'm sorry to keep you waiting, Inspector," Anthony Tipton apologized as he ushered the two policemen into his office.

"Not to worry, sir," Witherspoon replied. "It wasn't very long."

"Please make yourselves comfortable." He gestured to the chairs in front of his desk. Tipton was of medium height, with a rather pudgy frame. He had thick, dark brown hair with a few strands of gray, and a boyish, unlined face.

"Thank you," Witherspoon said as he took his seat. "I'll try not to take up too much of your time, but I'm sure you know why we're here."

"Of course." Tipton picked up a pair of spectacles, put them on, and tapped his finger on the file lying on the desk. "I've got Michael's will right here. But I don't think you'll find the contents helpful. He didn't have any direct heirs, but there are several beneficiaries. The rest of his estate is being disbursed among a dozen different individuals, charities, and institutions."

"Before we get into the particulars of his estate, we'd like to ask you some questions," the inspector said.

Tipton took off his spectacles. "Yes, I suppose you would." He sighed heavily and looked down at the desk. "Michael Provost wasn't just my client; he was my friend. This has been a very difficult time for me. But I'll do anything in my power to bring his killer to justice." He lifted his chin. "So ask me whatever you like."

"Mr. Tipton, when you spoke to the chief inspector, why didn't you mention that Mr. Provost was conducting an investigation into the disappearance of Ernie Grigson?"

"I know I should have mentioned it." He smiled sadly. "But, as I said, Michael was my friend, and frankly, I was afraid that if I brought up the Grigson matter, your chief inspector wouldn't take the matter seriously. For God's sake, he was out and about and playing detective because he so admired that fictional detective fellow . . . Oh, what's his name?"

"Sherlock Holmes," Barnes supplied.

"That's the one." Tipton looked at the inspector. "I didn't want anyone thinking Michael was foolish, because he wasn't. Perhaps I should have told the police everything I knew straightaway, but as I'm in the legal profession, I know something about police procedures."

"And you thought we'd take the information more seriously if we found it out ourselves," Witherspoon guessed.

"That's correct," Tipton replied. "But that wasn't the only reason I said nothing. I was also very concerned because Michael had been sending letters informing the police of his suspicions and detailing his activities for weeks. Those letters were never answered. That was most disturbing to me. As a matter of fact, a few days before he was murdered, I met Michael for lunch and offered to take the matter to my godfather to see if he could help."

"Who is your godfather, sir?" Witherspoon inquired.

"Lord Pennifrey. He's a cousin to Her Majesty," Tipton replied.

Witherspoon nodded. Lord Pennifrey

wasn't just related to the queen; he was also highly placed in the government. He'd worked in the Foreign Office and held several ambassadorships.

"But Michael told me to wait a few days before I contacted him. He said he'd found out something, and that if he was correct, he'd have all the proof he needed that Ernie Grigson had been murdered."

"Did he tell you what that proof might be?" Barnes asked.

"No." Tipton's shoulders slumped. "I should have insisted he tell me more about the whole wretched mess. But I didn't, and obviously Grigson's killer caught wind of the fact that Michael was on to him. Now poor Michael's dead, and I can't help but feel responsible."

"You mustn't blame yourself, sir," the inspector said kindly.

"Why did Mr. Provost think that joining the Wentworth Club would help him find out what happened to Grigson?" Barnes asked.

Tipton looked surprised by the question.

"His cook overheard Mr. Provost mentioning that to you over dinner one evening last October," the constable explained.

"Oh, yes, now I remember. We were having supper on the terrace, and I'd asked him if he'd made any progress," Tipton replied. "But, again, he didn't tell me any details. You must understand, I didn't approve of what he was doing. I thought it rather foolhardy and, well, we'd had some harsh words over the matter. So when I pressed him, all he would say was that his joining the Wentworth was going to help him find out what had happened to Mr. Grigson."

"I understand that Mr. Provost and Mr. Grigson were at medical school together. Is that correct?" Witherspoon wasn't sure that was what he'd meant to ask. But it was easy to get confused. He'd discussed the case with Mrs. Jeffries while eating his breakfast that morning, and now there were dozens of different questions whirling about in his head.

"That's correct. On the surface it would appear strange that they'd remained friends over the years."

"How so, sir?" Witherspoon asked.

"Michael Provost lived a very orderly, predictable life. Ernie Grigson drifted from place to place and job to job. He was from quite a wealthy family on his mother's side. But his father managed to gamble most of it away. Michael thought that was why he left medical school without receiving his degree — he ran out of money. Grigson took a position as a salesman for a pharmaceutical company, and his sister became a governess. I think that's how he and Michael kept in touch. For a brief period, they were both in the same business."

"If he had no money, how'd he end up buying the pub?" Barnes asked.

Tipton shrugged. "I've no idea. The only thing I ever knew of the man was what Michael told me." He flipped open the folder. "I don't suppose this will be very helpful, but there is one thing you should know. According to the terms of his will, Michael left Mr. Grigson a sum of two thousand pounds. It was willed to him directly."

"And does that mean that if Mr. Grigson is dead, the money would go to his next of kin?" Barnes asked.

"That's right." Tipton nodded eagerly. "That means the money will go to his sister, Edith Grigson."

CHAPTER 6

"I'm so delighted you came over," Ruth Cannonberry said as she ushered Mrs. Jeffries into the morning room. "Please sit down. Would you care for some tea?" She gestured toward the gold-colored velvet love seat.

Tall, fair-haired, elegant, and middle-aged, Lady Cannonberry was still as slender as a girl. She was the widow of a peer, but her upbringing as the daughter of a country parson had given her not only a sense of social justice, but a genuine belief in the equality of all persons. Her sense of egalitarianism extended to her relationship with the household of Upper Edmonton Gardens, and she insisted they address her by her Christian name.

"That's very kind of you, but I've just had breakfast." Mrs. Jeffries sank down onto the cushions. She waited until her hostesss had taken her seat, and then she got right to the point. "Ruth, do forgive me for being blunt. But we need help on a case, and as you're here in London, I was hoping I might prevail upon you for assistance."

Ruth clapped her hands in delight. "Of course. I'd be honored to help. You know that. Is it this dreadful Provost drowning? I know it's upset Gerald greatly. He told me last evening when he came over after supper that he didn't think he'd ever get it solved." She laughed. "But he will, especially with our help. Oh dear, I'm so excited; I'm babbling like a green girl."

"I'm afraid it isn't just the Provost murder that we've got on our plates," Mrs. Jeffries explained. "It's a bit more complex than that." She told Ruth everything. Even though she tried to be concise, by the time she recounted every fact, suspect, idea, or bit of gossip they'd uncovered, fifteen minutes had passed.

When Mrs. Jeffries had finished, Ruth said, "I don't know Sir Edmund Cleverly, nor do I recall ever hearing any of the names you've mentioned. But I am well acquainted with Isabella March. She's a member of my women's group. She's quite an intelligent woman." Ruth looked puzzled. "And quite strong willed. I can't imagine she'd allow her brother to dictate whether she could become engaged. Wait a minute." She leapt up and dashed across the small space to the fireplace. A cream-colored envelope was propped against a silver candlestick. She grabbed it, tore it open, and pulled out the card. "Yes, I thought so." She walked back to the love seat and held out the card so that Mrs. Jeffries could read it.

"It's an invitation." Mrs. Jeffries squinted at the small, elegant writing. "To a reception at the Cadogan Club."

"It's for Mrs. Mellows," Ruth explained as she retook her seat. "She's giving a speech on women's suffrage before the reception. As I've only just got back to London a few days ago, I wasn't planning to attend, but now I'll go. The reception's this afternoon. I'm sure Isabella March will be there. She's a great supporter of the suffrage movement. This will be the perfect chance to speak with her."

"Excellent. That's a very good place to start," Mrs. Jeffries agreed.

"What should I ask her?" Ruth's expression grew serious. "I mean, I know I can't just go blurting out questions about poor Mr. Provost, so what do you think would be the best approach?"

Mrs. Jeffries thought for a moment. "We don't know if Miss March knew Mr. Provost. She probably didn't. Her brother was a member of the club, but he didn't play whist. Ask about her brother's accident."

"I will. Let's just hope that she's in a chatty mood today."

"It's about time you showed up." Blimpey Groggins waved Smythe onto the empty stool opposite him. "I was begining to think you fell off the face of the earth. I've got a lot of information."

"I came by yesterday, but you were out." Smythe sat down.

Blimpey sighed theatrically. "Nell wanted me to take her to Liberty to have a look at a new bedroom suite. There's nothin' wrong with the one we've got, but Nell has some bee in her bonnet that we need new furniture. Anyways, you're not 'ere about my domestic concerns; you're 'ere about your Mr. Provost. Do you want a pint?"

"It's a bit early for me," Smythe replied. "Uh, about Provost, there's something you need to know. Provost was . . ."

"Investigatin' the disappearance of Ernie Grigson." Blimpey finished the sentence for him. "I know. I also know that Grigson and he were good friends, that he used to play whist in Grigson's pub, and that Edith Grigson, Ernie's dear sister, has moved in and taken the place over, lock, stock, and barrel. But that's not all I've got to tell ya."

"I didn't think it would be." Smythe grinned. "I should have known you'd tumble onto what Provost was up to pretty quick."

Blimpey laughed. "When you goin' to get it through your thick head that I'm ruddy good at what I do? This is goin' to cost you a bit more, you know that, don't ya. After all, I'm workin' on two crimes now instead of just one."

"I didn't think you were doin' it for free," Smythe replied. "What makes you think there's two crimes here? Grigson has just disappeared; we don't know that he's not gone off of his own free will. He's supposedly one of them that has the melancholia."

"Don't be daft. No one walks away from a freehold pub in London. Especially one on the river. And the only person who claims he's got the depression sickness is his sister. None of my sources found any evidence that there was a bloomin' thing wrong with the man's mind. Take my word for it — Grigson's dead. You'll know I'm right when you hear the rest."

"Alright, what else is there?"

"For starters, Grigson wasn't just a publican: He was also a bookie. He took bets on the horses. He'd been doin' it for years," Blimpey said. "Secondly, right before he disappeared, he was braggin' to one of his associates, another bookie, that he had made a killin' on that filly that won the Ascot Gold Cup."

"La Flèche? Lots of people made a bit on that one."

"Yeah, but Grigson made his wad on the Hardwicke Stakes, the race that La Flèche didn't win."

"I remember." Smythe smiled ruefully. "Ravensbury won by half a length. I had a fiver on La Flèche."

"So did everyone else in London," Blimpey said. "Including some punters that had given Grigson a fortune for her to win. But she didn't, and Ernie Grigson made a fistful of lolly."

"So Grigson had a lot of cash just before he disappeared," Smythe said thoughtfully. "That would explain why he's not turned up. Someone probably robbed him."

"It wasn't cash that he had," Blimpey said. "The punter made some comment like, 'You'd best take a big purse with ya when you take your lolly to the bank.' Grigson laughed and said not to worry, it wasn't lolly he had but somethin' even better, and that

190

he could carry it to the bank in his coat pocket."

Smythe drew back, his expression skeptical. "No offense, Blimpey, but is your source a good one? I've never heard of a bookie that didn't want cold hard cash to take a bet."

"Then your education has been woefully inadequate," Blimpey replied. "There's plenty out there that will take anything of value if that's all the punter's got — jewels, coins, paintings, Dresden figurines. I even knew one bloke that ended up owning a canal boat. If the punter loses, then the bookie keeps the goods and gets to sell what he's got. If the punter wins, then he gets his goods back as well as the cash value of the bet."

"Ya learn something new every day, I guess," Smythe mused. He considered himself quite knowledgeable about such things, but apparently he wasn't as well versed as he had once been. "And this was right before Grigson disappeared?" Smythe clarified. "That same day?"

Blimpey looked uncertain. "I can't guarantee that part, but my source said that if it wasn't the same day, it was close to the time."

"Did your source say where he'd seen

Grigson?" Smythe shifted his weight on the hard stool.

"At the Iron Anchor, Grigson's pub. He remembers it so clearly because Grigson was all dressed up that evening. He was all spit and polish, with a brand-new gray summer suit, a white shirt, and a red cravat with a fancy silver stickpin in the center."

Witherspoon and Barnes stood inside the elegant foyer of Charles Capel's Knightsbridge house and waited for the butler to return. But it wasn't a servant who came down the staircase: It was the master of the house himself. Capel was a man of medium height with wispy brown hair receding from a high forehead, a long nose, and a very sharp chin. He wore a pair of navy blue trousers and a white shirt with the cuffs undone and the collar open. A blue and gray striped tie was draped around his neck, and the ends bounced against his shirt as he stumbled down the stairs. He moved so quickly that both policemen stepped forward, fearing the poor fellow was going to fall.

"Not to worry, I'm alright." He grabbed for the banister, steadied himself, and slowed his pace. "I'm Charles Capel." He reached the bottom stair and took a big gulp of air. "I understand you wish to speak to me."

"I'm Inspector Witherspoon, and . . ."

"I know who you are," Capel interrupted quickly. "Sorry, didn't mean to be rude, but I'm in a bit of a hurry. Lots to do today and all that."

"When was the last time you saw Michael Provost?" Barnes asked.

Capel swallowed. "Let me see. I guess it was Tuesday last. The eight of us played whist as we always did on Tuesdays and Thursdays. But I didn't know the man very well. He played at the other table."

"Do you know of anyone who might have wished to harm Mr. Provost?" Witherspoon asked.

"Of course not," Capel replied. "That's a ridiculous idea."

"But Mr. Provost was asking questions," the inspector said. "Questions about a certain Mr. Ernie Grigson. Had he ever asked you about someone by that name?"

"Never heard of the fellow." Capel rubbed his left eye. "As for Mr. Provost going about and asking questions, well, what of it? Lots of people ask questions. Frankly, I thought that Mr. Provost's behavior was simply a matter of being overinquisitive. I've a cousin who has the same habit. Is this going to take much longer? I've got an appointment with my tailor."

"What time did you leave the Wentworth that night?" The constable noticed that Capel's eyes twitched.

"As soon as the game ended, I came home. You can ask my manservant if you need some sort of confirmation." He looked up the stairs and shouted, "Blakely, do come down here."

Blakely appeared on the landing. "Yes, sir?" he said.

"Tell these policemen what time I got home last Tuesday night," Capel ordered.

"Very good, sir," Blakely replied. He focused his attention on the inspector. "Mr. Capel arrived home at twenty past ten."

"You remember it specifically?" Witherspoon asked.

"He always arrives home at twenty past ten," Blakely replied. "I brought his whisky to his room at half past the hour, so he could have it when he retired for the night."

"You see," Capel cried triumphantly. "I told you I came straight home. You may go about your duties, Blakely."

"Did any of the other servants see you when you came in that evening?" Barnes asked.

"No, they'd all retired. Blakely's the only

one I need that late. Is there anything else?" Capel reached up and tried to fasten the top of his shirt, but he kept pushing the stud against the fabric and not into the opening.

"How did you get home that night?" Witherspoon thought this one of the oddest statements he'd ever taken. But at least the fellow was cooperating.

"Hansom cab. I always take a cab home." He edged toward the door. "I'm sorry to be so blunt, but you'll have to leave. I really must be going."

"We're almost through here, sir," Barnes said softly. "Are you sure you've never heard of Ernie Grigson? Never heard Mr. Provost mention that name?"

"Never." Capel grabbed the handle and yanked the door open. "I don't wish to be rude, but I've no more time."

The two policemen stepped outside. Barnes started down the stairs, but the inspector turned and said, "If we've more questions, we'll be in touch. Good day, sir."

"Yes, yes, I'm sure you will. Good day." Capel closed the door firmly.

"This is right nice of ya," Jim Evans said as the barmaid brought the two pints and put one in front of him and the other in front of Wiggins. "I don't see how I can help ya, but if ya keep buyin' me pints, I'll answer your questions."

Wiggins stared at his latest source and hoped he'd not made a mistake. Jim Evans was a gawky red-haired lad with a pale complexion and deep-set brown eyes. He'd spotted the young man coming out of Rollo Barrington's Knightsbridge home, followed him, and struck up a conversation. Luring him to the pub with the tale of being a private inquiry agent had been dead easy. "I don't have all that many to ask. What do you do for the Barrington household?"

Evans took a quick sip of his beer. "I don't work there regular-like. They just send for me when they need a bit of heavy work done or a repair. They called me to come over today because Mr. Barrington had the floors sanded, and they wanted the rugs to be put back down."

Blast a Spaniard, Wiggins thought. Evans wasn't even a member of the Barrington household. This was a blooming waste of time. He'd make this quick, then. If he hurried, he could get to the Odeon a bit early. "Puttin' down a few rugs doesn't sound like it's very taxing work."

"It wouldn't be for a proper household," Evans replied. "But there's only the old cook and two housemaids. Those big rugs are heavy. They couldn't lift 'em. It took both me and my mate to get them up the narrow back steps and into the drawing room. Mind you, whoever cleaned the bleedin' things didn't do a good job, but that's not surprising. Barrington was probably too cheap to have them done properly."

"Our information is that Mr. Barrington is wealthy," Wiggins said. The question was purely for show.

"Whoever's tellin' you such things is wrong." Evans snorted. "Barrington pretends he's got lots of money. He's always actin' high and mighty, and sneers at those of us that have to work for a livin', but he's had plenty of people dunnin' him to make good on his notes."

"What do you mean?" Wiggins asked. "What kind of notes?"

"I mean just what I said. Once he owed a bookmaker so much money, the man come to the house before breakfast and threatened to take him to the law," Evans said eagerly. "I know that for a fact, because I was standing right there fixin' the lock on his desk when the bloke come stormin' in, demanding his money." Evans laughed. "You should've seen Mr. Barrington. His face turned red, and his eyes bulged out like he was goin' to explode."

"What happened then?" Wiggins took another sip of beer.

"Oh, his brother showed up and they shooed me out the door, but Letty — she's one of the housemaids there — told me later that when the man left, the two brothers stayed in the study and got through a whole bottle of whisky that morning." He grinned triumphantly. "Not what a rich man would do, now, is it."

Wiggins nodded. "When did this happen?"

Evans thought for a moment. "It's been a couple of years back — no, I tell a lie. It was about three years ago. I remember because my niece was born that night and she's just gone three. But that's not the half of it. He pinches things, too."

"You mean he steals?"

"That's right. Letty told me he's got a hidey-hole up in his bedroom where he puts the stuff he takes."

"Just because someone has a secret place they put their special things doesn't mean they're a thief," Wiggins said. He put his treasures in a cigar box under his bed.

"That's not the only evidence he's a ruddy thief. Letty told me she's seen him come home and empty his pockets of all sorts of things: china figurines, snuffboxes, silver spoons. He helps himself to whatever catches his fancy. She once saw him steal a gold stickpin off his friend's coat as he was drapin' it over the bloke's shoulders."

"Are you sure this Letty isn't having a laugh at your expense?" Wiggins said. "It doesn't make sense, does it."

"What you talkin' about?" Jim protested.

Cor blimey, Evans was as thick as two short planks, Wiggins thought. "Think about it. Where could Barrington wear the jewelry he pinches? People would notice if he strolled into a dinner party wearing a pin he'd stolen off someone's lapel, and he couldn't have anyone over to visit if his drawing room was full of other people's china figurines, could he."

"Don't be daft. He's not a fool. Letty says he takes the stuff he pinches to Birmingham and sells it. But he doesn't sell everything. Letty says he keeps most of the jewelry to wear for when he goes out of town on one of his trips."

"Letty knows this for a fact, does she," Wiggins charged. This Letty sounded like a right clever lass. He wished he'd been able to speak to her instead of Evans.

Evans shrugged. "She's never followed him to Birmingham, if that's what yer askin', but she's seen him when he comes back." He leaned closer to Wiggins, his expression earnest. "When he returns from one of his trips, he goes right to his hidey-hole, takes whatever jewelry he was wearin' that day out of his pocket, and puts it back. He puts money there as well. Where was he gettin' pound notes if he wasn't sellin' stuff?"

"Maybe he had business dealings in Birmingham," Wiggins suggested.

"Rubbish," Evans snapped. "The only work the man's ever done in his life is a bit of thievin', and the only kind of business dealing you have with that is findin' a pawnshop that don't ask too many questions."

"Mr. Harkins, I assure you, our inquiries won't take much of your time." Witherspoon slipped into a wingback chair. He and Constable Barnes were in the drawing room of Percy Harkins' Mayfair town house. Harkins had frowned at the two policemen when the butler had shown them in, but he had decent manners and had asked them to sit down.

Percy Harkins was a small, slender man in early middle age, with thinning blond hair and a handlebar mustache. "I've no idea what you think I might be able to tell you.

The last time I saw Michael Provost, he was alive and well." He glanced at the closed drawing room door. "Can you please make this quick, Inspector? My wife will be home any moment now and, frankly, finding the police here would be very upsetting for her."

"We'll be as brief as possible," the inspector replied. He wondered whether Mrs. Harkins was of a nervous disposition or whether she'd be unduly worried by what her neighbors would think. In one of those moments that happen without warning, Witherspoon had a true insight into the nature of the world. Rich people and criminals had a lot in common: Neither group liked talking to the police, and they certainly didn't appreciate the officers showing up on their doorsteps. "What time did you leave the Wentworth Club the night Mr. Provost was murdered?"

Before he answered, Harkins glanced pointedly at the gold carriage clock on the mantel. "When the game ended. It was about ten o'clock. I said my good nights, and then I left."

"Did anyone leave with you?" Barnes flipped through his little brown notebook to a blank page.

"William Marston and I left together. We shared a cab home."

"Mr. Marston lives close by?" Witherspoon said.

Harkins nodded. "That's correct. He's only two streets over."

The inspector decided to switch tactics. "Do you know of anyone who might have had reason to want Mr. Provost dead?"

"No. He was a very ordinary sort of person. He didn't even argue about cards, Inspector." Harkins walked over and sank down onto the sofa next to the inspector's chair. "He played the hand he was dealt and didn't complain when luck went against him, which is more than you can say for the other three in that group."

"Did you always play with the same partners?" Barnes stopped writing.

"Always. William's my partner. Charles Capel and Octavius Delmar play together. The Barringtons are always together, and Cleverly gets whoever is making up the fourth at their table."

"The same four are always playing at separate tables, then?" Barnes asked curiously. He'd played a lot of cards over the years and wouldn't have ever played with the same partner every time.

"That is correct. We've been playing whist for fifteen years. Marston and I can practically read each other's minds. That's the advantage of playing with the same partner all the time." Harkins smiled smugly as if he had forgotten that only moments ago he'd been trying to get the two policemen out of his drawing room.

"So Michael Provost and his partner would have been at a disadvantage, right?" Barnes pointed out.

"Perhaps." Harkins shrugged. "But it didn't seem to hinder Provost's play. They won their fair share. But Cleverly is good at partnering with outsiders. He's done it a number of times before. They have trouble keeping a fourth at that table."

Witherspoon shifted his weight again. This chair was beautiful, but very uncomfortable. "Had Mr. Provost had any difficulties with any other club members recently?"

"No, I've heard of nothing. I think I saw him having a word with Lord Barraclough last week, but other than that, unless he was playing cards, he kept to himself." Harkins got to his feet. "Is this going to take much longer?"

Barnes glanced at the inspector. Harkins was lying. Why?

"How did you know Mr. Provost?" the constable asked softly. He grinned as he watched the inspector fidgeting about in that chair, trying to find a position that didn't flatten his backside.

"I don't understand the question," Harkins said. "I've just told you — I didn't even play at the same table as Provost, and I didn't know him all that well . . ."

"But you and Mr. Marston nominated him for membership," Barnes interrupted. "So surely you must have known him previously. You didn't just drag him in off the street to make up a fourth."

"Of course not," Harkins replied irritably. "I didn't understand what you meant. I nominated him because William asked me to be the second. You must have two members nominate you in order to gain admission to the Wentworth."

"So it was William Marston who actually knew Michael Provost and wanted him to become a member?" Witherspoon clarified.

"I believe he met Provost when they played a casual game together in a pub," Harkins replied. "But they weren't old friends or anything of that sort. After all, Provost was in trade. But William said he seemed a decent enough fellow, and they needed a fourth at the other table, so he asked me to lend a hand with the nomination, which I did. Now, you really must go —"

"Were you still on the premises when Mr.

Provost left the club?" Witherspoon cut Harkins off. He was tired of being asked to leave, and he didn't want to lose sight of his "timeline," so to speak.

Harkins glared at him. "Provost was talking to Rollo Barrington when we left. They were the last two in the card room."

"So you've no idea how Mr. Provost might have decided to go home that night?" Barnes asked.

Harkins looked surprised by the question. "I expect he went home the same way he always did: He walked."

"Walked?" Barnes repeated. "But the Wentworth is a good two miles from the Provost house."

Harkins looked puzzled. "Didn't you say you'd spoken to Charles Capel? Surely he must have mentioned this to you. Michael Provost believed in the virtues of walking, of fresh air, and of plenty of exercise. He claimed it kept one healthy. He always walked home."

Her many years in service had given Mrs. Goodge dozens of connections into the households of upper-crust London, but the only link she'd been able to find to this case was Mabel Bonner, and it was a weak link at best. For starters, Mrs. Goodge barely

205

knew Mabel, as they'd worked together for only a brief time. But Mabel was all she had, so Mabel would have to do.

"I'm so glad you were able to come." Mrs. Goodge put the plate of scones onto the table and slipped into her seat. "I've been trying to get in touch with some of my old er . . . acquaintances."

Mabel Bonner was a tiny woman with graying blond hair, blue eyes, and a sharp, pointed chin. She was dressed in a well-cut brown suit, with a brown and gold checked blouse and a brown bonnet with a matching ribbon around the brim.

She stared at Mrs. Goodge for a few moments before she answered. "It took the wind out of my sails when I opened that envelope and saw your note. We didn't work together very long. I was a young scullery maid, and you were the cook. I'm surprised you even remember me."

"Oh, nonsense." The cook forced a laugh. "Of course I remember you. You were always so quick-witted and clever." She held her breath, hoping her ruse would work.

Delighted by the compliment, Mabel smiled broadly. "That's very kind of you."

Mrs. Goodge relaxed. Gracious, it was true: People would believe any sort of foolishness as long as it flattered them. She didn't recall Mabel being anything other than a chatterbox back in the old days. "Not kind — truthful. You were always very observant as well, and you kept your ears open. All of us used to rely on you for information about what was going on upstairs."

"It's important to take an interest in what goes on around you." Mabel dipped her head modestly. "You know, I left service years ago and took a position as an undermatron at the Home for Deaf Children. I retired from there last year, and now I live with my daughter in Shepherd's Bush. Her husband works on the railways and he's gone a lot, so I help her with the children. It works well for both of us." She looked around the kitchen. "You're still working, then?"

The question wasn't unkind, so Mrs. Goodge didn't take offense. She knew that someone her age still being "in service" was unusual. Truth be told, she found that working for a living gave her an advantage. If she could get people to feel sorry for her, she could get them to talk. Pity worked as well as flattery in loosening tongues.

"I didn't have much choice." She sighed. "I didn't invest my wages properly, and when I lost my last position, I was lucky enough to find work with Inspector Wither-spoon."

She was exaggerating, but it wasn't that far from the truth. What she wasn't telling Mabel was that since coming to work for the inspector, she'd saved and invested every penny she earned and now had a tidy sum put away. "Actually," Mrs. Goodge continued, "I rather like working for him. His cases are ever so interesting."

"Really?" Mabel helped herself to a scone.

Mrs. Goodge nudged the butter pot closer to Mabel's plate. "Oh, yes. As a matter of fact, he's working on a very complicated matter right now. It involves the upper class, and you know what that means! It's too bad that you've left service — I'll bet that with your keen eyes and ears, you'd know plenty about the people my inspector is investigating."

Mabel froze for a moment, her hand hovering over her teacup. "What are their names?" she demanded. She picked up her cup. "I've got family still in service, and my ears work perfectly. You know as well as I do that gossip never stops, so I hear plenty."

Mrs. Goodge reached for her own cup. Mabel had taken the bait; now it was simply a matter of reeling her in and finishing the job. "You're right about that — gossip does make the world go round. But I doubt you'd have heard of any of these people —"

"Don't be so sure," Mabel interrupted. "Come on, give me the names, and we'll just see if I've heard of them or not."

"Let me see . . . There's two brothers by the name of Barrington. Both of them have big houses in the Marylebone area. And then there's a Mr. Charles Capel. He lives in Knightsbridge." The cook watched Mabel carefully as she recited every name she could think of that had been mentioned during this case. But, as Mrs. Goodge had suspected, only the last name sparked a reaction from Mabel. "And one of them is a knight, or he might even be a baronet. His name is Sir Edmund Cleverly."

"My niece works for him," Mabel cried triumphantly. "And a miserable piece of work he is, too. She hates it there, but she's not been in service long and has to stay enough time to get a proper reference. I know all about him."

"What have you heard?" Mrs. Goodge asked eagerly.

"He's got a terrible temper." Mabel took a quick sip of tea. "He's a screamer, you know, just like Mr. Pilchard. Remember him? Remember how we used to hide when he'd go into one of his rages and start throwing things?"

"Who could forget him?" Mrs. Goodge replied. The two of them had worked together at Horatio Pilchard's Mayfair mansion. "I hope Sir Edmund isn't as mean and nasty as that awful man. He died from a stroke, and I heard that it was brought on by one of his temper tantrums."

"Good. He deserved whatever he got. He made our lives miserable." Mabel snorted faintly. "Sir Edmund Cleverly isn't as bad as Pilchard. These days, you can't get away with treating staff like that. But the man can be very spiteful when someone crosses him."

"What do you mean?"

"Jennie — that's my niece — told me that last week he came home in the middle of the afternoon and stormed into his study. He was in a foul mood. One of his cousins came in right behind him. Now, mind you, Jennie was polishing the wooden panels in the hallway, so she couldn't help but overhear them. She said he was shouting so loudly, you could have heard him in the attic. So she wasn't eavesdropping on purpose or anything like that. Mrs. Mays — that's Cleverly's housekeeper — had given her a bottle of Adam's Furniture Polish to use on the wood, which I don't think is very good housekeeping, but then again, no one asked my opinion. Back when I was a girl, you used a paste of beeswax and elderberry juice to polish panels, but these days no one wants to do anything the old way. Even my daughter buys all her housekeeping supplies at the shops."

"What was Cleverly on about?" Mrs. Goodge prompted. "What had upset him?" She'd forgotten that along with being a chatterbox, Mabel had the habit of telling you every single detail, whether it was pertinent to the story or not.

Unoffended by the interruption, Mabel laughed. "His nose was out of joint because he'd been kept waiting for hours by his fiancée's brother. Jennie said all the girls below stairs had a good giggle over it. Especially as, even after all that waitin', he never got in to see the man."

"That's rather rude," Mrs. Goodge murmured. "Why would Sir Edmund wish to marry into a family with no manners?"

"He's the one without any manners," Mabel argued. "He barged into Jonathan March's place of business without so much as a by-your-leave and then had the nerve to complain because the man was too busy to see him. Jennie said that Sir Edmund ranted and raved about it for hours when he got home that afternoon. He was shouting that he'd make Mr. March pay for humiliating him. Even his cousin couldn't get him to quiet down."

"What's the cousin's name?" Mrs. Goodge asked. She hoped she remembered all these details.

"Jennie never said, but he and his brother come around fairly often," Mabel replied. "The servants don't like them. Not only is Sir Edmund bad tempered, but he's usually late with the quarterly wages. Isn't that awful? Not only is it a miserable place to work, but half the time they're a week or two late getting the pay they've earned. As soon as Jennie gets a bit more experience, she's leaving there."

"What do you think, sir?" Barnes asked as soon as they were in a hansom.

"I think it odd that Harkins claims that Provost kept to himself. Why would he lie about that? We already know that Provost did not keep to himself. When he wasn't playing cards, he was pursuing his investigation and asking all sorts of questions." Witherspoon grabbed the handhold as the cab lurched forward. "And I also think it odd that Charles Capel didn't bother to tell us that Provost had a habit of walking home from the club. But of course, Capel, like Harkins, was in a hurry to get us out his front door."

"Capel seemed very nervous. Do you think he was hiding something?" Barnes asked. "He seemed awfully eager to prove that he'd come straight home the night Provost was murdered."

"His type is very much like the criminal classes, Constable," Witherspoon said wisely. "Not only does he not want the police coming to his home, but once we're there, his only ambition is to get us out as quickly as possible. I don't think his agitated manner means anything sinister. His connection to Michael Provost was peripheral at best, and we've no evidence that he even knew Ernie Grigson. Asking his manservant to provide him with an alibi was simply his way of getting rid of us quickly."

"You're probably right, sir." Barnes wasn't so sure, but he decided to let the matter rest. However, he made a mental note to have a quick word with Mrs. Jeffries about Capel. His policeman's senses had gone on full alert when they were talking to Capel, but unfortunately he wasn't sure what they were trying to tell him. "Interviewing the Wentworth Club members again today was a good idea, sir. They all live close to one another."

"Yes, it was," Witherspoon agreed. "But once we finish with Rollo Barrington, we ought to check back at the station. I want to read the rest of the reports. Who knows, Constable, we might get lucky, and one of the lads might have found us a witness!"

Barnes didn't think it likely, but he let that pass as well.

Rollo Barrington was home and, like the others they'd visited that day, not overly pleased to see the two policemen the young housemaid led into the drawing room.

"It's the police, sir," the girl said as she threw open the double doors. "They want to speak to you."

Barrington, who was sitting on the sofa reading a newspaper, started in surprise and then glared at the girl. "Letty, how many times must I tell you that you're to announce people before you bring them into the room."

"Sorry, sir, I forgot." Letty ducked her head apologetically. "Should I take 'em back out?"

"No, no, no." He put down the paper and sighed audibly. "I'll see them. But close the door behind you when you leave."

"Yes, sir." She bobbed a quick curtsy and darted out, slamming the door behind her.

"What is it, Inspector?" Barrington asked. "Why have you come here? I've already given you my statement."

"No, sir, I'm afraid you haven't. You've made no formal statement whatsoever."

"Don't argue with me, man. I answered your questions when you were at the club," he snapped.

"You answered some of our questions, sir." Barnes stared at Barrington, meeting his gaze and holding it with a hard look that had sent many a felon scurrying for cover. "But that doesn't constitute making a formal statement. Furthermore, we've received additional information regarding Mr. Provost and his relationship with the members of the Wentworth Club." This was a bluff, but a good one, judging from the color that crept up Barrington's fat face, Barnes thought.

Barrington broke eye contact first. "Alright, then, get on with it. What do you want to know?"

"I understand you were one of the last people in the card room with Mr. Provost that night, is that correct?" Witherspoon shifted his weight and tried to lean unobtrusively against the doorjamb. He was fairly certain they weren't going to be invited to take a seat.

"Who told you that?" Barrington demanded.

"Mr. Harkins." Witherspoon pulled off his gloves and shoved them into his coat pocket. "He said that you and Mr. Provost were the last two people there. Is that not true?"

Rollo thought for a moment. "Yes, I suppose it's true."

"What were you and Mr. Provost discussing?" Barnes asked.

"We weren't discussing anything that I can recall," Barrington replied. "I think he was simply saying his goodbyes."

"Who left the building first?" Witherspoon unbuttoned his coat.

"I don't see the point of this questioning, Inspector." Barrington hauled himself off the sofa. "What difference does it make who left first?"

"It makes a substantial difference, sir," the inspector responded. "We know that Mr. Provost always walked home. Therefore, if we can determine who might have come out of the building behind him, we might be able to find out if someone was following him that night."

"Oh, yes, I see." Barrington nodded. "Provost did enjoy walking. He was always going on about the beneficial effects to one's health. He claimed he walked two

216

miles every evening. But I've no idea if anyone followed him that night. He was still standing by the cloakroom door, waiting for his coat, when my brother and I left. George's house is on Portland Place, so we shared a hansom home."

"The porter fetched the hansom for you?" Barnes asked softly.

Barrington shook his head. "No, he was getting a cab for another member. My brother and I didn't feel like waiting, so we walked to the corner and got our own. It was annoying, but despite our complaints, the club won't put another porter on night duty. They say it costs too much."

Mrs. Jeffries stood on the creaking wooden dock and stared at the crumbling stone steps leading down to the Thames. The Chelsea Vestry Wharf was old, rotting, and soon to be demolished, as new construction and modern embankments crept farther and farther down the river.

The ebb and flow of the tide kept the commercial ships firmly anchored until evening to the big docks to the east, but the river traffic was still crowded as barges, skiffs, and working boats vied for the best position on the current.

The afternoon was overcast, and the cold

air coming off the water sent the damp straight to her bones. Mrs. Jeffries tightened her cloak and moved closer to the steps. The tide was low, yet the water was all the way up to the second-topmost stair. At high tide the river would be much deeper.

She surveyed the area, trying to assess it from the eyes of the both the assailant and the victim. No doubt the murderer thought that all he'd need do was to shove his stunned victim into the water and hold him down. But Provost, despite being coshed on the head, must have struggled hard, or at least hard enough to force his killer to use enough pressure holding him under to leave bruises on his neck and shoulder.

She lifted her head and looked around. Down the road was a busy stretch: private residences, pubs, and hotels. But here there were only the rotting wharves and a derelict warehouse. Still, the murderer had taken an awful chance. There could easily have been witnesses that night. Did that mean the killer was desperate and felt he had to get rid of Provost immediately? Or did it mean that he'd seen Provost alone here and seized the opportunity to commit the murder?

She turned away and stepped carefully across the old wood to the road. It was getting late, but if she hurried, she could get to the Iron Anchor pub before she had to start back for their afternoon meeting.

She wasn't sure whether this was a good idea. She hoped only that Inspector Witherspoon didn't decide to pop in for a quick one today as well.

Chapter 7

Mrs. Jeffries dashed into the kitchen. She shed her bonnet and her cloak as she hurried toward the coat tree. "I'm so sorry to be late. I'd no idea it would take me so long to get back." She tossed her garments onto the pegs and then took her place at the head of the table.

"I only arrived myself a few minutes ago," Ruth Cannonberry said cheerfully.

"Take a moment and catch your breath," Luty said. "We can wait a bit before we start."

"I'm fine, really, just a bit winded from rushing." Mrs. Jeffries nodded approvingly when she saw that Mrs. Goodge had already poured the tea. "As we're all here, who would like to go first?"

"Why don't you," the cook suggested. She put a cup of tea in front of Mrs. Jeffries. "You've been out and about. Tell us what you've learned."

"Thank you," she replied. "I will." She told them about her trip to the Chelsea Vestry Wharf and how she'd stood on the dock and imagined how the murder might have been done. "Then I went to the Iron Anchor pub."

"This is becoming a habit with you," Mrs. Goodge warned mockingly. "You went to a pub the other day as well." It wasn't long ago that the very idea of the housekeeper's going into a riverside pub would have filled the cook with horror. "Next time, you must invite me to go along. I haven't been in a pub in years."

"It's a very nice pub, and I had a whisky," Mrs. Jeffries replied. "It made me a bit light-headed. The place was very crowded. I can see why Edith Grigson isn't keen on finding out what happened to her brother. She's making money hand over fist in that place."

"Did you speak with her?" Hatchet asked.

"Actually, I avoided her. I did strike up a conversation with one of their regular customers and found out some very inter-esting information." She picked up the cream pitcher and poured a small amount into her tea. "I spoke to a man named Mr. Roberts this afternoon. He's been a regular at the Iron Anchor for years. He was there the night Grigson disappeared. He claimed that Grigson seemed very excited about something and that Grigson mentioned he was expecting visitors. Mr. Roberts told me that after last call, Grigson instructed the staff to go on home and that he'd do the cleaning. The odd part is that Grigson was all dressed up that night."

"So he was going to wash glasses and mop spilled beer while he was wearin' his Sunday best? That don't make sense," Luty declared.

"Mr. Roberts thought it strange as well, especially as this was the last time that either he or any of the other regulars recall seeing Grigson."

"One of my sources said the same thing," Smythe added. "Grigson was all spit and polish that night. My source gave me some other interestin' bits, but I'll wait until Mrs. Jeffries is finished . . ."

"That's alright," the housekeeper said. "The only other thing I found out was the name and address of Ernie Grigson's best barmaid."

"I thought you already spoke to the barmaid." Smythe looked puzzled. "You know, on your other trip to Tadema Road."

Mrs. Jeffries laughed. "This one is supposedly more than just a barmaid to Mr. Grigson. She was — well, how shall I put it? She was very close to him."

They all knew what that meant.

"Right, then. I'll tell you the rest of my bit," Smythe said. "Ernie Grigson wasn't just a publican. He was also a bookmaker." He recounted everything he'd learned from Blimpey Groggins, referring to Blimpey only as his source. When Smythe finished speaking, there was a moment of stunned silence.

"This is an extraordinary turn of events," Mrs. Jeffries murmured.

"Could this case get any more mixed up?" Luty complained. "Now we find out that Grigson was a bookie. Where there's money changin' hands, there's bad blood. Half of London might have wanted him gone."

"True, but I still think we ought to proceed on the assumption that Mr. Provost's murder is connected to Grigson's disappearance and to the Wentworth Club. That ought to narrow down our field of suspects. It's getting late; let's move on." Mrs. Jeffries glanced around the table. "Ruth, as this is your first time with us on this case, have you anything to report?"

"I'm afraid I've nothing. Isabella March wasn't even at the meeting today," she explained. "But I've sent her a note asking if I can see her tomorrow. I hope that's alright. I'll be very discreet, I promise."

"That's perfectly fine," Mrs. Jeffries assured her.

"If it's all the same to everyone, I'll go next," Mrs. Goodge volunteered. "I had a nice chat this afternoon with one of my old colleagues." She told them about her visit from Mabel Bonner. She took her time in the telling and made sure she remembered to mention everything. "And that's really all I found out today," she concluded.

"Very good, Mrs. Goodge," Mrs. Jeffries said.

"I 'eard a bit today," Wiggins said quickly. So far he'd not contributed much to the investigation, and he was eager to make up for it. "I met up with a lad named Evans today. He does occasional work for Rollo Barrington."

"There seems to be a lot of that sort of work in London," Smythe muttered, thinking back to his trip to the Swan's Nest and his talk with Jerry Carter. Blast a Spaniard, there was something that really bothered him about that whole little incident. But what was it? He felt a soft touch on his arm, and he blinked, smiled at Betsy, and forced his attention back to the footman.

"Evans seemed a decent enough lad," Wiggins continued. "And even though he doesn't work regular-like at the Barrington household, he has a lot of contact with one of the housemaids there, and she seems like a right clever little lass." He told them about his meeting with Evans, making sure that he recited the conversation as close to word-for-word as possible. When he'd finished, he took a deep breath. "And that's what I found out today."

"So Barrington pinches things from his friends." Hatchet laughed softly. "I'll bet he makes a pretty penny on it as well. You'd think people would notice that something valuable disappears every time Rollo stops by for a cup of tea."

"He might be a thief, but is he a murderer?" Mrs. Jeffries wondered. "And how does his thieving relate to the Grigson problem?"

"Maybe Grigson found out about it and threatened to expose Barrington," Betsy suggested. "Maybe he murdered Grigson to keep from being ruined socially. I don't think Rollo Barrington would get many invitations if it got out that you have to hide the silver when he comes to dinner."

"But how would Grigson have found out about Rollo Barrington's nasty little habit?" Smythe asked. "All we know for sure is that Provost was convinced Grigson's disappearance had something to do with the Wentworth Club, but there's over seventy members there, and we don't even know that Grigson knew Barrington."

"That's true." Betsy sighed. "I'm grasping at straws. I didn't find out anything today. Like Mrs. Jeffries, I went to Iron Anchor, but I got there too early and there was no one in the place, so then I tramped all over Marylebone. The only thing I heard about the Barringtons was that they're always late paying their bills."

"Not to worry, love, tomorrow will be a better day for ya." Smythe grabbed her hand and squeezed it under the table.

"My day wasn't particularly good, either," Luty admitted.

"Mine was." Hatchet grinned at his employer. "I paid a visit to an old friend." He told them about his visit with Reginald Manley. "But the best part was when Manley's wife came home."

"Bet you got an earful from her," Luty muttered.

"Indeed I did," Hatchet exclaimed. "Most of it was the same gossip we've already heard, but I did find out that the Barringtons were terrified Isabella March wasn't going to marry their cousin, Sir Edmund. Mrs. Manley said that she overheard

Rollo telling George that if the marriage didn't take place, he was absolutely going to be ruined."

"I don't suppose she heard why he'd be ruined?" Mrs. Jeffries asked hopefully.

"Unfortunately, no. The lady was eavesdropping on a private conversation at a dinner party two weeks ago," Hatchet replied. "They moved too far away for her to hear anything else. Pity, really. You'd think people would have more consideration for others."

Just before the inspector and Constable Barnes were ready to pack it in for the day, a young officer stuck his head in and said, "May I have a word with you, sir? It's very important."

The two policemen were in the inspector's office at the Walton Street police station. "It's awfully late, McClement," Barnes said. "Can it wait until tomorrow? What are you doing here, anyway? You're assigned to T Division."

"I know it's late, sir." Police Constable McClement hesitated. He had the barest hint of a Scottish burr. "Sorry to disturb you. I'll come back tomorrow."

"No, no, come on in, lad. I've worked with PC McClement," Barnes said to the inspector. "And he's a good copper, observant and honest. I expect if he's got something to tell us and he's come all the way over here from T Division, it's important."

"I'm sure it must be." The inspector put down the report they'd been discussing and waved the constable over. His eyes felt as dry as old bones, and he was dreadfully tired, so he hoped this wouldn't take too long.

McClement didn't waste a moment. He stepped inside and quietly closed the door behind him. He was a tall young man in his early twenties, with curly brown hair and blue eyes. "Thank you, sir."

"McClement." Witherspoon knew he'd heard that name recently. "Ian McClement? Is that you?"

"That's right, sir." The lad began to blush, flattered that the illustrious Inspector Witherspoon had heard of him.

"You've just had a commendation for bravery." Witherspoon beamed proudly. "Well done, young man! Are you recovered from your injuries?"

"Yes, sir, I am. But they weren't that bad." McClement's blush deepened. "Just a knife wound or two."

"Don't be so modest, lad," Barnes said with a laugh. "You've earned your bragging rights. You kept that girl from being stabbed to death. It's too bad the tough that knifed you got away, but you've given a good description and every copper in the city is on the lookout for him."

Last October, Ian McClement had stepped in and saved a young woman from being robbed and possibly murdered. In the process he'd been stabbed and almost bled to death.

"Now, what is it you want to tell us?" Barnes asked curiously.

"It's about those letters, sir," McClement began. "The ones that pertain to the Provost murder. I know where they are . . . I mean, I know where they were sent and who's got them."

Witherspoon's exhaustion vanished. "Where are they?"

McClement took a deep breath. "They *were* at the Chelsea police station, sir. The one on the Kensington High Street."

"I know where it is," Witherspoon said. "What do you mean, 'they were'? Where are the letters now?"

"I don't know where he's taken them," McClement blurted, "but they're not at the station anymore. I know, because I've just come from there and they've been taken out of the evidence locker."

"Who are you talking about?" Barnes

asked, his voice deadly soft. "Who took them out of the evidence locker?"

McClement looked pained. "I don't want you to think I'm accusing another policeman of doin' something wrong, but I know who I gave them to when they came into the station. They put me on the reception counter when I first came back to work, because my arms were still a bit raw . . ."

"We understand all that," the constable interrupted. "Go on, tell us the rest."

"You both know what workin' reception is like. One of my duties was to sort the mail and make sure it got to the right person —" He broke off and took another deep breath. "I remember those letters because the handwriting was so easy to read. They were all addressed to the 'Officer in Charge,' and during those weeks, Inspector Nigel Nivens was our acting superintendent. The actual superintendent, Mr. Williams, was out on medical leave — he'd had the hernia operation, and it hadn't gone well."

Witherspoon's heart sank. He wondered how this case could get any more complicated. "How many letters were there?"

"Six in all, and I gave each of them to Inspector Nivens."

"Are you absolutely certain the letters were sent by Michael Provost?" Witherspoon asked.

"I can's say for sure about the first one," McClement replied. "But I know the last five came from him. They were always in heavy cream-colored envelopes, so they were easy to spot. After I gave Inspector Nivens the first, whenever I took another one in to him, he'd pull a face and make a nasty remark. That was when I started taking notice of the return name on the back. The last five were from Michael Provost."

"And his handwriting was easy to read," Barnes muttered.

"I hope you don't think I've come running here tellin' tales about a superior officer." McClement spoke directly to Witherspoon. "I kept waiting to hear that you'd got the letters in your possession, sir, but every time I asked the lads here at Walton Street, they were still missing. These letters are evidence in a murder, so I had to step forward. I couldn't just let them sit in an evidence locker."

"You acted correctly, Constable." Witherspoon gave him a reassuring smile. He could tell by the anguished expression on the young man's face that stepping forward had been very hard. This development might cause trouble for the Metropolitan Police Force, but the lad had done right and mustn't suffer in any way for performing his sworn duty. "How often did a letter arrive at the station?"

"It seemed like they came once a week, or maybe it was every two weeks."

"Do you remember when you received the first one?" Barnes asked.

McClement thought for a moment. "They let me back on duty by the end of November, but I'd been there awhile before we got the first letter. I can't be certain, but I recall it arriving sometime near the middle of December. I didn't pay any attention to that one. It was when the second one arrived that I started taking notice. I handed it to Inspector Nivens, and he started sneering when he saw the return address."

"Do you recall what Inspector Nivens actually said?" Barnes inquired. They were going to need all the ammunition they could get if it came to an interdepartmental fight with Nivens and his supporters. Once word got back to Nivens that McClement had come to them, Barnes had no doubt that Nivens would go after the young police constable and make him pay dearly. But Barnes was a wily old copper — he knew a thing or two about the world and about how to cover one's backside.

McClement blushed again, only this time

it wasn't because he was being unduly modest. "It wasn't very nice, sir. I don't know that I ought to repeat it."

"Tell us what he said," Witherspoon ordered harshly. Then, more kindly, he added, "Don't worry, Constable McClement. No matter how disrespectful his words might seem, I'm sure we've all heard worse."

"He tapped the envelope against the desk and told me the man who wrote it was 'an interfering little sod who thought he could do a better job of it than the police.' "

"That's not too bad," Barnes remarked.

"That's not the worst of it, sir. Then he said, 'And I hope the bastard gets his arse kicked for sticking his nose in where it didn't belong. I've looked into this case, and there's nothing to it.' " McClement shook his head sadly. "Poor Mr. Provost. He ended up a lot worse than just getting his backside kicked. He ended up dead."

"And that's precisely why the letters disappeared from the evidence locker," Barnes murmured.

McClement picked up his helmet and slipped it onto his head. "That's all I've got to report, sir." He adjusted his chin strap. "Thank you for hearing me out." He nodded and started for the door.

"Are you still assigned to the Chelsea station?" Barnes called after him. "In case we need to ask you more questions?"

"I'm there, sir." He grinned. "But I'm finally off that ruddy desk."

"Thank you for coming, Constable Mc-Clement," Witherspoon yelled.

As soon as they closed the door behind McClement, Barnes looked at the inspector. "Now we know why Nivens was so keen to try and fob this off as an accident. That's one mystery solved."

"But what I don't understand is why the letters were sent to the Chelsea station in the first place," Witherspoon said.

"Because it's closest to the Iron Anchor pub," Barnes replied. "And it was Ernie Grigson's disappearance Provost was investigating. We're only operating out of here because it was a constable from Walton Street that found Provost's body."

"So I expect Nivens will try to say that because the two stations are in different divisions, he hadn't heard we needed Provost's letters." Witherpoon sighed. "Honestly, I didn't think this case could get any messier, but it has."

"Maybe not, sir," Barnes said. "At least now we can get our hands on the letters. They might point us in the right direction."

Witherspoon couldn't think of a delicate

way to say it, so he blurted out the words. "Let's keep our fingers crossed that Inspector Nivens still has them."

"He still has them, sir," Barnes said flatly. "He might lie and say that he can't find them, or that McClement is mistaken and the letters were never in the evidence locker. But he'll not have done away with them. I don't like or respect the man, but he is still a copper, and even he wouldn't destroy evidence." Barnes hoped he was right.

When Witherspoon got home that evening, he was tired, but that didn't prevent him from telling Mrs. Jeffries everything that had transpired that day. The recitation took an hour and two glasses of sherry, and continued over dinner. By the time he'd finished his meal, he felt so much better that, he told Mrs. Jeffries, he was sure he'd fall asleep the moment his head touched the pillow. She wasn't sure she'd be able to sleep — the inspector had given her so much information, she was worried she might forget an important fact or detail before the household's morning meeting.

Her concern was so great that when she found herself wide-awake in the middle of the night, she got up and made a list of everything he'd said. Satisfied, she blew out her small table lamp, got to her feet, and started back to bed. Her blinds were up, so she paused and looked out into the night, fixing her gaze on the gas lamp across the road.

She now had an extraordinary amount of information about both Provost and Ernie Grigson. But what did it all mean? Nothing seemed to be connected or make any sense. Charles Capel was nervous when the police interviewed him. Why? Had it been just a normal reaction to a visit from the police, or was it something more? And Ernie Grigson wasn't just a publican; he also was a bookie. Perhaps he was murdered by someone who owed him a great deal of money, or perhaps it was because he couldn't come up with the cash to pay out a bet someone had won. Or perhaps being a bookie had nothing to do with either his disappearance or with Provost's murder. Maybe when the inspector got hold of the letters, they'd know more. If, of course, that miserable Inspector Nivens hadn't destroyed them in order to save his own skin. Witherspoon was sure the letters were still intact, but Mrs. Jeffries wasn't convinced. Nivens wasn't going to care whether a murderer escaped justice, as long as his precious career wasn't damaged.

She sighed, tore her gaze away from the gas lamp, and turned toward her bed. Perhaps tomorrow or the next day she'd make sense of it all. She got into bed and snuggled down in the bedclothes. Just as she was drifting off, an idea flashed through her mind, but before she could catch the slippery thing and give it a good going-over, she fell asleep.

The next morning, when they were all gathered around the table for their meeting, Mrs. Jeffries didn't need her list. The information flowed out of her so easily, the inspector himself might have been standing beside her, whispering the words into her ear.

When the others learned of Inspector Nivens' additional involvement in the case, they were as upset as she'd been. "But not to worry," she said quickly, before they could all complain about him at once. "The inspector is going to see Nivens this morning, and I'm sure that he'll get it all sorted out properly. But now we know why Nivens was so quick to label Provost's death as an accident."

"Humph." Betsy snorted delicately. "Nivens didn't want to admit he'd made a mistake by ignoring those letters. He hoped it would all be swept under the carpet and forgot about."

"Constable Barnes is going with Inspector Witherspoon, isn't he." Hatchet asked.

"Of course," she replied.

"Good. Barnes is a crafty old fox — he'll keep Nivens under control," Luty said. "Wouldn't ya just know that Nivens would be the one that had them letters. No wonder no one could find hide nor hair of 'em."

"Will the inspector bring the letters home tonight?" Betsy asked eagerly. "Or will he have to lock them up at Walton Street?"

"I don't know," Mrs. Jeffries admitted. "They're evidence, so I think they'll have to go into the evidence locker. Unlike Nivens, our inspector respects the rules." Sometimes she wished he didn't.

"So there's a good chance we won't get to see them ourselves, and we'll have to rely on the inspector to find out what Provost actually wrote," Smythe said.

"Were you able to put a few ideas into his head?" Mrs. Goodge asked. "We learned quite a bit ourselves yesterday. It's important that he knows what we know."

"I planted a few seeds," Mrs. Jeffries replied. "And I had a brief chat with Constable Barnes, so if my hints didn't work properly, we can trust the constable to help push the inspector in the right direction." She glanced at the carriage clock on the pine cupboard. "Oh dear, time is getting on, and we've much to do today."

"Thank goodness the inspector came up with more clues for us." Betsy stood up. "I know we had plenty of our own, but now I've some new ideas about where to concentrate my efforts. I'll try to find out why Charles Capel was so nervous."

"Excellent idea," Mrs. Jeffries agreed.

"And I received a note from Isabella March inviting me for morning coffee," Ruth announced proudly. "Perhaps I'll have something very valuable to share this afternoon."

"I just hope I have somethin' to report," Luty declared. "I've spent a lot of time chasing down a few whiffs of gossip, and findin' nothing. But I've got a good source lined up for today."

"And who would that be?" Hatchet asked.

Luty grinned. "Wouldn't you like to know?"

Smythe took Betsy's arm as they cut across the garden to the gate in the side wall. It was a cold, clear morning, and they had the place to themselves. "Mind you, be careful today," he warned. "It's them nervous ones like Charles Capel that you've got to watch." He was talking nonsense, but he was worried himself. Something Blimpey had said was nagging at the back of his mind.

She laughed and patted his hand. "I'm always careful. Besides, I'm just going to ask a few questions. I'll not be sneaking into the man's house and pawing through his desk drawers or reading his diary. Come to think of it, now that I've said it, that does sound like a good idea."

"Don't even joke about that." He stopped in the middle of the path, swung her around to face him, and regarded her with his sternest expression, the one that kept the toughs at the pub minding their own business and sent lazy stable lads scurrying for cover. But it had no effect on Betsy.

She giggled and put her hands on her hips. "What's got into you? You've been watching me like I was a pot of peas ready to boil over. What's wrong?"

"Why won't you set a wedding date?" he blurted out. He knew he shouldn't press her, but ever since Blimpey had brought up the subject, it had been festering in him like a blood blister on the bottom of his foot.

She looked at him, her expression incredulous. "What are you talking about? I have set a date. We're getting married in October."

"But you 'aven't set the day," he complained. "Is it because you're not wantin' to marry me?"

"Oh, for goodness' sake." She rolled her eyes and started walking. "I haven't set the day because it's only February, and October is months away."

He hurried to catch up with her. "What's that got to do with it? We can still set a day."

"Then let's do it the second Saturday in October." She stopped, and so did he. "I didn't realize this was upsetting you. Why didn't you say something earlier? I don't want you walking about thinking I don't love you. You should have said something, Smythe. You should have told me. If I didn't want to be your wife, I'd have mentioned it long before this."

His whole world suddenly shifted, and everything became right again. "I didn't want to press you." He grinned broadly. "After what happened, I didn't want to push too hard, but now it's alright."

"Men," she muttered as she started off again. "Who can understand them? They bend your ear for hours with all sorts of silly nonsense, but when it comes to something important, they get as tongue-tied as

241

a green boy. Where are you going today? You never did say."

He was feeling so good, he told her. "I'm going to track down a woman named Bernadette. I spoke to her in a pub a few days ago, and the minute I mentioned Provost's name, she took off like the hounds of 'ell was on her heels." As the days had passed, he'd not been able to get her off his mind.

Betsy's eyebrows rose. "Who is this woman, anyway? Should I be keeping a closer eye on you?"

He gave an uneasy laugh, hoping she was only kidding. "You can trust me; you know that. She was someone I spoke with in a pub near Provost's house. But the odd thing was, she was real chatty and friendly-like, until I mentioned Provost's name."

"And you're just now tracking her down? Why'd you wait so long?"

"This is a bit 'ard to explain, but at the time it happened, the lad I was talking to made some comment about her not wanting trouble and" — he shrugged — "that sounded reasonable to me. But I keep remembering the expression on her face when she heard Provost's name, and now that the days have passed, I'm not so sure she took off just because she'd heard he'd been murdered. I think there's more to it

242

than that."

"You think she knows something about the murder?" Betsy asked. She was surprised at her own feelings — that finding out he chatted with women when they were "on the hunt" bothered her just a tad. She knew she was being silly: Smythe would never be untrue to her. Besides, when it came to getting information, she wasn't above flirting, either.

"I'm not sure," he replied. "Maybe the poor woman doesn't know a ruddy thing, and I'm wasting my time."

"Nonsense," Betsy said briskly. "You must try and find her. You've got good instincts about people, Smythe. You're not the kind of man to get fanciful over nothing. She's important to this case; I know it."

"Your home is lovely, Miss March," Ruth Cannonberry said as she sank down onto the couch. It was upholstered in a stiff white satin, but was surprisingly comfortable. She glanced around the cavernous drawing room. The furniture was French Empire style and upholstered in various shades of white, yellow, and cream. The walls were done in white and gold fleur-de-lys-patterned paper, and gold velvet curtains with long, elegant fringes draped the windows. A crystal chandelier hung from the ceiling. At the far end of the room was a marble fireplace.

"Thank you." Isabella March smiled graciously. She was in her midthirties, with a pale complexion, a turned-up nose, and a wide, generous mouth. She wore a dark green wool dress with a high-collared white underblouse. "I was so delighted to get your note, Lady Cannonberry. Harriet Blackburn mentioned that you were asking about me at the meeting yesterday."

"Oh dear, I do hope my inquiry didn't offend you," Ruth said quickly. "And please, do call me Ruth. It's just that I was so hoping to see you. I wanted to speak with you about Michael Provost." She broke off and bit her lip. Drat, this was not going as she'd planned. Sometimes she forgot that most people didn't share her egalitarian views, and insisting they use one's Christian name was considered offensive. She hadn't meant to blurt out Provost's name, either. She'd meant to be subtle and discreet and drop it in the course of a civilized conversation. It had been a long time since she'd helped on one of Gerald's cases. "That didn't come out as I wanted, either. I'm so sorry, Miss March."

Isabella March regarded her with amusement. She didn't look in the least offended. "You must call me Isabella if I'm to call you Ruth," she said with a laugh. "But I'm afraid I don't know much about Mr. Provost. I met him only once. I heard that he was dead, and I'm very sorry. I understand he was murdered. That's terrible. He came to the house last week, but it was to see my brother, not me."

"I see," Ruth replied. Her mind went completely blank. Honestly, she ought to have written some questions on a slip of paper and tucked it up her sleeve.

"Are you asking about him for your friend the police inspector?" Isabella inquired curiously.

Ruth wasn't certain how to respond. On the one hand, she didn't wish to prevaricate, nor did she want to offend Isabella by insulting her intelligence. On the other hand, she didn't want to be completely indiscreet. She looked at Isabella and came to a decision. "Yes. If I can pass him some unofficial information as gossip, it might help catch a murderer. Of course, I don't tell him I'm trying to help. I don't want him to feel that I'm interfering in his work or implying that he can't do his job properly himself. That might make him feel bad."

"You were married, weren't you?"

245

Ruth was surprised by the abrupt change of subject. "Yes, I was. My husband died eight years ago."

"And you've never remarried," Isabella said thoughtfully. "Now, it's my turn to apologize. Do forgive me. I shouldn't be making personal comments. Now, feel free to ask me your questions about Michael Provost."

Ruth suddenly understood. "You're having doubts about accepting Sir Edmund's proposal, aren't you?" It was common knowledge in their women's group that Sir Edmund Cleverly had proposed.

"It's awkward. Edmund keeps pressing me for an answer, but after seeing the silly ways married women behave to keep their husbands happy, I'm not certain it's the right course of action for me," Isabella confessed. "I don't want to spend the rest of my life kowtowing to a husband. I'm very independent, and I enjoy living here with my brother. Jonathan minds his own business."

Ruth stared at her, surprised. "But I heard that . . ."

"I know what you heard," Isabella interrupted. "Everyone thinks it's my brother who didn't want me to accept the proposal. But I was the one that started that rumor. Jonathan thinks Edmund is a fool, but even so, he'd never interfere with my decision. Goodness, I don't know why I'm burdening you with my concerns —"

It was Ruth's turn to interrupt. "Don't apologize," she said gently. This sort of conversation happened to her all the time. Even strangers on trains told her their troubles. "Sometimes it's easier to speak freely in front of those who know us the least. It's obvious that this situation is of great concern to you. Perhaps discussing it will help you understand what you really wish to do."

"You're very kind." Isabella smiled ruefully. "I know I must come to a decision. It's not fair to keep him waiting for an answer. As I was saying, I was the one who started the rumor that my brother opposed my marriage to Sir Edmund. I did it only because I was trying to be considerate. I'm not in love with him, nor is he in love with me. But I didn't want to hurt his pride, and it's easier for a man to think that someone in the woman's family is opposed to the match rather than that the woman herself isn't sure."

"You mustn't marry him if you don't love him." Ruth leaned forward. "And as for why I didn't marry again, it's very simple: I didn't love anyone."

"What about your policeman?"

Ruth relaxed back against the sofa and laughed. "We're taking our time. Lord Cannonberry and I were friends for seven years before he got up the nerve to court me properly and we realized we were in love. It often works that way, you see. You're friends for ages first, and then you realize you want to spend the rest of your life with that one person."

Isabella eyed her speculatively. "You really were in love with your husband?"

"Oh, yes. You must love your husband. It's the only way an intelligent woman can possibly put up with the male of the species. They can be very vexing."

Laughing, Isabella rose, went to the bellpull, and gave it a good yank. "I'm so glad I talked to you. You've made me feel much better. At least now I know that love is a genuine possibility for a woman, even for someone my age."

"Love can happen at any age," Ruth said.

"I've rung for our coffee." Isabella crossed back to the couch. "You like coffee, don't you."

"The few times I've had it, I've enjoyed it," Ruth replied. She hoped that when they met again, Isabella wouldn't regret this conversation. Occasionally, when people confided in you, they were uneasy or embarrassed the next time you ran into one another. She didn't think that would be the case here. Isabella was a sensible woman who didn't appear to be at the mercy of her emotions. If she'd not wanted to discuss such a personal matter, she wouldn't have mentioned it in the first place.

The drawing room door opened, and a maid entered, pushing a tea trolley. She wheeled it over to Isabella. "Will there be anything else, ma'am?" she asked.

"No, Greta. Thank you." Isabella reached for the silver coffeepot.

"It smells delicious," Ruth commented.

"I'll let you add your own cream and sugar." Isabella poured the coffee into a blue and gold china cup-and-saucer set, and passed it to Ruth. "No one can ever get the proportions right."

Ruth picked up the cream pitcher. "Why did Mr. Provost come to visit your brother?"

"I'm not completely sure." Isabella finished pouring her own coffee, and took her seat again. "I think it had something to do with Jonathan's accident. When Mr. Provost arrived that day, Jonathan was quite surprised to see him. They aren't friends or even close acquaintances."

"But don't they belong to the same club?"

Ruth asked. She reached for the tongs and put a lump of sugar into her cup. She couldn't recall how much she'd used the last time she'd had coffee, so she helped herself to two more lumps.

"Yes, but Jonathan joined the club only because Edmund insisted," she replied. "He considers the place a boring waste of time and money. Even if I marry Edmund, he'll not renew his membership next year."

Holding her saucer carefully so that she wouldn't spill the liquid on either herself or, God forbid, her hostess' furniture, Ruth eased back onto the sofa. "Do you recall exactly what day it was that Mr. Provost came to see your brother?"

Isabella thought for a moment. "I believe it was last Tuesday. Yes, I know I'm right. I was coming down the staircase when he arrived. I was going into the library to write a letter. It was the housekeeper's day off, so Jonathan answered the door himself. I heard Mr. Provost say that he was sorry to barge in, but that he had to speak with my brother."

"And you think Mr. Provost came to speak to your brother about the accident?" Ruth took a sip of coffee. It still tasted a little bitter, but the sugar helped.

"I heard him say so," she replied.

"Can you recall his exact words?" Ruth had noticed that the others were very detailed when they made their reports at the afternoon meetings.

"He said, 'I heard about your accident, and it's imperative that I speak to you about it.' Jonathan seemed taken aback for a moment, but then he said, 'Let's go into my study.' At that point, Mr. Provost looked at me, and Jonathan introduced us. The two of them went off to the study, and I continued on to the library to write my letter."

"How long did Mr. Provost stay that day?" Ruth inquired. She hoped she was asking the right questions.

"Quite a long time," Isabella replied slowly. "Now that I think about it, that's odd, because my brother is a very busy man. He doesn't waste time. Michael Provost must have had something very important to share with him; otherwise Jonathan would have found a way to get rid of him." She grinned. "My brother is good at that sort of thing. It infuriates Edmund."

"Exactly what did happen to your brother?" Ruth asked. "I mean, what sort of accident did he have?"

"It was dreadful. He was almost killed. Jonathan was standing on the corner of a very busy intersection, waiting to cross,

251

when he felt someone shove him from behind. He flew out into the road just as a cooper's van came roaring around the corner. He would have been trampled to death had it not been for his quick reflexes. He threw himself to one side just as the horses bore down on him, but even so, he ended up getting kicked on his leg."

Ruth was genuinely horrified. "That's awful. Your poor brother."

"Luckily, Jonathan is very fit. He used to box, so he's got excellent reflexes, which probably saved his life. But, still, his leg took a terrible bruising. I suppose we must be grateful it wasn't worse."

"When did this happen?"

"Let's see . . . Mr. Provost came on a Tuesday, and Jonathan's accident was the previous Saturday. Yes, that's right — he'd gone to Knightsbridge that day to look at a piece of property. That's when it occurred. When he got home that afternoon, his clothes were dirty and his trousers were ripped."

"Did he tell the police?" Ruth took another sip. The coffee wasn't bad at all.

"I wanted him to." Isabella frowned. "But he refused. He said he couldn't prove that someone had pushed him."

"But weren't there witnesses?"

"Only to the accident," Isabella explained. "Dozens of people saw him going into the street, but no one would admit to seeing him pushed. One man even said it looked to him like Jonathan had started across and then tripped over his own feet when he saw the van flying around the corner." She cocked her head to one side, her expression thoughtful. "He told me later that when he mentioned the accident to the people at the Wentworth Club, he sensed that no one believed him. He said it was almost as if someone had gone behind his back and said he was making up tales."

Ruth thought she understood exactly what had happened. "Jonathan believed someone was deliberately trying to ensure that no one took his accident seriously?"

Isabelle nodded. "Yes, but why on earth anyone would say or do such a thing is utterly mystifying. Jonathan is an unsentimental, hardheaded businessman who hasn't got the imagination or the inclination to make up such nonsense."

"You believe he was definitely pushed in front of that van, don't you." Ruth pressed. She wasn't sure that Isabella fully understood the implications of what she'd just said.

"Absolutely."

"That means that someone deliberately tried to harm your brother," Ruth warned.

Isabella froze for a brief moment. "Oh my God, you're right. I've been such a fool. I should have seen this before. I must warn Jonathan." She put her coffee down on the trolley and started to get up.

"Where is your brother now?"

"In France," Isabella replied, her expression worried. "He's on a business trip. He took the late train from Victoria the same evening that Mr. Provost came to see him. Oh my goodness, he's no idea that Michael Provost was murdered."

"If he's in France, then he's probably perfectly safe," Ruth assured her. "Remember, Provost was murdered that night, after your brother had already left the country. The killer is in England. But think back — try to remember any other details about that day."

"You think that's important?" Isabella asked.

"It must be," Ruth insisted. "Provost was murdered after he spent several hours with your brother. When is Jonathan due back in England?"

"Not until next week," Isabella answered. "But I can send a telegram and ask him to come home."

Ruth said, "Don't do it as yet. Let me talk to Inspector Witherspoon."

"Won't he want to know what my brother and Mr. Provost discussed? I can't believe I've been such a fool. I should have seen that there was some connection between Jonathan's accident and Mr. Provost's murder." She shook her head. "It never occurred to me until we started talking about it. Now it seems so clear." She got up and began to pace the room.

"Can you recall anything else about that afternoon?" Ruth asked. "Anything — any little detail might be a useful clue in solving this matter."

Isabella stopped and stared at Ruth. "There was one thing. I saw Jonathan handing Mr. Provost an envelope as they came out of the study. But that's all. Oh, and just before he left for the train station that night, Jonathan asked me if I'd made up my mind about the engagment. When I told him I hadn't, he asked me to wait until he got home before I told Edmund my decision. As a matter of fact, he made me promise not to say anything until he returned."

CHAPTER 8

"I thought it important to reinterview everyone who saw Mr. Provost that night," Witherspoon explained as he and Barnes stood in the entry of George Barrington's home in Portland Place.

"Quite right, sir," Barnes agreed. He turned his head and pretended to study the hall rather than let the inspector see the amusement on his face. The poor man had spent half the morning convincing himself and Barnes that he wasn't trying to avoid a confrontation with Nivens but was instead taking formal statements.

Barnes didn't much blame the inspector. Facing Nivens and asking for Provost's letters wasn't going to be an easy task. "Are we to see Mr. Marston next?"

Witherspoon hesitated a fraction of a second and then pulled out his pocket watch. "It's already eleven o'clock. We'll go see Inspector Nivens when we're finished here. I might as well get that over and done with."

"Yes, sir," Barnes replied. They'd have to take a hansom back to the Yard, and that would give him a chance to put another bug in the inspector's ear. Thank goodness for Mrs. Jeffries and her little band of helpers: They dug up information twice as fast as the police. Thus far, not any of the people he and Witherspoon had interviewed had seen fit to mention that Grigson wasn't just a publican but a bookmaker as well. If he'd not taken a few moments for a quick cup of tea with Mrs. Jeffries this morning, they'd still be in the dark about that fact. Barnes turned as footsteps pounded on the stairs.

"What is the meaning of this intrusion?" George Barrington asked. He'd dressed in a hurry and not done a very good job of it. His shirt was hanging out of his trousers and half the buttons were still open.

"We need to speak to you, sir," Barnes said. He wondered whether everyone from that silly gentlemen's club spent their mornings lounging about in their nightclothes.

"You've already spoken to me." Barrington stopped on the bottom step. "I don't have anything further to add to my statement."

"You didn't make a statement," the constable replied. "You merely answered a few questions. The inspector has a few more to ask."

"We'll try not to take up too much of your time," Witherspoon interjected cheerfully.

Barrington crossed his arms over his chest. "Go ahead. I've not got all day."

"On the night Mr. Provost was killed, how did you get home?" Witherspoon asked.

Barrington blinked in surprise. "How did I get home? The way I usually do: I took a hansom."

"Does the porter always get the cab for you?" Barnes asked.

"Not always," he replied. "Sometimes there's a queue and I don't wish to wait, so I get my own. The porter was getting someone else a hansom when my brother and I were ready to leave. So we went off and got our own."

"Did you see Mr. Provost depart?" Barnes watched Barrington carefully. So far he wasn't telling any obvious lies. The porter had already said he'd seen the two Barrington brothers leave on their own.

"No."

"That's odd, sir, considering you've just admitted you waited to leave with your brother, and he was the last one seen with Mr. Provost in the card room."

"Provost was still hanging about the cloakroom when we left," he said. "I'm sorry the man is dead, but I don't see how I can help you."

Barnes ignored the outburst. "What time did you arrive home that night?"

"I don't recall." Barrington sighed heavily. "There was a lot of traffic, and it took longer than usual."

"Why don't you ask your manservant what time it was that you came in," Witherspoon suggested.

"I'd told the servants not to wait up for me," Barrington replied. "All of them had retired by the time I arrived home. I checked that all the doors were locked, and went upstairs. I imagine it was about half past ten." He began tucking his shirt into his trousers.

Witherspoon considered speaking to the servants but thought the better of it. The inspector was ashamed of himself. Coming here had been a cowardly attempt to postpone the confrontation with Nivens. "Thank you, Mr. Barrington. We appreciate your cooperation."

Barrington's pale eyebrows rose. "You're welcome," he muttered as the two policemen turned and went to the front door.

As soon as they were outside, Witherspoon

said, "Do you think Nivens will be at the Yard or at the Chelsea station?"

"The Chelsea superintendent is back from medical leave. Nivens is at the Yard." Barnes had already checked.

Witherspoon hurried down the short walkway to the road. "Right, then. Let's get a hansom and get this over with."

Smythe poked his head through the door of the Swan's Nest pub and noted that it was crowded enough to give him a bit of cover. He stepped inside and rushed to an empty spot at the end of the bench along the wall. As he slid into the space, he examined the room closely, studying the women as his gaze moved from table to table and group to group. But he didn't see her. He hoped his quarry hadn't disappeared completely from the neighborhood.

He cast his eyes around the pub again, looking for a likely candidate for what he needed done. He had to be careful. Even flashing a bit of money about wouldn't guarantee that someone wouldn't tip her off.

He spotted an old woman dressed in a threadbare brown coat so thin in spots that he could see the lining from his place at the other end of the bar. She looked as though she could do with a quid or two. He stood up and moved in her direction, when the door suddenly opened and Bernadette Healey entered.

She started for the bar, but something, perhaps some movement on his part, made her turn her head and see him. Their gazes met, and her mouth dropped open as she recognized him. In an instant, she turned on her heel, dashed for the door, and disappeared as quickly as she'd come. He gave chase, but he was on the other side of the room, and by the time he maneuvered around the obstacles between him and the exit, she'd had a jolly good start on him. He flew out onto the narrow pavement, almost falling, but he righted himself and then turned in a wobbly circle to see whether he could catch a glimpse of her. But she was nowhere to be seen. "Blast," he muttered.

"She's gone to ground," a voice said from behind him. "But I can help you. I know where she's dossin' these days."

He whirled about. A girl who appeared to be no more than ten stood staring at him. She was a blue-eyed little blonde, painfully thin and dressed in clothes that were barely rags. Her blue jacket was patched on both sleeves and held together at the neck with strings. The hem along her limp gray skirt was torn and dragging the ground, and the green wool cap holding her stringy hair off her face looked as old as she was.

She stared at him with a hard, speculative expression that chilled him coming from one so young. "You deaf or somethin'? Didn't ya 'ear me? I said I can 'elp ya. I saw ya chasin' her out of the pub."

Smythe wanted to speak to Bernadette Healey, but he wasn't going to use this poor girl to find her. She looked as if she'd been used enough in her short life. He knew there were thousands of girls like her in London, girls who'd been tossed out of workhouses or abandoned by parents and left to fend for themselves. Every quarter, he gave all of his coachman's salary and a lot more besides to charities that helped the city's destitute, especially poor children. But this child didn't look as if anyone had ever helped her.

He reached into his pocket and pulled out a handful of coins. Holding the money out, he stepped toward her. "Well, give us yer hand, girl," he ordered softly when she simply stared at him.

She lifted her hand and spread her fingers, and he dropped the money onto her grimy palm. Her eyes widened when she saw how much he'd given her. She raised her head and met his gaze. "I ain't told ya nothin' yet."

"And I don't want you to," he replied gently. "Take this money and buy yourself a good coat and a pair of shoes. Then get a decent meal. That's the best I can do for ya."

Confused, she closed her fingers over the coins and stepped back. "Why ya doin' anythin' for me?"

"Because you remind me of someone," he replied. If life had been just a little bit different, this could have been his Betsy. "Now go on and get some food."

The girl began backing away. "You ain't the only one lookin' for Bernadette," she said. "There's another one, only he ain't nice like you."

Smythe's jaw dropped in surprise. But before he could recover and ask her what she meant, she'd turned and taken off running. Despite his good intentions about not wanting to use the child, he thought about giving chase. But then he realized that would frighten her to death, and he guessed she'd known enough fear in her life.

Besides, there were other, easier ways of finding out who else was searching for Bernadette Healey — and more importantly, why they were looking.

■ ■ ■ ■

Witherspoon's footsteps slowed as he and Constable Barnes approached the small office on the third floor where Nivens was reading burglary files. They stopped in front of the door, and the inspector turned to Barnes and said, "Would you mind waiting out here? This might be awkward for Inspector Nivens."

"Of course, sir," Barnes replied easily. He took no offense; Witherspoon was merely being a gentleman about the matter. "I'll be right outside."

"I appreciate your understanding, Constable." Witherspoon took a deep breath, turned, and rapped gently on the door.

"Enter."

"Call out if you need me, sir," Barnes said as Witherspoon went inside.

A moment later, half a dozen doors to the long corridor opened, and police constables appeared. They moved silently, saying nothing and simply standing in the door frames.

Earlier, while Witherspoon had been ascertaining Nivens' whereabouts in the building, Barnes had slipped down to the canteen and spread the word that Witherspoon was confronting Nivens and that it might get ugly. Every constable in the room had volunteered to come up and stand at the ready in case they were needed. Witherspoon was much loved and admired by the rank and file. Nivens was universally loathed.

Inside the office, Nigel Nivens looked up from the report on his desk and frowned. "Good Lord, what on earth are you doing here?"

"Forgive me for disturbing you, Inspector," Witherspoon began politely.

"State your business quickly, then," Nivens cut him off. "I've a meeting with Chief Inspector Barrows about these St. John's Wood burglaries, and I need time to prepare for it."

Inspector Witherspoon hated confrontations, but he was no coward. Nivens had treated him with contempt and hostility at every turn, and though Witherspoon had tried to be reasonable and have a decent working relationship, the man made it utterly impossible. "Then I'll get right to the point, Inspector. I want the letters that Michael Provost sent you when you were acting superintendent at the Chelsea police station."

Nivens drew back. "Letters? What letters? I've no idea what you're talking about,

Witherspoon," he blustered.

"Don't be foolish, Inspector. You know exactly what I'm talking about." Witherspoon kept his voice down. "I've sent out notices to every station in the London area, asking for the letters Michael Provost wrote the police in the weeks before he was murdered."

"What makes you think I have them?" Nivens asked.

"Because you're the one who received them," Witherspoon replied. "Provost sent them to Kensington, and the constable on duty handed each and every one over to you."

Nivens snorted. "Don't be absurd. Whoever told you this nonsense is lying."

"I don't think that's the case," Witherspoon replied. "We have it on good authority that the letters were given to you. They were then put into the evidence locker, and now they're gone. You're the responsible officer, so I'm asking you to produce them, as they are now evidence in my investigation."

Nivens leapt to his feet. "Are you accusing me of taking evidence? That's a damned serious accusation, and I'll not have you bandying that about and destroying my reputation," he yelled.

Witherspoon held his ground. "You can either turn the letters over to me quietly, or I'll go to the chief inspector and request an official inquiry."

"How dare you!" Nivens shouted. "How dare you speak to me like that! How dare you take the word of some upstart constable over me!"

"My source is very reliable and was only doing his duty. Furthermore, I suggest you be a bit more discreet when attending social occasions, especially dinner parties. Discussing current cases that are being actively investigated is frowned upon." Witherspoon turned on his heel. "You've got until tomorrow," he warned as he left.

Outside in the hall, the constables slipped back into the offices and quietly closed the doors as Witherspoon appeared. He nodded at Barnes and turned toward the stairs.

"Are you all right, sir?" Barnes asked as the inspector marched down the corridor.

"I'm fine, Constable." He gave Barnes a grateful smile. "As you may have heard, Inspector Nivens didn't take it very well."

"That was to be expected, sir," Barnes replied. "Where are we going now?"

"We really should go see Mr. Marston, but, frankly, I don't think I can stand taking another statement from one of those Wentworth members. Let's go to the Iron Anchor pub. I want to ask Edith Grigson if her brother had a solicitor."

Barnes chuckled. "Do you think she'll tell you the truth, sir?"

"Oh, I doubt it, but we've got to ask." They started down the stairs. "But it doesn't matter. We're also going to visit the other pubs in the neighborhood. It occurred to me over breakfast this morning that if Edith Grigson had sacked all the people who worked for her brother, some of them had probably found employment at other pubs close by the Iron Anchor."

Betsy stopped under a tree and watched as the young maid plopped down on a damp wooden bench. It looked as if the girl was crying, but Betsy couldn't be sure; she was too far away, and the girl's head was bowed. She was staring at either the toe of her scuffed black shoes or the footpath. Betsy hesitated. She wasn't sure what to do. She'd seen the girl coming out of the servants' entrance of the Capel house, and followed her here to Hyde Park. But approaching her now might not be a good idea. The poor lass looked so miserable, and Betsy didn't want to intrude. But, then again, she re-membered the days when she'd first been on her own, how lonely she'd been, how sometimes she'd wanted so badly to share her troubles that she'd have spoken to strangers if any had been handy.

Betsy walked down the path. When she got to the bench, she said, "Do you mind if I sit down?"

The girl raised her head and stared at Betsy in surprise. Her blue eyes were red-rimmed with tears. She had brown hair tucked up under her maid's cap, a pale face, and nice even features. "Go ahead," she mumbled as she shifted to one side. She swiped at her cheeks with a gloved hand and went back to staring at her toes.

"I'm a housemaid as well," Betsy said as she sank down next to the girl. "I can see that you've got troubles, and I remember what it was like the first time I was on my own. Sometimes I'd get so lonely, I'd have talked to a toadstool if I'd thought it could listen."

The girl said nothing, but Betsy could see her lips twitch as she tried not to smile. "No, really. Once I was so sick of having no one to talk to that I smuggled a saucer of milk outside to coax the neighbor's cat into standing still long enough for me to have my say."

The girl giggled. "Go on, you're making

269

that up."

"I am," Betsy admitted. "But I have been lonely and I have been troubled. I'm not trying to intrude."

"I'm not lonely — well, I am, but that's not why I'm crying." The girl sounded a bit irritated. "I'm afraid I'm going to get the sack, and that's enough to make anyone cry. By the way, my name's Lizzie Stark."

"Short for Elizabeth." Betsy laughed. "Then I'm a Lizzie, too, only everyone calls me Betsy. Pleased to meet you. Why are you afraid you're losing your job?"

Lizzie shrugged. "That's the awful part — I don't know. The man I work for is a decent enough sort. Truth to tell, Mr. Capel's more than decent: He pays well, doesn't work us hard, and keeps his hands to himself, if you know what I mean."

"I do." Betsy nodded vigorously. She'd been lucky for most of her working life: The inspector would never in a million years behave in a less-than-gentlemanly fashion to any woman. But she knew there were many households where that wasn't the case. "There's no mistress in the household, then?"

"Mr. Capel's single, and he's not real particular about the cleaning. Like I said, it's a good place to work." Lizzie smiled wryly. "Leastways, it was until a few days ago."

"What happened?"

"He come home from his club one evening, lookin' over his shoulder like he was scared the devil himself was goin' to come through the drawing room window," she replied. "He just about wore a hole in the carpet going back and forth between the drawing room and the front windows. Mrs. Palmer finally asked him if everything was alright, and he said he was just feeling a bit off-color. But I know he was lying. You don't pace the way he was unless you're worried to death about something or other."

"And you think he's going to sack you because he's upset?" Betsy rubbed her hands over her arms in an attempt to keep warm.

"He won't be just sacking me," Lizzie exclaimed. "It's all of us, the whole household. That's one of the reasons I'm sitting here bawling like a newborn babe. I'm not sure what to do. I'm the only one that knows, and I'm not certain if I should tell the others. What if I'm wrong, and he wasn't serious about closing up the house? What then? I'd have got everyone all upset and bothered about nothing."

"Come on; it's cold out here." Betsy stood

up. "There's a teahouse on Oxford Street, and we could both do with something hot to drink."

Lizzie gaped at her. "Haven't you been listening to me? I might be out of a job soon, so I'll not be wasting any money at a teahouse."

"And I'm inviting you as my guest." Betsy grabbed her arm and pulled Lizzie to her feet. "I've got plenty of coin, and I could use some company. It's my day out, and I'm tired of being on my own. The tea is hot, and they've got the loveliest buns as well."

"Oh, I really couldn't let you do that," Lizzie protested. But she didn't sit back down.

"Don't be silly. You'll be doing me a favor." She took Lizzie's arm and tugged her gently along the path to the park entrance. Betsy kept up a steady stream of chatter as they walked, and by the time she and Lizzie were sitting at a table in the nice, warm tea shop, the girl looked considerably more at ease.

"This is ever so nice of you." Lizzie smiled shyly as she picked up her cup.

"Considering I bullied you into coming here, it's the least I can do." Betsy grinned. "Now, why do you think everyone in the household is going to be sacked?"

"Because I overheard Mr. Capel talking to Mr. Martin — that's his good friend from across the road — and he was telling Mr. Martin that he had to go away."

"Go away?" Betsy repeated. "You mean leave town?"

"That's right." Lizzie bobbed her head to emphasize her point. "He said that something had come up, and he needed to get away as soon as possible. He told him he was going to shut up the house as soon as he could lay his hands on some cash. He'd already instructed his broker to sell some of his shares, and he said he was going to see his banker to arrange for a letter of credit as soon as the shares sold."

"No wonder you're upset." Betsy regarded her sympathetically. She knew what it was like to suddenly be without employment or a roof over your head. "But maybe he's not planning on being gone long. Maybe he was just planning a holiday."

"He's not going on holiday. I know what I heard," Lizzie replied. "I was just outside his study, polishing the floor, and I could hear every word. Neither Mr. Capel nor Mr. Martin was bothering to keep their voice down. They had a right nasty old row over the matter. Mr. Martin was furious because he and Mr. Capel had planned to go to a house party together in the Lake District next month. When Mr. Martin reminded him of it, Mr. Capel told him he'd have to go on his own, that he wouldn't be back by then."

"Did he say why he had to leave?" Betsy took a sip of her tea.

"No, and that sent Mr. Martin round the bend. He kept asking where he was going and when he'd be back. Mr. Capel told Mr. Martin that he couldn't say, and that he might be gone for a long time. He made Mr. Martin promise not to tell anyone he'd gone. Absolutely no one." Lizzie's eyes filled with tears. "And that means I'm out of a job."

"Don't cry, Lizzie." Betsy patted her arm. "Even if the worst happens, there are plenty of positions about. You'll find another job."

Lizzie shook her head. "Not someone like me. I'm not trained properly. This is my first position. Mr. Capel is a bachelor. All he wants us to do is keep the dust off the furniture, his clothes cleaned, and the whisky decanter filled. If it weren't for the housekeeper, the place would be a real pigsty."

"You've every right to be upset," Betsy said. "You said you thought your Mr. Capel was scared of something. Do you have any idea what it might be?"

"I don't know, but everyone's noticed he's been acting strange. He's all nervous and twitchy-like."

"How long has he been that way?" Betsy wasn't certain how far she could push this conversation. There was a very thin line between listening to Lizzie with a sympathetic ear and asking one question too many.

"For a few days now," Lizzie replied thoughtfully. "I think I noticed it Wednesday afternoon, when he come home from his gentlemen's club. That's right — that was the first day he started watching out of the drawing room windows. Should I tell the others?" she asked. "We're not a big household, but there is Mr. Blakely — he's the butler, but he doesn't do much except shine Mr. Capel's shoes and press his clothes. It's Mrs. Palmer, the housekeeper, that runs the place. Then there's the cook, and two other housemaids besides myself."

"You seem pretty sure about what you heard," Betsy replied. "So, yes, you should tell them. They'll need to find work as well."

"You again." Edith Grigson picked up a wet glass and began drying it with a towel. "What are you doing back here? Having the police tramping in and out of my establish-

275

ment isn't good for business."

"I thought this pub belonged to Ernie Grigson," Barnes said. "It's his name on the license. As to why we're here, the inspector has more questions for you. Don't you want to find out what happened to your brother?"

"Nothing has happened to Ernie," she insisted. She put the glass down on a tray and pulled another out of the basin of rinse water lying on the lower counter beneath the bar. She gave the glass a shake and continued with her drying. "He's gone off on one of his little escapades, and he'll come walking in here any day now."

"If you really believe that's true, Miss Grigson, then why did you sack his staff and hire your own people?" Witherspoon asked.

Taken aback, she went still and stared at him. "I don't need to explain my actions to you . . ."

"Yes, I'm afraid you do," Barnes cut in. "Or, if you prefer, we can have a word with the local council about the name of the publican licensed to operate this establishment." It was a bluff — as a family member, she was perfectly within her rights to run her brother's business in his absence — but the constable hoped she wouldn't know that.

"There's no need to do that," she said quickly. "Alright, I'll admit I sacked a few of his staff. But only because they were lazy and playing my poor brother for a fool. It wasn't because I wanted to take over his business or because I think he's not coming home. Ernie isn't a good judge of character; he lets people take advantage of him."

"Did he let his bookmaking customers take advantage of him as well?" Witherspoon watched her face, hoping to tell by her expression whether he'd hit the mark. On the way over, Barnes had mentioned that he'd heard a rumor Grigson was a bookmaker. Miss Grigson's reaction might confirm the gossip.

Startled, Edith almost dropped the glass, but managed to grab the handle before it hit the wood. "I don't know what you're talking about. You shouldn't believe everything you hear."

"Oh, come now, Miss Grigson, wasn't bookmaking the way your brother got the money to buy this place?" Barnes said.

"What of it?" she replied.

"We have it on good authority that your brother was a bookmaker," Barnes continued. "So please don't waste our time denying it. What we need to find out is if you know of anyone who lost a great deal of money to your brother."

She put the glass on the counter and

tossed the drying cloth next to the basin. "I'll admit Ernie took a few bets, but it was only a side business. As for anyone losing heavily or owing him a lot of money, I'd not know about that. I only found out about the bookmaking when I got here. My brother and I weren't close. I'm the only family he's got, but he couldn't be bothered to keep in touch with me, couldn't be bothered to find out if I needed anything or if I was happy." Her eyes filled with tears. "You'd think a man would be a little concerned about his sister, wouldn't you. Look at this place." She waved her arms in a circular motion. "He could have asked me to come here. I'd have kept house for him, helped him to run this business."

Witherspoon stared at her sympathetically. "How did you find out your brother had disappeared?"

She swiped at her eyes. "I got a telegram."

"Who sent it?" Barnes asked in a kindly tone.

"Michael Provost," she said softly. "One of Ernie's staff went to Mr. Provost when he didn't open up the pub. Mr. Provost came over and searched the place. When they couldn't find hide nor hair of Ernie, he sent me a telegram the next morning."

"Miss Grigson, why didn't you mention

this before now? Your brother has disappeared, and Mr. Provost is a murder victim. Didn't it occur to you that the two events might be connected?"

"Why should it?" She glared at him defiantly. "All Provost did was send me a telegram. Other than the time he come around asking all his nosy questions, I'd nothing to do with him."

"Does your brother have a solicitor?" Witherspoon asked.

"What would he need with a solicitor?" She picked up the drying cloth and draped it on her shoulder.

"He might have done up a will," Barnes suggested.

"What for?" She reached for another wet glass. "The only things he had to leave were this pub and a silver stickpin like mine." She jerked her chin toward the silver owl pin on her lapel. "Ernie had one just like it. Our mother had them made for us. The eyes are diamonds, but they're only chips. Ernie wears his all the time."

Barnes glanced at the inspector and saw by Witherspoon's expression that he was thinking the same thing. The woman simply wouldn't believe that something bad had happened to her brother.

"Where were you last Tuesday night?"

279

Witherspoon asked.

The door from the back room opened, and a young man with a keg of beer on his shoulder stepped out and made his way down the narrow space behind the bar.

"I was right here on Tuesday night," she replied. "Where else would I be?" She glanced over her shoulder. "Put that keg underneath, Tom," she instructed. "But don't hook it in yet. We'll not need it till this afternoon."

"You were here all evening on Tuesday?" Barnes pressed. "You didn't go out?"

"I was here until after midnight." She stepped aside to give Tom room to shove the keg into place. "I never left the pub."

"Oh, yes, you did, Miss Grigson," Tom said cheerfully. "You said you had the headache and were going for a walk along the river. Don't you remember? You left at ten o'clock that evenin'. We closed up without ya that night."

"The only things I heard today were what we already know." Luty was disgusted. "Honestly, you'd think the quality of gossip in this town would be a little better. But all I found out was that the Barrington brothers live off the income of a trust set up by their mother. Rollo lives in the family home,

280

and it's worth a pretty penny, but that's about the only asset he's got. George Barrington was married years ago, to Vanessa Harcourt, but she died. Her family had better lawyers than his did." Luty ran her fingers over the handle of her teacup. "They set it up so that George got a lifetime right to live in the Harcourt house — but when he dies, it reverts back to the Harcourts. So even though he married rich, he's got nothing to show for it. Neither brother has ever done a lick of work in his life. I hope someone else has heard something useful, because my day was sure wasted."

"Don't say that," Mrs. Goodge comforted her. "We knew a little about the Barringtons, but we didn't have the details you got for us. Besides, you've done better than me. I've fed half of London in this kitchen today, and the only bit I heard was that Sir Edmund Cleverly owes money all over town. A lot of people extended him credit when they heard he was engaged to Isabella March."

"Oh dear, then they're all going to have a dreadful time collecting what they're owed," Ruth interjected. "He was never actually engaged to Miss March. I had coffee with her this morning, and I'm certain she's made up her mind not to accept Sir Edmund's proposal." Ruth told them everything she'd heard from Isabella. She took care to mention every detail, no matter how small. When she'd finished, she glanced around the table, and then relaxed when she saw the expressions of approval on everyone's faces.

"Well done, Ruth," Mrs. Jeffries said. "Now we know where Michael Provost went when he left his office early that day."

"And whatever he and Jonathan March discussed, it was enough to make him get his sister to promise not to go ahead with the engagement," Betsy murmured.

"But what does it all mean?" Mrs. Goodge complained. "Is Jonathan March's accident connected to Provost's murder? If so, then it probably doesn't have a thing to do with Ernie Grigson. Grigson didn't even know March."

"I don't know what it means," Mrs. Jeffries admitted. "But I've a feeling it is all connected in some sort of way we can't see as yet."

"Maybe this will 'elp put the puzzle together a bit more," Smythe volunteered. He told them about his return to the Swan's Nest pub, his sighting of Bernadette Healey, and his encounter with the young girl. "And I think the little lass was tellin' the truth," he concluded. "I'd already given her a handful of coins, so she had no reason to lie to me."

"She might not be lying, but children do have very vivid imaginations," Hatchet suggested. "She might have imagined she saw someone that wasn't really there."

"Are you going to try and find Bernadette?" Betsy asked.

"We've no choice," Smythe replied. "If someone's really after Bernadette Healey, it's because she knows something. We've got to find her before anyone else does."

"Should we tell the inspector, then?" Mrs. Goodge asked. She cast a quick glance at Wiggins out of the corner of her eye. The lad was staring at the floor, looking for all the world like he'd just lost his best friend.

"Give us a day or two," Smythe said quickly. He'd already given the task to Blimpey. His boys could find both the girl and Bernadette a lot faster than the police. "I've got a source or two I can tap."

"Excellent," Mrs. Jeffries said briskly. "It seems as if we're moving forward on this matter quite admirably. I also found out something which I hope will turn out to be useful."

"You spoke to Ernie Grigson's 'special friend'?" Luty grinned broadly.

"Indeed I did." Mrs. Jeffries helped herself to another slice of Madeira cake. "I told her that I was a friend of Dr. Bosworth's, and that it was due to the good doctor that the police took Provost's death seriously. After that, she was quite candid with me."

"What did you find out?" Smythe asked.

"Not much more than we already know," Mrs. Jeffries said. "She confirmed that he was a bookmaker and that he'd made a great deal of money on the Hardwicke Stakes and the Ascot Gold Cup. She also said that he was planning on meeting someone that night and he was very excited. But he wouldn't tell her the details or who he was expecting. But he did say that after that evening, neither of them would ever have to work again."

"Too bad she didn't have a name or two handy," Betsy said. "Because what I found out today will confuse things even more. Charles Capel is scared to death about something, and is leaving town." She told them about following and then having tea with Lizzie Stark. Like the others had, Betsy recounted every detail of the conversation and took care not to leave out anything. "So poor Lizzie is sure she's going to be unemployed, and I don't think she's exaggerating one little bit."

"Lizzie first noticed Capel being nervous on Wednesday last," Mrs. Goodge said. "That's the day he found out Provost had been murdered."

"Maybe he knows why Provost was killed?" Hatchet suggested. "Or if he doesn't know for sure, he at least has strong suspicions about someone."

"We'll need to get this information to the inspector as quickly as possible," the cook said bluntly. "If Capel scarpers off, he'll take what he knows with him."

"He's not going for a day or two," Betsy reminded them. "Like I said, he's waiting for some shares to sell."

"What does this all mean?" Ruth asked. "We've so much information, but nothing seems to fit properly in any sort of pattern."

"Nothin' fits yet, but it will," Mrs. Goodge declared. "Mrs. Jeffries will sort it out. She always does."

Mrs. Jeffries wasn't so sure of that. "I'm flattered by your faith in my abilities, but at this point, I must admit I agree with Ruth. It is all still very confusing. Furthermore, I'm not the only one who puts the puzzle together — we all do. Now, does anyone else have anything to report?"

"I'm afraid my sources were sorely lacking in information today." Hatchet smiled ruefully. "But I have some excellent ideas for tomorrow."

Mrs. Jeffries glanced at the footman. The lad hadn't said a word during the whole meeting.

Wiggins saw her looking at him. "I've not found out anything," he said. He was miserable and depressed and, worst of all, he couldn't tell anyone how he felt, because then they'd know he'd not been doing his fair share. "But I'll be out on the hunt again tomorrow."

And tomorrow he wouldn't bother wasting his time hanging about the Odeon Opera House, waiting for a minx of a lass to tell him she couldn't have tea with him!

The Lion's Head pub was just around the corner from New Scotland Yard and was, as to be expected, filled with policemen. It was a nicely furnished place, with wood paneling on the walls, etched glass in the windows, and plenty of tables.

The scents of beer and cigar smoke drifted through the air. Constables and detectives crowded around the tables and stood two deep at the bar. Noisy laughter rang out from time to time as stories were told and jokes exchanged.

But the man at the table on the far side of

the room wasn't a recipient of any good-natured jests or interesting tidbits of gossip. Inspector Nigel Nivens didn't often come to the Lion's Head, but tonight he'd been desperately in need of a whisky and perhaps, if he was truly honest with himself, a bit of company.

He picked up his glass and took a sip. This was his third, but he didn't care. He wasn't on duty tonight. He sat alone at a table big enough for four and knew that, barring a miracle, no one would ask to join him.

Nivens surveyed the room. There were three other inspectors sitting by the wall, but they'd avoided looking his way. Two plainclothes detectives, both of whom he'd worked with, stood at the bar with their bodies at awkward angles so that they could keep from making eye contact with him. Every constable in the house shunned him as though he carried the plague.

Everyone hated Nivens, and usually that didn't bother him. But tonight it tasted bitter. He took another sip and grimaced as the harsh taste hit the back of his throat. He looked to his left as a shout of laughter erupted from a nearby table. A plainclothes detective was holding his sides and another was laughing so hard that there were tears streaming down his cheeks. Everyone else at the table was laughing as well. But no one even so much as glanced at him.

Nivens turned away, picked up the whisky, and drained the glass. He caught the barman's eye and gestured for another one. Just then, the front door opened, and Ian McClement and another constable entered the pub.

Nivens was sitting slightly behind a post, so he could see the entrance clearly, but he wasn't in their line of sight. He watched as McClement headed for a group of his mates at the far end. By the time the two newcomers had reached their destination and joined their friends, Nivens realized that every copper in the room had either nodded respectfully at the young constable or offered to buy him a pint.

Nivens' lip curled, and he looked away. McClement might be respected and admired, but that didn't get you anywhere in this life. Once a bit of time passed, everyone would forget that McClement was a hero, and he'd go right back to being a lowly constable walking a miserable beat. He'd stay that way for the rest of his life. That wasn't going to happen to Nivens. He had plans, and if achieving his ends meant that the rank and file didn't like him, he couldn't care less.

"Your whisky, sir." The barman set the glass down in front of him, and Nivens shoved some coins at the man and waved him away.

Nivens took a quick drink and saw another constable put a half pint of beer in front of McClement. From where he sat, the inspector could see McClement protesting amiably.

Stupid git, Nivens thought. He doesn't know how lucky he is. Wish someone would buy me a drink. But that wasn't going to happen, and Nivens knew it.

Nivens drained his glass and put it back down on the table. Being respected by your peers wasn't important. What mattered was getting ahead, getting noticed, making sure you had all the best information and the right connections. Moving up the ladder till you reached the top — that was what mattered.

That was the only thing that mattered.

Another burst of laughter erupted, this time from the group of lads surrounding McClement. Nivens got to his feet and started toward the front door. No one said anything to him — not a word of greeting, not a hello or a "how are you," nothing. He might as well have been invisible.

He paused and glanced over his shoulder.

He ought to do something about Mc-Clement. He knew the little sod had gone running to Witherspoon about those wretched letters. Nivens patted the pockets of his coat. He had plans, and his plans didn't include getting his career ruined by a snot-nosed constable who should have minded his own business. Nor did Nivens intend to be humiliated by that fool Witherspoon. It was time to do something about those letters.

Nivens stepped outside into the cold night air. He turned and headed toward the river.

CHAPTER 9

Witherspoon was very tired when he got home that evening, but over a glass of sherry, he relaxed and told Mrs. Jeffries everything that had happened that day. When he finally went in for his dinner, he felt much better, but the same couldn't be said for Mrs. Jeffries.

Later that night, when everyone had retired and the household was finally quiet, she slipped into her seat at the table. Suddenly, Samson, the cook's cat, leapt into her lap, startling her. "Good gracious, what's all this about, then? Has Mrs. Goodge closed her bedroom door on you?"

Samson wedged his fat backside underneath the edge of the table and tried to curl up into a ball. Mrs. Jeffries eased her chair out to make more room, and he settled in her lap like a big furry lump.

She liked animals, but in truth she was a bit frightened of this one. Samson scratched, clawed, bit, and was generally bad tempered with everyone except the cook, who adored him.

"You must really be feeling lonely, to come keep me company." She gingerly petted his back. He twisted his big, broad face to give her a sharp look, but he didn't move to bite her or raise his claws toward her fingers. She relaxed a little. "I don't think we're ever going to get this case solved," she murmured aloud. After everything she had learned today, she was more confused than ever. Perhaps talking it out with Samson, as it were, would help. It certainly couldn't hurt.

"We've got two possible murders here, and I'm sure they're connected, but I can't determine what the trigger might have been for Provost's death." She stroked Samson again and was rewarded by a faint purr. "Grigson might have been made to disappear because someone wanted to nullify a wager. If what Smythe told us is true — that some bookmakers take collateral for their clients and front the cash themselves — then it's possible that Grigson's killer came back hoping to reclaim his property. That makes sense, doesn't it." Samson purred a bit louder.

"But, then again, we don't know for certain that the killer had anything to do with Grigson's bookmaking. Perhaps it was something entirely different. After all, his sister certainly benefited from his disappearance. Perhaps she murdered Provost to keep him from asking so many questions. We know that she was walking along the river on the very night Provost was drowned."

Mrs. Jeffries discussed the case with the cat for another half hour. Samson, despite his many other faults, was an excellent listener. By the time she put him on the floor and went up to her own bed, she was no closer to an answer, but the bits and pieces were making more sense to her. The beginnings of a picture were starting to emerge, but it was still just the barest outline, very much of a sketch rather than a complete image.

Mrs. Jeffries put the inspector's breakfast plate on the table, made sure the silver cover was firmly in place to keep his food warm, and then went out into the hallway. Witherspoon was at the top of the staircase as Mrs. Jeffries emerged from the dining room. There was a knock on the front door.

"I'll get it, sir. You go in and have your breakfast while it's still hot," she exclaimed as she raced down the hall to the foyer. "It's probably Constable Barnes. I'll bring him right in."

But it wasn't Barnes who stood there: It was a very disheveled Inspector Nivens. His coat was open and his tie undone; his eyes were red-rimmed as though he'd been weeping; and his trousers were damp up to the knees. Mrs. Jeffries almost didn't recognize him. "Inspector Nivens?" she said warily. "Is everything alright?"

"Good day, Mrs. Jeffries." He whipped off his bowler hat. His hair stood up in tufts. "Forgive my intrusion at such an early hour, but I need to speak with Inspector Witherspoon."

She was tempted to slam the door in his face, but as Witherspoon was now right behind her, she didn't dare. "Of course, Inspector." She stepped aside and nodded for Nivens to come inside.

"Gracious, this is a surprise," Witherspoon said. "I'm just about to have breakfast. Would you care to join me?"

"No, thank you." Nivens swallowed. "But a cup of tea would be most welcome."

"Come along, then." The inspector led his guest to the dining room. "We've plenty of tea."

"I'll just nip down and have Betsy put the kettle on," Mrs. Jeffries called out as she charged for the back stairs. She took the steps two at a time and flew into the kitchen. "Smythe, I need for you and Wiggins to come to the landing and stand at the ready. Inspector Nivens is here, and he looks a terrible fright. I don't know what he wants, but I don't trust him an inch." Without waiting for their reply, she turned and went back up.

The dining room door was shut, but she went in anyway. "Do you need anything, sir?" she asked. Witherspoon was tucking into his breakfast, and Nivens had a cup of tea in front of him.

"No, we're fine, thank you." The inspector smiled reassuringly.

She had no choice but to leave. "Very good, sir," she replied, closing the door firmly behind her as she left. She took care to walk hard enough that the two policemen would hear her footsteps as she retreated.

Wiggins and Smythe were standing on the landing.

"What's 'e doin' 'ere?" Smythe asked.

"I'm not sure, but stay close. I don't think he means our inspector any harm, but he was in a state when he arrived. I'm going back to see if I can hear anything."

Downstairs, Betsy glanced at Mrs. Goodge, who was sitting in her chair with

Samson curled in her lap. "What's going on up there?" Betsy whispered. "Does Mrs. Jeffries think that Nivens might get violent?"

"I think that was her concern," the cook replied. "I wish Hatchet and Luty were here. Luty's got a gun."

"Yes, but she doesn't always carry it." Betsy looked worried. "Perhaps I ought to go up as well. I could take the sugar hammer with me."

Just then, there was a knock on the back door.

"Thank goodness, that's probably Luty and Hatchet." Betsy dashed for the back door and threw it open with a relieved smile. A lad who looked no more than eight stood there.

"I've got a message for Smythe," he announced. He pulled off his cap and bobbed his head respectfully. "Can you go get him, please? It's important."

"Give it to me," Betsy ordered. "He can't come to the door now."

"Bloomin' ada, the guv's not gonna like this." He shoved an envelope at her. "But I can't hang about all day waitin'. If he can't come to the door, make sure he reads the note right away. The guv said it was important." The lad slapped his cap onto his head, turned, and nipped off.

Betsy ran back to the kitchen. "Someone's sent Smythe a message. I'll take it up to him."

"For goodness' sake, what is going on?" The cook was so agitated by everything happening at once that she forgot about her beloved cat and leapt to her feet. Samson tumbled to the floor. He yelped and stalked off.

Upstairs, Mrs. Jeffries had crept back to the dining room door and put her ear against the wood. Witherspoon and Nivens were talking in low tones, but her ears were sharp enough that she could make out some of what was being said.

"I've been up for most of the night, Witherspoon," Nivens said. "I walked along the river for hours and watched the sun come up. I've done a lot of thinking, especially about our current dilemma."

The inspector said something in reply, but he spoke so softly, she couldn't hear what he said.

"I know what people think of me," Nivens continued. "And for the most part, I don't concern myself with the opinions of others. But I am still a policeman."

"Of course you are," Witherspoon replied.

"Do you ever think about the point of it all?" Nivens asked, his tone philosophical.

"Why are we here? What's our purpose? Are we just here to express the glory of the Almighty, or is there another, more meaningful reason for the individual soul to exist?"

Mrs. Jeffries frowned. What on earth was he going on about? She heard a faint rustling and a soft murmur of voices behind her. Glancing over her shoulder, she saw that Betsy had come up and joined the other two at the top of the stairs. What was going on?

"Are men judged by their achievements or their character?" Nivens continued. "That's truly the great question. Are we rewarded for how high we've climbed, or are the voyage itself and our conduct on that journey more important?"

Mrs. Jeffries thought she might lose her breakfast. She peeked over her shoulder again, and this time Smythe had disappeared. But Betsy and Wiggins were still on the landing. When Betsy caught Mrs. Jeffries' gaze, she smiled and raised her arm. She was holding the sugar hammer.

Inside the dining room, Witherspoon was talking, but once again his voice was so low that she couldn't understand what he was saying. Drat.

"You're a decent sort, Witherspoon." Nivens broke off and started coughing.

Mrs. Jeffries rolled her eyes in digust. What a performance. The man sounded as if he was coming down with pneumonia.

"You won't ruin me because of our past differences," Nivens continued in a quavery voice. A chair scraped against the floor, and she drew back, preparing to make a run for it if she had to, but instead Nivens started speaking again. "All the letters are here. Do with them as you wish. Like I said, Witherspoon, despite what everyone believes about me, I'm a policeman."

The chair scraped again, only this time she also heard the creaks and squeaks people made as they pushed back in their seats and rose from the table. She frantically motioned for Wiggins and Betsy to disappear and then scurried down to the landing, arriving just as the dining room door opened and the two inspectors stepped into the hallway.

Mrs. Jeffries swung about and pretended she'd just come up from the kitchen.

But neither man paid any attention to her presence as they continued down the hall to the front door. When they reached the foyer, Nivens grabbed the handle, turned to Witherspoon, and said, "My fate as a police officer is in your hands, Witherspoon. I pray you're a better man than I've been."

"Don't worry, Inspector," Witherspoon said kindly. "I've no grudge against you. You've my word of honor that I'll do my best to use the letters only as evidence in a murder, not as ammunition against a fellow officer."

Mrs. Jeffries wanted to box Witherspoon's ears. How could he make such a promise? This was his chance to get rid of the wretched man. She didn't believe for one minute that Nivens was sincere. Thus far, the fool had been lucky that he hadn't already lost his postion. Having friends in high places could help only so much when you were as incompetent an officer as Nivens. And what's more, Nivens knew he was useless as a detective. He'd bungled more cases than any detective on the force! His whole performance today was simply a ploy to keep his precious career from being further damaged by his own selfish stupidity. Selfish. Incompetent. Inept. The words echoed in her mind as she suddenly understood what had so flummoxed her from the beginning about this case.

Nivens stumbled backward as the front door was pushed from the other side.

"Oh, sorry, sir." Barnes stuck his head inside. "I thought the thing was jammed."

"Come in, Constable." Witherspoon held the door wide open. "The inspector was just leaving."

The two policemen nodded to each other as they passed in the doorway. Witherspoon waited until Nivens had reached the street before he quietly closed the door.

"Do go back in and finish your breakfast, sir," Mrs. Jeffries suggested. "I'll bring up a fresh pot of tea. I'm sure the constable would enjoy a cup on such a cold morning." She turned and hurried toward the back stairs before the inspector could reply. She had to find out what had caused Smythe to disappear.

Smythe stood on the landing of the attic floor of a run-down lodging house in Battersea. He put his ear close to the door. He wanted to make sure she was alone. It would be awkward if she had company, and Smythe didn't fancy getting into a fight just because he wanted to have a word with the woman. He waited for several minutes, then knocked softly on the wood.

"I told you I'd have the rent in a day or —" Bernadette Healey's voice broke off as she threw open the door and saw Smythe. Her mouth rounded in surprise, and panic flashed across her face. She flung herself against the door, trying to slam it shut. But he stuck his foot in, grabbed the knob, and pushed hard from his side. She stumbled backward, and he muscled his way into her room.

"Get out of here before I start screaming," she cried. "I've done nothing wrong! Do you hear me? Nothing!"

"I just want to talk to you." He closed the door and leaned against it. It wouldn't do to be interrupted now that he'd found her.

"You've got no right to come here forcin' your way into my room," she charged. She was backing away from him. Her eyes were wild with fear, her face deadly white.

"I'm sorry I 'ad to push in on ya, but I've got to speak to ya," he said, trying to keep his tone gentle and reasonable. She looked terrified. "I mean you no harm. I just want to ask you a few questions."

"You're goin' to hurt me," she shouted. "But I'm not givin' in without a fight. I warn you — you come any closer, and I'll scream my head off."

"I promise, I'm not going to lay a hand on you," he replied. "But someone else might. That's why you're so scared. You know someone is after you. I swear it's not me. I just need to talk to ya."

She stared at him warily. "How do I know

I can trust you?"

"You don't, but if I was goin' to hurt ya, would I be breaking in 'ere in daylight? Your landlady's right downstairs, and she's the one that let me in. If I meant you any harm, I'd not have let her or anyone else in the neighborhood see my face," he replied.

Bernadette said nothing for a moment. Then she shrugged and sank down onto her bed. She pointed to the only chair in the room. "You can sit there."

He sat down. The room was small and shabby. Limp gray curtains hung at the tiny window, a stained beige coverlet lay across the narrow iron bed, and a green-gray threadbare rug was on the floor. "Why did you take off when I was askin' about Michael Provost that day in the pub?" Smythe asked.

"I didn't want trouble." She laughed harshly. "But ever since that night, it's been nothing but misery for me. I'm a decent woman, you know. I've never had to take to the streets like some have. But havin' to hide out and not work has cost me every penny that I've got — and my job."

"How long have you been hidin'?" he asked.

"Long enough." She snorted delicately. "I first spotted the bloke that was huntin' me the day I saw you in the pub. I thought the two of you were workin' together."

"We're not," he said. "You want to tell me about it, or should I just keep askin' questions?"

"I might as well save us both a bit of time." She smiled bitterly. "That'd be the fastest way to get rid of you."

"It would," he agreed.

"I work at the Railway Hostel, just off Lotts Road. I do the dirty work, the washin' up and the heavy cleaning, but I don't mind. It's better than the streets, and at least I can go to church on Sundays with a clear conscience. Not that I blame the women that have to go on their backs. It's not their fault — they've got to do what they can to survive, and most of 'em don't have a choice, but that's neither here nor there." She scooted back so she could rest against the wall. "I work nights because Mario — that's the owner — pays three bob a week more if you do the nights. I've no family, so it doesn't matter to me when I work. I usually get off a little after ten, and then I walk to my lodging house."

"Where're your lodgings?" he asked.

"On Tetcott Road, behind the Royal Brewery. I share a room with three other women," she said. "That night I was walking down Lotts Road, and all of a sudden this gent come up to me and asked me if I'd like to earn five pounds." She pushed a lock of hair off her cheek. "I told him I wasn't a street woman and to try his luck elsewhere. He said that wasn't what he was looking for, that what he needed was someone to help him play a joke on one of his friends. Then he took out a fiver and waved it under my nose."

"Were you standing under a gas lamp?" Smythe asked.

"There was one close by, and it was one of them nights with a lot of low cloud cover. It was real easy to see, and I could tell it was a five-pound note." She looked at Smythe. "Do you know how long it takes me to earn that kind of money? That was more than I make in a month. So I asked the toff what he wanted me to do."

"And what did he say?"

"This is the odd part." She crossed her arms over her chest. "All he wanted me to do was stand on the old wharf. He said I was to stand there and wait until another two blokes come walking close, and then I was to disappear."

"How long were you supposed to stand on the dock?"

"He said his friends would be by within

five minutes." She scratched at a rough patch of skin on her hand. "And that I'd know when to take off, because one of the blokes would wave his bowler hat at me when they got into position."

"You didn't think this was a strange sort of joke to play on someone?" Smythe asked.

"Don't be daft. Of course I did," she protested. "But he was flashing that fiver at me, and I needed the money desperately. I've not had a new pair of shoes in years. So I took the money and went down to the dock and just stood there."

"What did the bloke do?" Smythe asked. "Where did he go?"

"He took off like the hounds of hell was on his heels. He went running up Lotts Road and disappeared down a side street."

"Then what happened?" Smythe prompted.

"I stood on them old wharves by the Vestry dock, and sure enough, two blokes appeared from round the corner and came toward me. They were some distance away, but I've got good eyesight, and when the one waved his hat at me, I scarpered. I went to the Swan's Nest and had a gin. I had more than one, if you want to know the truth. Then I went on home. But I couldn't sleep."

"Why? What made you so suspicious?"

She shrugged. "There was something about the whole situation that didn't sit well. I laid there listening to Nancy and Stella snoring up a storm. I told myself that what a bunch of toffs did to each other was none of my business, and that I was a fool to be worryin' so. But finally I couldn't stand it, so I got up and went back."

"What'd you see?"

Her eyes filled with tears and her lips trembled. "Oh, God, it was dreadful. The poor man was in the water. He was floating by the piling with his arms out to the sides and his face down in the drink. I knew he was dead. What's worse, I knew they'd used me in some way to lure the poor bloke there and put him in."

"You could see him that clearly?" Smythe clarified. He wished Mrs. Jeffries were here. He knew this was important.

"I already told you — them clouds were almost like mirrors. He was easy to see." She made a face. "But I wish to God I'd not gone back; I wish to God I'd never taken that bloody fiver."

"What happened then?" he asked.

"I knew what I had to do, didn't I. He had to be found. I wasn't goin' to let them toffs get away with usin' me to kill someone.

307

They didn't think he'd be spotted till the morning, but I put an end to that plan." She laughed harshly. "I wanted him to be found, but I wasn't going to go find a copper and drag his arse back to the dock, that's for sure. I knew they'd never believe my story, and I'd be the one arrested. So I came up with another way to get the police there. It was dead easy. I stood on Lotts Road until the constable on patrol came round the corner. As soon as I knew he'd seen me, I took off running like the devil himself was after me."

"That was clever." He looked at her approvingly. "The police always give chase when they see someone running away."

"That's right." She grinned. "I'm a good runner, but I let the constable get close enough so that he could see me when I tossed a piece of wood into the river. I didn't throw it until I was right near the dock where the poor bloke was floating. My aim was true, and the constable looked in the right direction. He saw the body right away. Once I knew that he'd seen it, I kept on going. I didn't stop till I was back at my lodging house."

"But that wasn't the end of it, was it." Smythe said. "Someone's been after you?"

"I thought it was you," she admitted.

"Right after you come round to the Swan's Nest asking about Mr. Provost, Mario said a big brute of a fellow had come to the hostel and wanted to know when I was working next."

Smythe didn't particularly like that description, but he could understand how it would fit him. "It wasn't me. I didn't know where you were workin'."

"I wasn't takin' any chances," she replied. "This is murder, and if they could kill that fellow, they'd not think twice about killin' the likes of me."

"I think you ought to go over them yourself, sir," Barnes said as he poured himself a cup of tea from the fresh pot Mrs. Jeffries had just put on the table.

Witherspoon raised his eyebrows. "You mean read them here?"

"Yes, sir." The constable flicked a quick glance at the dining room door and noted that it was cracked open just the tiniest bit. "These letters have disappeared out of the evidence locker once. It could happen again. At least if you've read them before you sign them in, you'll know what they contain."

Witherspoon considered it. "Do you really think it's necessary? Inspector Nivens brought them here voluntarily."

"He really had no choice. He knew we'd learned that he had the letters and that he was the officer in charge when they were delivered to Chelsea station. Besides, sir, what could it hurt? It won't take more than a few minutes to have a look at them."

"Let's go over them in order, then," Witherspoon agreed. He handed the constable half the stack, and he took the other half. A few moments later, the pages were neatly stacked in date order from the earliest letter to the last.

"They're each no more than a page," the inspector commented as he picked up the first note. "And Constable McClement is indeed correct: The handwriting is very easy to read. The first one is dated December eighteenth. It's only a few paragraphs."

He read the letter, handed it to Barnes, and then picked up the second one.

Barnes scanned the page quickly. "All it says is that Provost's certain something has happened to his friend Ernie Grigson, and he'd like the matter investigated. Provost says he's undertaken his own investigation but he will keep them informed of his progress."

Witherspoon handed the constable the second letter.

Outside in the hall, Mrs. Jeffries held a

sheet of paper to the wall and began taking notes as the two policemen discussed the letters. By the time they were finished, she had a cramp in her fingers, but she'd managed to jot down the important points from each message as it was read. When she heard the men finish their task and get up from the table, she tucked the paper into her apron and darted for the back stairs. Once again she pretended she was just coming from the kitchen when the two policemen stepped out of the dining room. "Are you on your way, sir?" she asked pleasantly.

"Indeed we are, Mrs. Jeffries." Witherspoon beamed proudly. "The constable and I have a very busy day planned. We're going to put these letters into evidence, and then we're going to have a word with Charles Capel."

"Shouldn't we wait for Smythe?" Betsy cast a fleeting look toward the back door. "He'll want to know what's in those letters."

"We don't know where he went or when he'll be back," Mrs. Goodge pointed out. "Once you gave him that envelope, he was out of here so fast, he didn't even take time to tell us where he was going."

"We really can't wait." Mrs. Jeffries pushed her tea mug to one side and pulled the notepaper out of her pocket. "We might need to take action quickly, and we must be at the ready."

"Go on, Hepzibah," Luty encouraged. "Tell us what them letters said."

"I only had time to write down the important points," she warned. "The first letter was dated December eighteenth. In it, Provost told the police he suspected foul play in the disappearance of Ernie Grigson. He also informed them that he was conducting his own investigation into the matter and that his inquiries had led him to the Wentworth Club, which he had now joined in order to pursue the matter further."

"Did the letter say what drew him to the Wentworth Club?" Ruth asked.

"If it did, the constable didn't read that part aloud," Mrs. Jeffries replied. "The second letter was dated January third. All it said was that Provost was sure Grigson had been murdered because he was a bookmaker."

"So Provost referred to it as murder, not as a disappearance," Hatchet murmured.

"Yes, Inspector Witherspoon commented on that as well." Mrs. Jeffries took a quick sip of her tea. "The third letter was dated January tenth, and revealed that Provost had learned that Grigson accepted bets from people who didn't have cash but who would instead sign over something of value that they owned. Provost told the police that Grigson didn't do it as matter of course but only for a select few clients."

"And I'll bet those clients were at the Wentworth Club," Mrs. Goodge said.

"The fourth letter was dated January seventeenth. In it, Provost said he'd narrowed down his list of suspects to the members of the Octet group of whist players. In this message, he also mentioned one of them, Charles Capel, by name. Provost wrote that Capel had been one of Grigson's customers and had introduced several others to Grigson."

"But the letter didn't give any other names?" Betsy asked. If Capel was their killer, poor Lizzie and the others would be unemployed.

"No. The fifth letter was from January twenty-fourth. Provost told the police he'd discovered that one of the Wentworth Club members had used an extremely valuable item to secure a wager, and that Provost knew what the item was."

"But he didn't mention in the letter what it was?" Mrs. Goodge asked, her tone incredulous. "Why not?"

"I don't think he had very much confidence in the police," Mrs. Jeffries explained. "I did hear Constable Barnes say that every letter included a plea for the police to investigate the matter. By the time Provost wrote the sixth letter, he was out and out accusing them of gross negligence and dereliction of duty."

"When did he send the last one?" Hatchet asked. "What's the date?"

"January thirty-first." Mrs. Jeffries smiled sadly. "He told the police he'd not made any real progress since his last letter, but that he was meeting with a dependable source of information and he'd write again the next week."

"But he never wrote that letter, because he was murdered the following Tuesday night," Betsy said.

Fred, who'd been sleeping quite peacefully on the rug, suddenly leapt to his feet and charged down the hall just as they heard the back door open.

Smythe could be heard gently scolding the dog. "Get down, Fred. Mind your manners. The lady is a guest."

Everyone turned as Smythe and a red-haired middle-aged woman came into the kitchen. "Sorry to burst in on you like this," he said. "This is Miss Healey, and she's goin' to help us with this mess."

"How do you do, Miss Healey." Mrs. Jeffries nodded politely as she got to her feet. "Please sit down. I'm sure you could do with some tea."

"Thanks, that would be lovely. Please call me Bernadette." She glanced uncertainly at Smythe, who took her arm and led her to an empty spot next to Ruth Cannonberry.

Betsy stared at Bernadette for a moment, and then she smiled. "My name is Betsy. Are you hungry? Would you like something to eat? We've plenty of food — there's brown bread and scones."

"I'd love something to eat," Bernadette admitted shyly. "Thanks ever so much. I've had nothing but a bit of mutton since yesterday lunch. I didn't dare go out, ya see. I was afraid he'd catch me."

Smythe gave Betsy a quick, grateful smile. "We need a place to hide Bernadette. She's a witness to what happened that night, but she's afraid she'll be the one arrested if she goes to the police straightaway."

"Why should she be arrested if she's only a witness?" Mrs. Goodge demanded. She looked at Bernadette and bobbed her head by way of introduction. "I'm the cook — Mrs. Goodge."

"Pleased to meet you," Bernadette replied.

"Because she's more than a witness,"

Smythe explained. "But she'd no idea murder was bein' planned that night. We've got to hide her until we can sort out what needs to be done."

"She can stay at my house," Luty volunteered. She grinned at Bernadette. "I'm Luty Belle Crookshank, and this here is Hatchet." She poked him in the ribs. "We'll keep ya safe until this is all figured out. Uh, Smythe, exactly what are you goin' to do to get it figured out?"

"Let me explain everything, and then we can sort out what needs to be done," he said. He told them everything Bernadette had shared with him about that night. When he finished, he looked at the housekeeper. "What do you think would be best to do now?"

Mrs. Jeffries thought for a moment. "The first thing is to get the inspector to have a word with the constable that chased Bernadette."

"What good would that do?" Bernadette asked as she helped herself to a slice of bread from the plate Betsy had put in front of her.

"It'll confirm your statement regarding the sequence of events, and prove that you were deliberately trying to guide the police to Provost's body," she replied. "That alone should be good-enough evidence that you were duped and had nothing to do with the murder itself. As a matter of fact, your actions that night were very heroic."

Bernadette looked at her hopefully. "Ya think so? Ya really think so? Oh, that would be such a comfort and a relief. I've felt lower than a snake's belly over what happened that night. If I'd not taken that bloke's fiver, poor Mr. Provost might still be alive."

"It wasn't your fault." Mrs. Jeffries rose from her chair. "But there's no time to lose." She looked at Luty. "Take Bernadette to your house, and keep her there until we're ready for her."

"That's easy enough," Luty said.

Mrs. Jeffries turned to Ruth. "Can you go see Miss March? We need to find out if she happened to mention to anyone at all that Provost had been to see her brother."

"You want me to go now?" Ruth asked.

"Yes, right away, and you've got to come back immediately and let us know what she says."

Ruth pushed her chair from the table and got up. "I should be back within the hour," she promised.

"Excellent," Mrs. Jeffries said. "I need someone to get a message to Constable

Barnes. He has to get the inspector to speak to the constable that discovered Provost's body, the one that chased Bernadette."

"But didn't the inspector say he was going to the Capel house?" Betsy reminded them.

"Yes, but he'll report in at the Walton Street station first," Mrs. Jeffries said. "And it's more important that he speak to the constable than that he talk to Capel."

"But Capel might be getting ready to leave town," Hatchet pointed out. "And it appears he's an important part of this investigation."

"True, but right now our first task is to make sure the inspector speaks to that constable. There are other ways we can ensure that Capel doesn't leave."

"I'll nip down to the station," Wiggins volunteered. He'd already been out once today, and what he'd seen had made him miserable as sin. He'd gone extra early that morning to Catherine Shelby's rooms, so that he could escort her to the Odeon, but when Wiggins got there, an older man was already at her lodging house door. When Catherine came out, she'd not only taken the old fellow's bouquet, but she'd also kissed him full on the mouth.

"What excuse will you use?" Mrs. Goodge asked. She'd seen Wiggins slip out earlier, and wondered what he'd been doing. But he was a grown man, and he'd tell her in his own good time. She only hoped he wasn't getting his heart broken. But he probably was, and there was naught the cook could do to help him with that.

"I'll think of something," Wiggins said as he got up from the table. He went to the coat tree and yanked his jacket from a peg. "Not to worry — I'll make sure Constable Barnes knows this is important."

As soon as he was gone, Mrs. Jeffries looked at the others. "Luty, do you have your Peacemaker with you?"

Luty patted the big fur muff in her lap. "Sure do. It's right here."

"Please don't encourage her, Mrs. Jeffries," Hatchet complained. "That weapon is terribly dangerous. Whoever heard of carrying a Colt .45 in London? It's positively uncivilized."

"Yeah, but it's come in handy a time or two," Luty shot back.

"And it may come in handy today as well," Mrs. Jeffries interjected. "Someone needs to protect Bernadette until she can make her statement to the police. I can't spare either of you" — she looked at Smythe and Hatchet — "so we must rely on Luty."

"Don't worry." Luty grinned at Bernadette. "I'm a right good shot."

"Oh my God," Bernadette muttered. She looked as if she might be ill. "What 'ave I got myself into?"

"What are we going to be doing?" Hatchet asked.

"You and Betsy are going to the Capel house. We must make sure he doesn't get away. Betsy can find out from Lizzie if he's sold his shares and managed to get his hands on enough cash to leave town. If you think he's on the move this morning, you'll need to barge into his house and find some way to delay him."

Hatchet's eyebrows rose. "I'm not certain I'm up to that task. What on earth am I going to say to the fellow?"

"You'll think of something," Mrs. Jeffries said reassuringly. "You're well dressed, and Capel is more likely to listen to you than to any of us." She turned to Smythe. "You must go to Howard's for the carriage. We must be ready to get Bernadette to the station quickly and be on the move if the need arises."

The kitchen at Upper Edmonton Gardens was now silent except for the sound of Mrs. Jeffries' bombazine dress rustling as she paced the floor. The others had been gone for more than an hour now.

"Do you think you've got it solved?" Mrs. Goodge put her rolling pin aside and sprinkled the pastry with more flour. She was making apple tarts.

"I think I know what happened, but I'm not absolutely certain who actually committed the murder," Mrs. Jeffries admitted.

The cook looked at the housekeeper over the rim of her spectacles. "Don't be offended, but that doesn't make sense."

"I know." Mrs. Jeffries stopped and took a deep breath, inhaling the aromas of cinnamon and sugar. The scents should have comforted her, but today she had far too much on her mind to enjoy the sweet odors. "I think I know the why and the how of the murder, but the who is just a bit murky."

"I'm back," Betsy called from the hallway. She ran into the kitchen and skidded to a halt. "It's a good thing you sent me over there. Lizzie said that Capel's managed to lay his hands on some money, and he's leaving town this afternoon. Hatchet said he'll keep watch, and if it looks as if Capel's going to clear out before the inspector arrives, then Hatchet'll find a way to delay him."

"Poor Hatchet," Mrs. Goodge murmured. "He's got a miserable task. What's he going to say?"

"He's clever." Betsy took off her hat and gloves. "He'll come up with something. Ruth's on her way in — I saw her coming across the garden."

But it was Wiggins who got there first. He was grinning from ear to ear. "Cor blimey, good thing I'm as fast as I am. I got there just in time."

"Were you able to get the constable alone?" Mrs. Jeffries asked. "Did you give him the message?"

Wiggins grinned broadly. "Course I was. I nipped in and told the constable on reception that I was from the Witherspoon household and I needed to see Barnes." His gaze fixed on the apple preserves the cook was pouring into a bowl, he headed for the worktable. "The constable come out, and I pulled him to the side and let him know what had happened. He promised me he'd take care of it, and told me not to worry. He said to be at the ready and that he'd get a message here to the house when it was safe to bring Bernadette to the inspector. Can I have one of these?" He reached for a slice.

Mrs. Goodge smacked his fingers. "Get off — I've barely got enough for my tarts as it is. There's some Madeira cake left in the larder if you're hungry." She was happy that the lad seemed to be in better spirits.

A few moments later, Ruth, her cheeks flushed with excitement, came rushing into the kitchen. "I saw Isabella March," she announced as she collapsed into a chair.

"Take a moment and catch your breath." Mrs. Jeffries slipped into the seat next to her. "You look like you've run a mile."

"I have," Ruth admitted. "I wanted to get back as soon as possible. I've got news. On the day Mr. Provost would be murdered, Isabella went to a tea at Imogene Sinclair's home and happened to mention that Michael Provost had come to visit her brother that afternoon." Ruth untied her bonnet strings and pulled the cap off. "She said half a dozen people probably overheard her."

"Were any of our suspects from the Wentworth Club in attendance?" Mrs. Jeffries asked.

Ruth nodded. "Rollo Barrington was standing right behind her when she was speaking. He probably heard every word. Oh, and Jonathan March is home. He arrived last night, and the first thing he did was make sure that Isabella hadn't agreed to the engagement with Sir Edmund."

"Is that why he returned early?" Mrs. Jeffries asked.

"No. He told Isabella he'd run into a friend who told him about Michael Provost's death. He came home straightaway." Ruth put her bonnet onto the seat next to her. "Jonathan March told Isabella that on the day Provost came to see him, after they talked, the two of them had jointly written a letter to the police. Only this time, they had a specific recipient in mind."

"Oh no, have we got to track down another letter?" Mrs. Goodge groaned.

"I don't think this one was ever posted," Ruth replied. "I think Provost's killer found it and destroyed it. You see, this one was written to a policeman who'd actually have done something about the matter. It was addressed to Inspector Gerald Witherspoon."

Chapter 10

"Before we go, sir, Constable Harridge wants to have a word with us." Barnes motioned the bemused young man into the small office. They were at the Walton Street police station. When Barnes had checked the report to find out which officer had called in the alarm on Provost, he'd gotten lucky. Constable Harridge was still on night patrol, and he had just gone off duty that morning when Barnes pulled him aside and insisted that Harridge tell them every detail of how he'd come to find the body.

"Is it urgent?" Witherspoon asked. He'd just slipped his arm into the sleeve of his overcoat. "Can it wait until we get back?"

"The constable's just got off duty. He's on night patrol." Barnes felt a rush of guilt, as he'd deliberately used the one thing that would persuade Witherspoon to listen to the constable now instead of later. The inspector wouldn't want a man who'd worked all night to have to come back before his next shift — and by the time Harridge was back on duty, Barnes and Witherspoon would be finished for the day. "You'll want to hear this before we get out and about, sir. He's the one who found Michael Provost floating in the drink and called in the alarm."

"Night duty, eh? Well, we can't have you tramping all the way back here to make a statement in the middle of the day, can we." Witherspoon slipped the garment off his shoulders and tossed it back onto the peg. "Now, Constable, I've read your report, but I take it you've something to add."

Police Constable Harridge was a tall young man with blond hair and blue eyes. He glanced at Barnes with a confused look on his face. "Well, er . . ."

"Go on, Harridge, tell him exactly what you told me," Barnes prompted. "Don't be alarmed — there wasn't anything wrong with your report. It's your impression of that night that I want you to tell the inspector. Police work is more than just facts. A good copper isn't afraid to trust his instincts, and what you just told me could be very important."

"Right, sir." Harridge gave the constable a relieved smile and then turned his attention to the inspector. "I was walking patrol on Lotts Road and keeping a sharp eye out, as there have been a number of commercial burglaries in the area."

"What time was this?" Witherspoon didn't recall seeing this information in the report, but, then again, he had rather skipped over the details of the discovery of the victim. He was a bit squeamish about corpses.

"It was very late, sir. I'd say it was close to three in the morning," he replied. "It had been a very uneventful night, but I'd not let my guard down. As I said, I was keeping a sharp eye out because of all the burglaries in the neighborhood. All of a sudden I saw a woman standing in the middle of the road. I thought she was acting as a lookout, sir, for the burglars, so I started towards her. But she must have heard me, because she suddenly took off running."

"Of course you gave chase," Witherspoon prompted.

"Right, sir, but she was very fast. She ran down Lotts Road; then, all of a sudden, she veered off onto them old wharves. Now it weren't a dark night, sir, if you know what I mean."

"I've worked a few nights myself, Constable," Witherspoon replied. "I know precisely what you mean. Go on."

"Anyways, she veered off onto the dock, and then I saw her raise her arm and toss something into the water. Naturally, I tried to make out what it was, and that's when I spotted the body. His arms were floating out to the side, and with that white hair and him being facedown, he was easy to see, even in the dark. I raced over to where he was, thinkin' maybe the poor fellow might be still alive. I shined my lantern on him, but I could tell right away he was dead."

"How could you tell?" Barnes asked curiously.

"I've walked the river beat for over a year now." Harridge smiled sadly. "And I've seen half a dozen or more drownings. After a while, you can tell just by looking whether they're gone or not, and I just knew this poor man was dead."

"What happened to the woman?" Witherspoon asked.

"She'd disappeared, sir," Harridge said. "When I looked around for her, she'd gone. That was the odd thing, sir. I had the strongest feelin' that she'd lured me there on purpose. That she'd wanted me to find the dead man."

"What do you think, sir?" Barnes asked as he and the inspector went out to Walton

Street in search of a hansom. Barnes had managed to send a note to Upper Edmonton Gardens, telling the household that Witherspoon had met with the police constable who had found Provost's body. Barnes wondered what was going to happen next.

Farther up the road, a hansom came around the corner and dropped a fare. Barnes waved at the driver.

"Constable Harridge's statement was very interesting," Witherspoon murmured. "Especially his feeling that the woman was deliberately guiding him to Provost's body. But was that because she wanted Provost found? Or was it simply an accidental sighting? I think perhaps I've been derelict in my duty here. Harridge mentioned the woman in his report, and I should have had more lads out trying to find her. Frankly, Constable, I never even gave the matter a thought."

"We've been busy, sir," Barnes replied as the cab pulled up to the curb. "You'd have gotten around to her."

"That's good of you to say, Constable." Witherspoon stepped inside and slid across the seat to the far side.

Barnes gave the driver Capel's address and then climbed inside. "And I don't know that the woman could have been found if we'd had a hundred lads out looking," he declared. "Some people just don't like that kind of trouble." He hoped that young Wiggins hadn't muddled the message and that the household wasn't being fooled by a clever woman who'd committed murder.

"I don't understand that attitude." Witherspoon grabbed the handhold as the cab pulled out into traffic. "If she's a witness, it's her duty to come forward. This is a murder case."

"Maybe she was acting as a lookout, or maybe she's scared," Barnes suggested. Wiggins had been in a hurry, and the constable wasn't sure he'd heard all the pertinent facts of the matter. He hoped he was on the right track here. "Or maybe she's waiting for the right moment, sir. It takes some people a bit of time to work up the nerve to walk into a police station."

Wiggins raced into the kitchen, waving the note that had just been delivered by a street urchin. He tore it open, read it, and grinned. "Barnes's managed to do it! Listen to this."

He cleared his throat.

"Constable Harridge confirms Bernadette Healey's statement that she lured the police to Provost's body. Going to Capel house now but will have W back at Walton Street after lunch."

"Good. I'll go get Bernadette and take her to the station," Smythe said.

"Let's hope that Charles Capel hasn't left town," Betsy muttered. She looked at Mrs. Jeffries. "Is it making sense yet?"

"I would like to think that it is," she replied, her expression thoughtful, "but I'm still not certain I'm right."

"You don't have to be right," Wiggins declared. "Now that Miss Healey can go to the police and talk to our inspector, she can identify the bloke that give her the five pounds that night. He's got to be the killer."

"Looks like we're just in time, sir," Barnes said as he and the inspector got down from the cab. "Mr. Capel appears to be getting ready to depart."

Across the road, a four-wheeler had pulled up in front of the Capel house. A stack of suitcases and a trunk were piled on the pavement next to the carriage. The driver was at the rear, shoving a small chest into the boot.

Blakely, Capel's butler, was coming out

331

the front door, a hat case under one arm and a carpetbag in the other. Charles Capel, dressed in a camel-colored overcoat and a brown fedora, followed the butler. He was carrying a black walking stick in one hand. His eyes widened in surprise as he saw the policemen approaching him.

"What do you want?" he asked.

"Are you leaving, sir?" Witherspoon gestured at the luggage.

"Yes, as you can see, I'm going out of town." Capel looked past the inspector. Blakely put the hat case and carpetbag into the carriage and then picked up the top suitcase from the heap. He handed it to the driver, who'd come around from the back of the carriage.

"Mind you take care with that," Capel warned.

"Where are you going, sir?" Witherspoon asked.

Capel pulled a pair of black leather gloves out of his coat pocket. "I've business to attend to, Inspector. Frankly, my business is no concern of the Metropolitan Police."

"I'm afraid it is, sir," Barnes said. As he turned his head, he thought he saw a familiar form in a black silk top hat dart from behind a slender tree trunk and hurry to the corner. "We're investigating a murder, and we've come across some additional information. We need to ask you some questions."

"I've already answered all your questions," Capel complained. He pursed his lips and concentrated on pulling on a glove. "Now get out of my way. I don't want to miss my train."

"Why didn't you tell us that you were the one who introduced Ernie Grigson to the other members of the Wentworth Club?" Witherspoon asked. He was still unsure of what this piece might mean, but he knew it was very important.

Capel started, and dropped the other glove onto the pavement. Blakely stopped loading the cases and hurried over to retrieve it. "Who told you that?" Capel demanded.

"Michael Provost," Barnes said softly. "He told us."

Capel turned white, and the Adam's apple in his throat bobbed as he swallowed. "Michael Provost is dead. He can't have told you anything."

"Oh, but he could. Mr. Provost wrote a number of letters before he died." Witherspoon put up a hand and motioned for the driver and the butler to stop loading the luggage. "And I'm afraid your name is rather prominently featured in several of them."

"I had nothing to do with his murder," Capel insisted. "Nothing, I tell you. All I did was make a few introductions."

"Then why are you in such a hurry to leave?" Barnes asked reasonably.

"This isn't fair," Capel cried. He balled his hands into fists and shook his arms furiously. "It's not right, I tell you. This shouldn't be happening to me. I don't deserve this. I shouldn't have to spend my life looking over my shoulder and wondering if I'm next."

"Next for what?" Witherspoon pressed.

"Are you a fool?" Capel stared at him as though he were a half-wit. "Why do you think I've sacked my staff, uprooted my life, and sold everything I could get my hands on to raise cash, and why I am now desperately trying to catch the noon train for Southampton? I'm scared they're going to kill me next." He looked at his butler. "Keep on loading those cases."

"They'll either come after you in Southampton or wait until you return," Barnes said quickly. "We can protect you, sir."

"The way you protected Michael Provost?" Capel laughed harshly. "That didn't work out so well for him."

"Mr. Capel, please come down to the station and make a formal statement. You have my word of honor that whoever killed Mr. Provost will be arrested, and that you'll have the full protection of the Metropolitan Police Force."

Capel glanced at the butler and then back at the inspector.

"Constable Barnes is correct," Witherspoon said softly. "If we don't bring the murderer to justice, you won't ever be free. Do you want to spend the rest of your days in fear? Or do you want to do what's needed to end this now?"

Capel closed his eyes for a brief moment. "Blakely, take the cases back inside. I'm not leaving."

Across the road, Hatchet peeked around the corner and saw the inspector and Barnes still standing with Capel. All of a sudden he saw the butler reach into the carriage and take out the cases that he'd just put into it. Hatchet watched long enough to see the luggage go back into the house and Capel leave with the two policemen. Hatchet wasn't certain what had happened. But he knew he had better get back to Upper Edmonton Gardens and tell the others.

■ ■ ■ ■

"Are you quite comfortable, sir?" Witherspoon sat down on the other side of the desk from Capel. They were back in the same small office at the Walton Street police station. Barnes sat on a straight-backed chair to one side, his notebook open and his pencil at the ready.

Capel had taken off his hat and coat. "Given the circumstances, I'm as well as can be expected. But you do understand that I shall hold you personally responsible if I end up dead." He broke off as he realized how silly his threat sounded. He raised his hand in a weary gesture. "Oh, let's just get on with this. What do you want to know?"

"Why don't you start at the beginning and tell us everything," the inspector suggested.

"Yes, I suppose that would be best." Capel gave a self-deprecating laugh. "God, I've been such a fool. I should have gone to you as soon as I heard that Provost had been murdered."

"You're here now," Witherspoon said kindly. "That's what matters."

"Right." Capel straightened his spine. "I have a quarterly trust as income, and I live quite comfortably. I like to gamble, Inspector, but unfortunately I'm not very good at it. My bookmaker was a man named Ernie Grigson. He took bets for me when I had cash, and when it was close to the end of the quarter and I was short on money, he took expensive household items to cover the value of the wager. The arrangement worked well for both of us: Grigson occasionally got a delightful Dresden figurine or a set of silver spoons, always worth more than the actual cash value of the bet, and sometimes I got my goods back as well as a fistful of cash." He broke off and sighed. "I feel wretched. Ernie was a decent chap. If I'd kept quiet, he'd still be alive, and so would Provost. But, like a fool, I had a bit too much whisky one night at the club, and I told the others about my very understanding bookmaker. Of course, they all wanted to meet him."

"Which others? Your entire card group?" Witherspoon asked.

Capel shook his head. "No, just the Barringtons and Cleverly. None of the others were interested. Marston and Delmar don't gamble much, and I think Harkins had already left. Hempel wasn't interested, either. Poor bloke was in enough trouble financially. He'd spent the whole evening telling us about a bad loan he'd made and how he was going to have to go to court to get his money back."

Barnes looked up from his notebook. "Who's Hempel?"

"He was the fourth at the other table," Capel replied. "Michael Provost took his place when Hempel emigrated to Canada to join his daughter. I never did hear what happened to his lawsuit."

"Go on."

"I did as they insisted and introduced them to Grigson."

"Where did the meeting take place?" Witherspoon pushed his spectacles up his nose.

"At his pub. I brought the three of them by one night last June. Grigson always took the wagers after hours." Capel drew little circles on the desktop with the end of his finger.

"Let me make sure I understand the facts of the matter," Witherspoon said. "You took the two Barrington brothers and Sir Edmund Cleverly to meet Grigson. Is that correct?"

"That's right." Capel smiled mirthlessly. "Those three like to gamble, Inspector, and none of them are any better at picking winners than I am, though they all like to pretend they're bloody experts. Fools. But the point is, I can afford to have losses. They can't."

"But they gambled anyway," Barnes said. "And Grigson took the wagers."

"Yes," Capel replied. "It didn't matter to me if I lost a silver candlestick or a hundred pounds. My quarterly allowance is more than adequate. Dear old Papa thought me an idiot and incapable of handling my own affairs, but as I was his only child, he made certain I was well provided for financially. But none of those three have any money."

"What did they use to make their bets?" Witherspoon leaned back in his chair.

"One of them could usually lay his hands on something valuable or on a bit of cash," Capel explained. "They always bet together, you see. I don't know why, but that's what they did. They took a real beating on the Hardwicke Stakes race. It was right afterwards that Grigson disappeared."

Barnes said, "Didn't that alarm you, sir?"

"His sister claimed he suffered from melancholia." Capel looked down at the toes of his shoes. "And I believed her. I guess I wanted to think she was telling the truth and that he'd just gone off somewhere. Then Michael Provost showed up and started asking questions. When Provost was murdered, I knew I was going to be next. I'm the last link, you see. I'm the only one who knew that three of the Octet group had been placing bets with Grigson."

"What about the other members?" Witherspoon asked. "You said you mentioned Grigson when you were all playing cards?"

"I did, but they took no notice. None of them were interested. When I think back, I don't recall that I specifically mentioned Grigson's name until later that night, when I was approached by the Barringtons and Cleverly." Capel sighed. "I should have known when Michael Provost showed up and began asking his questions that this would end badly."

"So Provost made his inquiries quite openly?" Barnes glanced up from his notebook.

"He tried his best to be discreet," Capel replied. "But he didn't quite succeed. The point is, most of the club members hadn't ever heard of Ernie Grigson. So when Provost was inquiring about, no one was able to give him any answers. But when I found out that Provost had been murdered, I knew right away that it was because he'd been conducting an investigation into Grigson's disappearance, and that he'd found out something that scared those three. I

340

knew I would be next. I was the only person left who knew that they had been placing bets with Grigson, and that they'd lost a big one. One they couldn't afford to lose."

Hatchet burst through the back door of Upper Edmonton Gardens and charged into the kitchen. "Charles Capel has gone to the police station with Inspector Witherspoon and Constable Barnes."

Mrs. Goodge, Wiggins, and Betsy were sitting at the table. The cook was drinking a cup of tea, Betsy was peeling potatoes onto an old newspaper, and Wiggins was at the far end sharpening the carving knives.

Mrs. Jeffries was pacing the floor. She stopped by the window. Her mind worked furiously, and she thought she understood what had happened. But she wasn't sure. Yet it was the only answer that made sense. It had to be one of them, but which one?

"Capel was trying to get away, but the inspector arrived before he got his cases loaded into the carriage," Hatchet continued.

"Did they place him under arrest?" Mrs. Goodge asked.

"I don't think so." Hatchet shifted his top hat from one hand to the other. "It looked as if Capel went off with them voluntarily.

But I wasn't close enough to hear anything. The inspector spoke with him for a few minutes, and then Capel ordered his servants to put his luggage back inside the house. I don't understand why he was going to leave town."

"If my theory is correct," Mrs. Jeffries replied, "he was leaving because he was afraid he'd be killed. I suspect it was Capel who introduced Grigson to his killer. When Provost was murdered, Capel probably thought he'd be next."

"You know who killed Provost?" Hatchet pressed.

"I'm not precisely sure which one it was," Mrs. Jeffries admitted. "But I think we'll all find out by the end of the day." She looked at the carriage clock on the sideboard. "Luty should have received our message by now. She's to take Bernadette Healey to the Walton Street police station right away. That ought to set the cat amongst the pigeons."

"We got a message from Constable Barnes that the inspector had spoken with the constable who found Provost's body," Wiggins explained. He blew gently against a blade and laid it back in the velvet-lined box. "So she'll not be arrested."

"We sent Smythe to Luty's with the message," Betsy added. "But he should be back by now."

"I'm right 'ere," Smythe called as he came into the kitchen. "Luty was at the ready." He grinned broadly. "She and Bernadette were chatting like old friends. Luty even sent for one of her solicitors to accompany Bernadette when she goes to make her statement. Mind you, the poor fellow did look a bit confused."

"Is madam accompanying Miss Healey to the police station?" Hatchet asked, his expression alarmed.

"No, Luty's droppin' her and the lawyer off down the road a piece and then comin' right back 'ere." Smythe slipped into the chair next to Betsy's and gave her a quick kiss on the cheek.

Mrs. Jeffries thought for a moment. "Good. That will give the three of you time to get to the Wentworth Club." She looked first at Hatchet, then at Smythe and Wiggins.

"What should we do when we get there?" Wiggins closed the lid of the carving box.

"It would be nice if one of you could get inside and keep watch," she replied. "But failing that, just try to see what happens when the inspector arrives with Miss Healey."

"You think he'll take her there?" Betsy

343

rolled up the newspaper with the potato peelings into a loose ball and set it to one side.

"Oh, yes, I'm sure of it. If my theory about the murders is correct, then it's the fastest way for the inspector to find out what he needs to know."

"Do you think he'll be alright, sir?" Barnes flipped his notebook closed and stood up. Charles Capel, accompanied by two constables, had just left to go home.

"He shouldn't be worried about his safety," Witherspoon said. "He'll have an officer with him until we make an arrest."

"Which one should we see first? One of the Barringtons, or Cleverly?"

"I'm not sure," the inspector replied. "I wish Capel had been able to give us a few more facts."

"Well, his statement has narrowed down the list of suspects," Barnes pointed out.

The door opened, and Constable Yates stuck his head inside. "Excuse me, Inspector, but there's a woman out here who is insisting on seeing you immediately. She claims to be a witness on the Provost case."

"A witness," Witherspoon exclaimed. "Gracious, it never rains but it pours. Send her in, Constable."

"She's got her solictor with her, sir," Yates replied. "Should I send him in as well?"

"That will be fine," Witherspoon said. As soon as Yates disappeared, the inspector looked at Barnes. "Why do you think she's brought a solicitor?"

Barnes thought he understood what was happening, but he couldn't be certain, so he merely shrugged and said, "Perhaps she simply felt the need for a legal advisor. It's just as well, sir. If she has her lawyer with her, we can't be charged with violating any procedures."

"In here, ma'am." Constable Yates opened the door and ushered inside a middle-aged woman and a man carrying a flat leather case. "This is Inspector Witherspoon," Yates explained. "He's in charge of the investigation."

"Thank you, Constable." The man stepped forward and extended his hand. "I'm Matthew Duxbury, and this is Miss Bernadette Healey. Miss Healey is my client, and she'd like to make a statement regarding the events that happened on Tuesday night, February fourth."

Witherspoon shook the man's hand and nodded politely at Bernadette Healey. He introduced Constable Barnes.

"Would you please be seated," he in-

345

structed. "Miss Healey can sit here" — he pointed to the chair in front of the desk, the one Charles Capel had vacated only minutes earlier — "and Mr. Duxbury can have the other one."

Barnes disappeared into the hallway and came back a few moments later with a third chair. He put it by the door, sat down, and took out his notebook again.

Witherspoon went behind his desk and sat down as well. "I take it that this statement pertains to the murder of Mr. Michael Provost?"

Bernadette looked at the solictor. Duxbury nodded. "Yes," she said, her voice barely above a whisper. "It does."

"May I ask why it's taken you so long to come forward?" Witherspoon regarded her closely. He had a strong suspicion as to who she was and why she was here. Her eyes were frightened, and she sat hunched over in her chair.

Bernadette kept her gaze on the floor for a long moment; then she raised her chin and looked Witherspoon directly in the eyes. "Why do you think? I don't trust the police." She crossed her arms over her chest and glared at the inspector. "I was afraid that if I told what I saw, you'd lock me up. But even though I'm scared to death, my con-

346

science won't let me keep quiet. Now, do you want to hear what I've got to say, or not?"

"Yes, as a matter of fact, I do," Witherspoon said gently. "Perhaps it would be best if I just let you make your statement and then I'll ask my questions. Is that acceptable?"

She nodded curtly. "Right, then. I'll tell it my own way, exactly as it happened." She took a deep breath and plunged straight ahead. She told them about walking home from work and being accosted by a man who'd offered her money to play a jest on his friend.

Barnes interrupted. "Would you recognize this man if you saw him again?"

"I'd know him in a heartbeat," she stated bluntly. "Anyways, like I was saying, I agreed because five pounds is more than I'd earn in a month," she continued. She told them the rest of her story, then sat back and stared apprehensively at Witherspoon.

"My client came forward of her own volition," Duxbury said quickly. "She could have stayed silent, but in the interest of justice, she voluntarily made a statement."

"We believe her," Witherspoon replied, but he kept his gaze on the worried-looking woman sitting in front of his desk. "And I want to add that I do understand why she was hesitant to speak up. Not everyone has reason to trust the police."

Bernadette sagged in relief. "Thank goodness. I've got to tell ya, I've been terrified. I'm glad I came in, but there's something else you need to know. Someone's been following me, and I don't think it's because he wants to give me another fiver."

Witherspoon stood up. "Would you be willing to accompany me? I think we can get this sorted out very quickly."

"Where we going to go?" she asked.

"Oh, it's very simple." He smiled. "We're going to find the person who accosted you that night."

As the group entered the Wentworth Club, they formed quite an interesting procession. Witherspoon held the front door open for Bernadette. She was followed by Barnes; by Duxbury, who could have left now that he knew Bernadette wasn't to be arrested, but who had tagged along anyway because this was a lot more interesting than his usual legal work; and by two constables. Three other officers had been instructed to wait outside and apprehend anyone who came running out any of the doors. Witherspoon had had that experience on previous cases, and he didn't care to repeat it.

The porter's mouth opened in surprise when he saw Bernadette Healey. "You can't come in here with a woman." He scrambled out from behind the tiny reception desk. "That's against the rules. Women aren't allowed."

"It's quite alright," Witherspoon said reasonably. "This is a police matter."

"Police matter! Oh, my stars and garters, that's even worse," the porter cried. "You really must wait here until I get Mr. Bagshot."

"We're not waiting anywhere," Barnes stated flatly. This was a murder, and he wasn't going to give the killer a chance to make a run for it. There were too many doors to these old buildings, and he wasn't sure that he and the inspector had covered them all. He pushed past the porter and started for the common room.

"I'm going to fetch Mr. Bagshot." The porter charged for the hallway. "Oh dear, he'll be most upset, most upset indeed."

Heads turned as the group stopped through the wide double doors of the common room. Witherspoon turned to Bernadette. "Take your time and have a good look around. If you see the man, point him out to us."

Bernadette moved farther into the room and surveyed the faces of the men reading their papers or sipping whiskies. As the members realized a woman was standing in their domain, a buzz of disapproval began to build. But by then, Bernadette had had a good look at everyone. "He's not here," she announced.

"Not to worry," Witherspoon said patiently. "We'll go to the card room next. Perhaps he'll be in there." He took her elbow, and they went back the way they'd just come. As they reached the foyer, Bagshot, followed by the porter, emerged from the hallway.

"Just what do you think you're doing?" Bagshot demanded. He stopped directly in front of them. His face was red with rage, and he was puffed up like an angry bullfrog. "Get that woman off these premises immediately."

Barnes moved ahead of the others and shoved Bagshot to one side. "You're interfering in police business," he warned. "Stay out of our way, or I'll have you arrested as an accomplice to murder."

Bagshot's mouth opened, but he stayed plastered up against the wall. "Your superiors will hear about this," he yelled as Barnes led the group past him.

"His name is Chief Inspector Barrows," Witherspoon called over his shoulder. "You can find him at Scotland Yard." If anyone was to get reprimanded for this, he didn't want it to be the constable.

Barnes stopped outside the card room and looked at Witherspoon. The inspector nodded, and the constable grabbed the handle and opened the door. Barnes and Witherspoon entered first, followed by Bernadette and then the two other constables.

Percy Harkins, Sir Edmund Cleverly, and the Barrington brothers were playing whist at one of the tables. Another man was reading a book.

"What's the meaning of this?" Sir Edmund Cleverly rose to his feet.

Witherspoon ignored him. "Do you see the man here?" he said to Bernadette.

She stared at them, her gaze moving from face to face. "That's him," she declared, lifting her hand and pointing at the table.

"That's ridiculous." Rollo Barrington overturned his chair as he leapt up. "I've never seen this woman in my life."

"That's him! That's him!" Bernadette cried. "I remember that voice. It's him alright."

"Constable, please escort Miss Healey outside," Barnes ordered. One immediately stepped forward and took her arm.

Then he and Witherspoon walked to the table.

"Rollo Barrington, you're under arrest for the murder of Michael Provost," Witherspoon said.

"I didn't kill anyone," Barrington yelled. "All I did was give the cow a fiver to lure him there."

"Shut up, Rollo," George Barrington ordered harshly. "You're only making this worse. Say nothing. They can't prove it."

"That's easy for you to say." Rollo glared at his brother.

"I'll get our solicitor straightaway," George replied. "Just keep your mouth shut."

Sir Edmund Cleverly was edging toward the small door on the far side of the room. Percy Harkins had got up as well, and the man who'd been reading the book had dropped it onto the floor.

"You're not the one under arrest," Rollo continued, "and I'm not taking the blame for this." He suddenly pointed at Sir Edmund. "This was all his idea."

Just then a tall dark-haired man burst into the room. He looked straight at the inspector. "My name is Jonathan March, and that man" — he pointed at Sir Edmund Cleverly — "tried to murder me. He also murdered

Mr. Michael Provost and a publican named Ernie Grigson."

Cleverly stopped edging for the door and broke into a flat-out run.

Barnes, Duxbury, and the remaining constable charged after him.

Witherspoon kept a firm hold on Rollo Barrington.

Duxbury reached Cleverly first. He dived for his legs and brought him down just as Cleverly's hand reached for the doorknob. Barnes and the constable each grabbed an arm and hauled him to his feet.

"I didn't do anything," Cleverly shouted. "It was Rollo's house deed, not mine. Why should I have murdered the man?"

"You only used my deed because you were already mortgaged to the hilt and Grigson knew it," Rollo screamed. "You're the murderers, not me. I didn't kill anyone." He looked at Witherspoon, his face frantic with fear. "I'll turn Queen's evidence and I'll tell you everything. Everything. I'm not going to hang for murders they committed. All I did was stand lookout. They're the ones that held him under."

CHAPTER 11

"It's all over," Wiggins announced as the three men hurried into the kitchen of Upper Edmonton Gardens. "You shoulda seen 'em bein' carted off. It was a regular parade!"

"Who was arrested?" Mrs. Goodge demanded.

"Don't tell us yet," Betsy pleaded as she grabbed the kettle. "The tea is almost ready. It'll only be a moment."

"Which should give Wiggins time to dash across the gardens and get Ruth." Mrs. Jeffries smiled at the footman. "She should be here as well."

"Alright." He slapped his hand on his leg and called the dog, who was sleeping in front of the cooker. "Come on, boy. Come with me. Let's go walkies." The animal wasn't as young as he used to be and sometimes didn't wake up when he heard the footman's voice. But Fred opened his eyes, spotted his beloved Wiggins, and leapt to his feet. The two of them dashed for the back door.

The others got the afternoon tea on the table. Betsy filled the pot with boiling water while Mrs. Goodge put the plates out.

Mrs. Jeffries took the time to give herself a stern lecture on the pitfalls of overconfidence. More than one person had apparently been carted off, so obviously she'd been wrong in her assumptions about who was the guilty party. She opened the sideboard drawer and took out a stack of serviettes.

She could hear in the background the excited chatter of the others, as the women teased the men and tried to find out what had happened. Everyone had worked very hard, she thought. Just because her vanity was a bit bruised was no reason to put a damper on their celebration of a job well-done.

"Are you alright, Mrs. Jeffries?" Betsy asked softly. She reached for the stack of serviettes. "You're awfully quiet. I'll put these out if you like. The tea's ready to be poured."

"I'm fine." Mrs. Jeffries forced herself to smile. "I'm tired, that's all." She handed Betsy the linens, took her place at the table, and began to pour. Wiggins and Ruth returned a few moments later.

"Alrighty, then," Luty said. "Everyone's here and everyone's got their vittles. Now talk. Tell us what happened."

"Shall I relate my part first?" Hatchet looked at Smythe and Wiggins, waited for their nods of assent, and then said, "The three of us arrived at the Wentworth Club only moments before the police. Smythe took a position across the road."

"I hid behind a grocer's cart. But I was close enough to keep an eye on the front door," the coachman said.

"Wiggins took a post on the corner," Hatchet continued.

"It gave me a good view of both the front door and the servants' entry," the lad clarified. "I could see 'em both from where I was hiding. Mind you, I was a bit concerned that there were other doors in that old building. But I couldn't actually see any from where I stood."

"And I managed to slip into the club itself." Hatchet grinned broadly. "It's amazing what the simple act of doffing a silk top hat will do. All I did was nod politely to the porter and make up some tale about being the guest of Lord Barraclough, and he let me pass without so much as a by-your-leave. From what I could see, Barraclough wasn't even on the premises. However, I digress. The inspector and his party arrived, and it was the most amazing thing I've ever seen. I'd hidden in an alcove in the common room when the police first burst in, and I saw everything. Miss Healey stood in the doorway and looked at every face before the inspector led her off to the card room."

"I'd have paid to see that." Mrs. Goodge snickered. "I'll bet the members were fit to be tied when they saw a woman standing in their precious club."

"They were indeed." He laughed and looked at Luty. "Matthew Duxbury acquitted himself very well. When we got to the card room, his quick action prevented Sir Edmund Cleverly from escaping."

Mrs. Jeffries gasped in delight. "I knew it! I knew it was him."

"It wasn't just him, Mrs. Jeffries," Wiggins added. "There were three of 'em bein' carted off. The Barrington brothers were arrested as well."

"The Barringtons," she repeated. "Oh dear, then perhaps I really did get it wrong."

"Nonsense. Your theory must have been somewhat correct. You sent us there knowing that an arrest would be made today," Hatchet pointed out.

"True." Mrs. Jeffries felt a bit better. "Go on, tell us the rest."

"When the inspector took Miss Healey into the card room, I slipped down to the servants' pantry and watched from a crack in the doorway. Miss Healey identified Rollo Barrington as the one who accosted her that night. He denied it, of course, but when he realized he was going to be arrested for murder, he started screaming that he'd only been the lookout. Then he pointed at his brother and Cleverly, and accused them of being the actual killers. That's when everything got very interesting. Cleverly made a run for it and was brought down by Mr. Duxbury. Duxbury tackled him just before he reached the door."

"I'm goin' to have to give that man a bonus!" Luty exclaimed. "Who'd have thought Duxbury had it in him."

"But that's not all," Hatchet continued excitedly. "Just then, Jonathan March burst into the room and accused Cleverly of trying to murder him. He then announced to all and sundry that Cleverly and the Barringtons were guilty of murdering Ernie Grigson and Michael Provost."

"Isn't this what you thought was goin' to 'appen?" Wiggins asked Mrs. Jeffries.

"I'd no idea that it was all three of them,"

she admitted. "I was fairly certain Cleverly was guilty, and I thought he might have an accomplice, but I didn't think it was quite this broad a conspiracy."

"Apparently Barrington had given Grigson the deed to his house as collateral for a wager, and they murdered him to get it back," Hatchet explained. "At least that's what I surmised from the outbursts and accusations that were flying about the card room when they were being arrested."

"Of course," Mrs. Jeffries murmured. "Of course I should have realized. Now it all makes sense. George Barrington doesn't even own the house he lives in. That house will revert back to his late wife's family when he dies."

"And Sir Edmund is already in hock up to his neck," Hatchet added.

Mrs. Jeffries almost cried in relief as it all came together in her mind. She hadn't been wrong — she'd simply not realized the scope of the whole situation. Her basic theory had been right!

"But what's any of this got to do with Jonathan March?" Ruth asked. "If I understand correctly, the Barringtons and Cleverly killed Grigson to get the deed to Rollo Barrington's house. Then they murdered Provost because he'd figured out that the three of them had slain Grigson. But what I don't comprehend is why Provost went to visit March, and how that had anything to do with Grigson. Jonathan March doesn't gamble, and according to his sister, he never has. She has never heard him mention the Iron Anchor pub, so he didn't even know Grigson."

Mrs. Jeffries took a sip of tea to give herself a moment to think. She wanted to ensure that she explained it correctly. "Provost went to visit March after he heard about March's accident. He'd deduced that March's being shoved in front of a cooper's van was no accident, but a deliberate attempt on his life," she said. She saw it all so clearly now. That was what had been nagging at her from almost the beginning of this case. The murders had been a means to an end, a way of resolving a troublesome situation. It was what these people did when they needed money, when they needed someone out of the way.

"They had trouble keeping a fourth." The words echoed in her mind, and she suspected she understood why that table was always having to recruit new members. Perhaps she'd have a quiet word with the inspector when things calmed down. She'd ask him to make sure that all those men

who'd allegedly emigrated to the colonies had actually boarded a ship. If she was right, at least one of them was probably at the bottom of the Thames. As Dr. Bosworth had said, homicide by drowning was very difficult to prove without a witness. Except for Michael Provost — even with a nasty head injury, he'd had enough strength to put up a fight and force his assailants to use so much pressure to hold him under that it left bruises on his neck and shoulders.

"Mrs. Jeffries," Betsy prompted. "What about Mr. March's accident?"

"Provost realized that Cleverly had tried to kill Jonathan March, and that this attempted murder was part of a pattern," she replied.

"A pattern." Mrs. Goodge repeated the word. "You mean something they'd done before?"

"Yes," Mrs. Jeffries answered, her expression thoughtful. "I don't think it started with Grigson's murder. They're cousins, you see, and none of them have anything to live on but the income from small trusts or, in Cleverly's case, an estate that has dwindled substantially as the years have passed. None of them are wealthy. Yet because of their background and their own conceit, all three feel entitled to live lives of ease and luxury."

"Our investigation did rather give us all that impression," Hatchet murmured. "However, many impoverished members of the aristocratic classes find themselves in less-than-favorable financial situations. The world has changed. But that hasn't made them killers."

"True," Mrs. Jeffries concurred. "Most people realize they have to adapt to different circumstances as time goes by. But not everyone accepts the reality of their situations. These three certainly didn't. George Barrington married Vanessa Harcourt, an heiress. He probably thought he'd never have to worry about finances again. But she died and, as Luty pointed out, her family had better lawyers than his. He was left with nothing but a lifetime right to reside in the Harcourt home. Poor Rollo wasn't able to make an advantageous marriage, and he's had to add to his income over the years by stealing from his friends and selling the goods."

"He didn't sell everything," Wiggins interjected. "According to the maid, he kept a lot of jewelry."

"Right, he liked to wear it." She smiled. "Vanity, vanity, all is vanity. But I digress. Let's move on. So then we come to Sir Edmund. He's the aristocrat of the bunch and hasn't done a day's work in his life. He's arrogant and vain. Remember what Mrs. Goodge's source told her? He swore vengeance on Jonathan March because the man was too busy working to make time to see him when Sir Edmund called at his office. If that isn't incredible self-importance, then I don't know what is. He was furious that a man who was in *trade* had the gall to ignore him."

"You think Sir Edmund tried to murder March because his pride was bruised or his feelin's hurt?" Luty asked incredulously.

"That was part of it," Mrs. Jeffries said. "But the real reason he wanted March dead was because Cleverly, like everyone else in London, thought that it was March who was standing in the way of Cleverly's engagement to Isabella March."

"You're right," Ruth said eagerly. "Isabella told me that she was the one who started the rumor that Jonathan disapproved of the match. She did it to spare Sir Edmund. But Sir Edmund didn't know that. He thought her reluctance to accept him was because of her brother's disapproval."

"Her effort to cater to Cleverly's pride almost cost March his life. In Cleverly's mind, if Jonathan was dead and buried, Isabella March would marry him. He'd be wed

363

to an heiress, and he'd never have to worry about money again," Mrs. Jeffries said.

"Perhaps I'm being dense, but I still don't see how that connects to Provost," Ruth argued.

"Ah, this is the difficult part to explain." Mrs. Jeffries wasn't certain she had the skills to express what she felt. But her instincts were right about this; she knew it. "Michael Provost had spent some weeks investigating Grigson's disappearance. Unlike us, he had no one to help him in his quest. But Provost was very intelligent, and he had discovered that Grigson's disappearance was, as I said, part of a pattern." She took a deep breath. "When he heard about March's accident, he knew that Cleverly was trying to kill March, to get him out of the way so Cleverly could marry March's sister. And if you think of Grigson's situation in a certain light, that's exactly what happened to him."

"Huh?" Wiggins said. "What's that mean?"

"Grigson and March both stood in the way of one of those three getting what they wanted, what they felt they were entitled to have. Grigson accepted Rollo's house deed as collateral for a wager. Barrington lost, but he wasn't about to give up his house."

"So that's what Grigson meant when he

said he'd never have to work again," Smythe muttered. "Property values being what they are, Barrington's house would have fetched enough to keep Grigson and his lady love for the rest of their lives."

"That's right." Mrs. Jeffries nodded approvingly, delighted that the others were starting to see the connections and that these weren't just figments of her own imagination. "March and Grigson were both in a position to seriously harm one of the cousins. Provost took a big risk by going to see March that day, but he knew he needed an ally in order for the police to take him seriously."

"So he went to see March and told him of his suspicions." Luty nodded in understanding.

"And it was that very night that Provost was murdered," Betsy said.

"Right after Isabella had inadvertently mentioned in front of Rollo Barrington that Provost spent half the afternoon with her brother," Ruth said. "Oh dear, poor Isabella will feel awful when she finds out. She signed Michael Provost's death warrant."

"No, she didn't," Mrs. Jeffries countered. "Provost was marked for death from the moment they found out he was asking questions about Ernie Grigson. The killers only acted that night because they were desperate. They knew that if March and Provost went to the police together, both Grigson's death and March's accident would be investigated very thoroughly."

"But did the murderers know that the two men had written a letter to Inspector Witherspoon?" Betsy asked.

"I don't think so," Mrs. Jeffries replied. "But if Provost still had it on him, they probably found it and destroyed it."

"Maybe he posted it before he went to the Wentworth that night," Wiggins suggested.

Mrs. Jeffries looked doubtful. "I don't think so. According to what Ruth learned from Miss March today, the letter was addressed to Witherspoon. If Provost had been able to mail it, the inspector should have received it by now. No, for some reason of his own, Provost must have put the letter in his pocket, and the killers found it."

"But why did Provost walk home alone that night if he knew he was in danger?" Smythe wondered. "Why didn't he take a hansom?"

"Because he didn't know he was in danger," Mrs. Jeffries said. "He had the letter safely in his pocket, and he'd no idea that the three of them were so suspicious that they'd decided to act. He didn't know that Rollo had heard about his visit to March's house."

"So Provost had no reason to change his routine, and he walked home as he always did," Mrs. Goodge said softly. "Poor man."

"You'd 'ave thought that when Rollo Barrington accosted him, he'd 'ave cottoned on to the fact he might be in danger." Wiggins helped himself to another bun. "He shoulda made a run for it. That fat old Barrington couldn't 'ave caught him."

"That's why they used Bernadette Healey," Smythe pointed out. "Barrington probably caught up with Provost and pointed to her standing there on the dock. Remember, she said that's all he told 'er to do."

"But why did they want her to stand there?" Wiggins asked.

Smythe shrugged. "I think we'll 'ave to wait until the inspector comes home this evening to find out that particular detail. But I suspect that he was usin' her in some way to allay Provost's fears and to keep 'im from running off."

Betsy looked at Mrs. Jeffries and asked, "What was the piece that put it all together?"

She laughed. "There wasn't any one piece this time. Frankly, if the inspector hadn't gotten those letters from Nivens and Smythe

367

hadn't found Bernadette Healey, I'd still be puzzled over several aspects of this case."

"But the letters didn't really tell us much," Betsy argued.

"They gave us Charles Capel's name," Mrs. Jeffries said. "And the only reason that Capel would be nervous and making a run for it was because he knew or suspected who the killers were."

"How did you know he wasn't the killer?" Luty asked.

"Because, unlike the others in that whist circle, Capel didn't need money," Mrs. Jeffries replied. "In all of the information we learned about the Octet whist group, we never heard that Capel was in financial difficulties. It was the Barringtons and Cleverly who were always late paying their grocery bills and their house servants. So I reasoned that, though Grigson was murdered to retrieve something of value, Capel could have simply made an arrangement with him to buy it back when Capel got his quarterly allowance. You'll notice it took him less than twenty-four hours to lay his hands on enough cash to leave town. Once Betsy told me that Lizzie had overheard Capel telling his neighbor he was going to sell some shares, I realized that Capel was running because he knew something, not because he'd done the murders."

"Well, we'll find everything out once the inspector gets home." Luty yawned. "I wonder how long that'll be."

Mrs. Goodge glanced at the oven. "I've got a joint of lamb cookin'. Do you think he'll be home in time for supper?"

"It's a very complex case," Mrs. Jeffries said. "I imagine he'll be quite late."

Luty got up. "Good. Then I'm goin' home. I told Duxbury to come there as soon as he'd finished takin' care of Miss Healey. I want to git a few more details out of him."

"And he did his task admirably." Hatchet went to the coat tree and got Luty's cloak. "We'll be back later," he promised as he draped the garment over her shoulders and turned her toward the back door.

"Dang right we will. I'm dying to find out what happened at the police station." Luty waved good-bye, Hatchet nodded, and they disappeared through the back door.

"If ya think the inspector's goin' to be a while, I'd like to get the rig back to Howard's." Smythe stood up. "The horses don't really like bein' kitted out in the harness. Truth of the matter is, they don't much like pullin' the carriage."

"God forbid your precious horses have to suffer," Betsy muttered. Then she smiled.

"Oh, go on. But, honestly, sometimes you're more considerate of those animals than you are of me."

"You know that in a pinch I'd pick you over them." He laughed, dropped a quick kiss on her cheek, and got to his feet. "I love it when you're jealous. Too bad it's over a couple of old nags," he teased as he disappeared down the hallway.

"I don't have a jealous bone in my body," she yelled. "Silly man. If I was really the jealous type, I'd have asked you a lot more questions about what you're up to when you're on the hunt," she muttered. But he'd already gone. "But I don't dare, because then he might start asking what I get up to!" She chuckled to herself.

The other women laughed as well.

Perplexed, Wiggins simply shook his head. He'd never understand women. "Since we've a bit of time before the inspector gets back, I'll move those big tins down from the top shelf in the larder," he said as he got up.

Ruth rose and went to the coat tree. "I must go as well. I've a guest coming for tea in twenty minutes. I invited her before this all began. But I will be back. I must hear the rest of the story."

"Uh, yes, yes, of course," Mrs. Jeffries

murmured.

As soon as Ruth had gone, Mrs. Goodge said, "You're worried about something. What's wrong?"

"I just realized we're not supposed to know anything about the arrests," Mrs. Jeffries said. "And the inspector probably won't be home until quite late this evening. How are we going to explain a kitchen full of visitors?"

"Maybe the news will be in the afternoon papers," the cook said hopefully.

On their other cases, one of them had usually had a reason to be at the station when the arrests occurred, or the inspector had arrived home early enough for them to pretend that Luty and Hatchet had just dropped by for afternoon tea.

"I doubt it," Mrs. Jeffries said.

"And we've got Ruth to explain." Betsy frowned. "If it was just Luty and Hatchet, we could always say they'd stopped on their way to a social function to drop off a recipe for Mrs. Goodge. We've used that excuse before."

"We'll think of something," Mrs. Jeffries stated. "The others have worked too hard on this case not to be here to hear the end of it."

"Good. Then I'll nip up and finish dusting the top floor," Betsy said. "It always pays to be at the ready. Who knows? We might get another case right away."

"I'm going to go to my room for a short nap," the cook announced. "The lamb's got another hour before it's done, and everything else is ready for when the inspector comes home."

"I'll go and check how Wiggins is getting on," Mrs. Jeffries said.

"See if you can get him to talk a bit. Something is bothering the lad. He's cheerful enough today, since he's been out and about and taken an active part on the case, but come tomorrow he'll be down in the dumps again if he doesn't let the misery out of his system." Mrs. Goodge looked worried. "Wiggins holds things inside, and that's not good for him."

"But you're the one he usually confides in," Mrs. Jeffries protested. The footman and the cook had become very close over the years.

"True," the cook agreed. "But this time I've a feeling he'll need to speak to someone who knows a little more about the affairs of the heart than I do." She headed for the short hallway off the back stairs that led to her suite of rooms, and then she stopped. "Being a spinster has its disadvantages. I don't think I can give him the kind of advice he needs right now. But you've been married, Mrs. Jeffries. You know all about romance and that sort of thing."

Mrs. Jeffries started to protest again, but Mrs. Goodge had slipped away before she could think of what to say. Still, the cook was right: Someone needed to speak to Wiggins and find out what was upsetting him. Mrs. Jeffries supposed it might as well be her.

She straightened her spine and marched toward the dry larder. Wiggins was on a chair, reaching for a tin of drinking chocolate on the top shelf. "Did you need something, Mrs. Jeffries?" he asked.

"No, I just wanted to make sure you were alright," she replied. "You've been very quiet recently. We've all noticed you haven't been yourself. Is there something wrong? Something you'd like to talk about?"

He turned his gaze back to the shelf, grabbed the tin, and then climbed down off the chair. He put the chocolate on the wide bottom counter and flopped down in the chair. "I've made an awful fool of myself," he said softly. "And I've let everyone here down as well. What's worse is that I did it all for a silly woman who wasn't worth one moment of a decent man's time."

"Oh dear. I'm sure it's not as bad as all that." Mrs. Jeffries stared at him sympathetically.

"Yes, it is," he said. "All those times you thought I was out huntin' for clues, I was really moonin' about the Odeon Opera House, hopin' she'd pay me a bit of attention, instead of doin' my duty. I'm a stupid fool."

"To begin with, you haven't let us down in the least. Regardless of your other activities during the course of this investigation, you contributed your fair share. And furthermore, there isn't a human being over the age of five that hasn't made a fool of themselves at one time or another."

He said nothing, simply stared down at his hands.

"Wiggins, there are no words that will make you feel better. You've obviously been hurt, and I know that you feel absolutely dreadful. I wish I could wave a magic wand and make you feel better, but I can't. The awful thing about this life is that none of us get through it without taking a few licks to our innermost hearts. But know this: Time really does heal all wounds." She hoped she was saying the right thing.

He lifted his head and looked at her, and her heart sank when she saw the unshed tears in his eyes.

"I really thought she liked me." He blinked hard to keep from crying. "But she didn't. She let me take her to tea and buy her lunch at the café, but all along she was seein' someone else."

"I'm so sorry, Wiggins," Mrs. Jeffries murmured. "You're a wonderful young man, and you certainly didn't deserve to be treated that way —" She broke off as she heard the sound of steps on the back stairs.

"Cor blimey." Wiggins swiped at his cheeks. "I'd know those footsteps anywhere. The inspector's home already."

"Hello, hello," Witherspoon called as he came into the kitchen. "Gracious, something smells wonderful."

"Good afternoon, sir," Mrs. Jeffries said as she raced in behind him. "You're home early today."

"We've made an arrest in the Provost case," he announced proudly. "And it's going very well, very well indeed."

Mrs. Jeffries tried not to panic. The others would have a fit if they missed hearing the particulars directly from him. "How wonderful, sir. I knew you'd do it. Uh, are you finished with all the paperwork and the details already?"

"No. We've arrested the two Barrington

brothers and Sir Edmund Cleverly. But they're all wanting to turn Queen's evidence on one another, so one of the undersecretaries at the Home Office has been sent for to help sort it all out."

Wiggins tiptoed behind the inspector and slipped silently toward Mrs. Goodge's room.

"Would you like some tea, sir?" Mrs. Jeffries banged her feet hard against the floor as she went to the cooker, trying to mask the noise the footman might make as he raced off to get the others. Then she realized that she needn't be quiet after all: The inspector had come home for one reason and one reason only. He wanted to tell them what had happened. He wanted to boast about his arrest and crow a little about his wonderful achievement.

"That would be lovely." Witherspoon sat down at the head of the table. "Don't you want to know what happened?"

"Yes, sir, I do, but could you please wait till the others are here? You know they'll be most upset if they miss hearing you tell us what happened. Mrs. Goodge is just in her room, and Betsy's upstairs doing the dusting. Oh dear, Smythe has gone to Howard's to return the carriage."

"Not to worry. I can wait. We've plenty of time. I'm not due back on duty until tomorrow. It'll take the undersecretary hours to decide what to do." Witherspoon beamed. "All three suspects made very comprehensive statements, so we've constables out gathering up the physical evidence. There's really nothing for me to do until it's all sorted out by the powers that be."

"You mean they all confessed?" Mrs. Jeffries asked.

"Oh, yes, they're vying with one another to see who can avoid the hangman." He sighed. "But I expect it'll be Rollo Barrington who ends up in prison for life. He didn't actually kill anyone. Ah, there's Mrs. Goodge." He smiled at the cook as she hurried into the kitchen. A few minutes later, they were joined by Betsy and Wiggins.

Even Smythe managed to make it home before the inspector had finished.

Luty and Hatchet weren't quite so lucky and had to hear the details of the case secondhand. Ruth had come back in time to have supper with the inspector and was still upstairs, so she heard it directly from the horse's mouth, as Luty so delicately put it.

"Thunder and tarnation," Luty exclaimed. "Who'd have thought he'd have gotten home so quickly."

"Well, at least we got the answers to our

questions," Hatchet pointed out. "We know that Capel was the one who'd introduced Grigson to the others, and that's why he was trying to leave town."

"Humph, the big coward." Luty patted her muff, which was lying on the table next to her. "Duxbury told us what happened in the card room." She laughed. "I'da liked to have seen that. Duxbury was right proud of himself."

"And well he should be," Mrs. Jeffries replied. "If Sir Edmund had made it through that door, he might have gotten away."

"I still don't understand how the three of 'em could afford to hire someone to find Bernadette Healey," Wiggins said. "What did they use for cash?"

"There was cash in Rollo Barrington's hidey-hole," Betsy reminded him. "The inspector said that when the constables searched his house, they found a wad of pound notes."

"And they found Grigson's stickpin," Hatchet added. "Rollo simply couldn't resist. He pinched it off him after the other two knocked Grigson unconcsious. Poor man. They're never going to find his body."

"True. They'd already planned Grigson's murder when they went to see him that night, and they brought stones to weigh him down before they dumped him in the Thames." Mrs. Jeffries pursed her lips in distaste. "They really are despicable human beings, and I, for one, am disgusted that any of the three might escape the hangman just because they've confessed."

"We don't know that they will," Smythe said. "Just because they're falling all over each other to turn Queen's evidence doesn't mean the crown will accept it."

"They're influential people," she replied. "Take my word for it: Not all of them will hang."

"But they'll be in prison the rest of their lives. That's even worse." Luty shuddered. "I'd rather be dead than caged up like an animal."

Mrs. Jeffries decided that this might be an opportune moment to put a rather interesting notion into the inspector's mind. If her general theory was correct and the murders of Provost and Grigson were part of a pattern, then wouldn't it be a good idea for the inspector to find out what had happened to all those other fourths who'd played at the Barrington-Cleverly whist table?

Mrs. Jeffries would bet her next quarter's wages that not all of those men had simply died or boarded a ship to emigrate to another country. As a matter of fact, Witherspoon had mentioned that the fourth before Provost, a Mr. Hempel, had been talking about a loan he wanted to collect on — and then he'd suddenly left the country.

She got to her feet and went to the sideboard. "I think I'll take another bottle of Harveys up to the inspector and Ruth. There wasn't much left in the other one. I'll be right back."

She went upstairs and stopped just outside the drawing room. The door was cracked open and she put her ear up to it, listening to make sure she wasn't interrupting at an awkward moment.

"Oh, Gerald, you must be so proud," she heard Ruth say. "You've solved a very complicated case."

"Thank you, dearest."

Dearest? Mrs. Jeffries drew back. Gracious, matters had progressed between these two. Good.

"I think this calls for a celebration," Witherspoon continued. "There's enough here in the bottle for a toast."

Mrs. Jeffries didn't wish to intrude, but she wanted them to have an adequate supply of sherry. She started into the room and then stopped when she heard the clink of glasses. Perhaps she ought to wait until they'd finished their toast.

"Let's raise our glasses, Ruth," the inspector said. "To Inspector Nigel Nivens. Without his help, this case wouldn't have been solved. It took real courage for him to hand over those letters."

Mrs. Jeffries' jaw dropped in surprise, and she jerked backward. A red mist of rage clouded her vision. Her stomach tightened in knots, and she had to force herself to stay still and not burst into the room and smash those raised glasses to the floor. She couldn't believe what she'd just heard! This was unbelievable. Giving that odious toad credit for doing his bloody duty!

She turned on her heel, tucked the unopened bottle under her arm, and charged back to the kitchen. She didn't care whether the inspector heard her.

The others looked up as she stomped into the kitchen. When everyone saw the expression on her face, they stopped speaking. But she didn't give anyone time to ask any questions. "Betsy, get some sherry glasses."

The maid cast a quick, worried look at Smythe and then got up and rushed to the cupboard.

"I thought you were taking that up to the inspector," Mrs. Goodge commented as the housekeeper slapped the bottle onto the table.

"He doesn't need it. We're going to have our own toast, and if the inspector objects, I'll buy him another bottle." Despite her fury, she knew Witherspoon would never begrudge them a sip of sherry.

"Uh, is everything alright?" Wiggins asked.

"Everything is just fine," she replied. She shoved the bottle toward Smythe. "Can you open this, please."

Betsy put the glasses down in front of Mrs. Jeffries. Smythe opened the bottle and handed it to the housekeeper.

Mrs. Jeffries poured the amber liquid into the tiny sherry glasses and nodded at Betsy to hand them around.

Everyone looked at her expectantly.

She picked up her glass and held it high. "Please raise your glasses and stand up," she commanded. "We're going to honor the person who has done the most in bringing these murderers to justice."

She waited till they all were standing with glasses raised, and then she gave the toast. "To Michael Provost. May he rest in peace. A good man and great detective. He was one of us."